BABY ZERO

PIERRE OUELLETTE

BABY
ZERO

A NOVEL

JORVIK
PRESS

ISBN: 978-1-7331007-8-6

Library of Congress
Control Number: 2024935025

Design and formatting: Keith Carlson

First edition

JORVIK PRESS
5331 S Macadam Ave., Ste 258/424,
Portland OR 97239

JorvikPress.com

Pierre Ouellette lives in the Portland Metro Area and is the author of eight previously published novels that span a diversity of subjects and settings. He served for two decades as the creative partner in an advertising and public relations agency focused on science and technology. Prior to that he was a professional guitarist and played in numerous pop bands and jazz ensembles, including Paul Revere and the Raiders, Jim Pepper and David Friesen.

ALSO BY PIERRE OUELLETTE

The Forever Man

A Shot Away

Haight St.

Bakersfield

The Deus Machine

The Third Pandemic

WRITING AS PIERRE DAVIS

A Breed Apart

Origin Unknown

*Dedicated
to the memory
of my brother,
Joe Ouellette.*

1

Something is wrong.

The embryologist knows it as soon as she brings up the display in the laboratory at NewLife Associates, a clinic in Boston dedicated to in vitro fertilization. It makes her put aside the spat she'd just had with her boyfriend over his uncouth behavior at the party last night. It makes her forget about her daily lunchtime reading of an old copy of *The Handmaid's Tale*, which has her hooked.

The display presents the outcome of a process that started yesterday, when ten eggs were extracted from the ovaries of a woman who wanted a baby but failed to conceive. Normally, an ovary produces a single egg, which drifts through the fallopian tube and into the uterus, where it hosts a party for several million sperm. If none show up, it fades away into oblivion. However, a full house means hundreds of thousands of suitors, all wanting a shot at making a baby. But not in this case. Somewhere along the way, something isn't working right.

The fix? Simple in concept, but complex and demanding in detail. It starts with a 36-hour hormonal bath that prompts an ovary to produce several eggs instead of one. Each resides in a fluid-filled cavity called a follicle, which is pierced by an aspiration tube introduced through the vaginal wall. Both fluid and egg are sucked out and into a culture medium, carefully kept at body temperature.

This is where the embryologist joins the process. She inspects the entire harvest under microscopic magnification for prime candidates. Those that pass are placed in individual incubators, where the sperm is introduced, and an 18-hour fertilization ritual takes place. When the party ends, she examines the results for each egg through a digital microscope. She looks for the telltale sign of successful fertilization: the appearance of two cells inside the egg. Soon, two will become four, and four will become eight, and the baby parade will be off and running on its way to 26 billion cells. Once a solitary egg, now a communal embryo.

But that's not what she sees today on the screen.

It presents the images of ten separate eggs in monochrome. None appear fertilized. Not a single nascent embryo out of the bunch. Extremely unusual. One possibility is low-grade sperm, but that's highly unlikely. The sperm were carefully sorted and evaluated before the process even began.

She again scrutinizes each image with the utmost diligence. In the embryonic journey, failures are common in the first few days. Sometimes, two cells never make it to four cells, or four to eight. Chaos breaks out, fragmentation sets in, asymmetries appear. And occasionally you would see what she now sees, a complete failure to fertilize. None would ever make the trip into the mother's uterine cavity to complete the pregnancy or undergo freezing to become a possible child of the future.

Ten failures in a row. All things considered; it seems much more likely a systemic failure than biological happenstance. In any case, she has to notify Dr. Emmet Rudolph, who both owns and manages this clinic, as well as two others. Past episodes have taught her that incidents like this do not bring out the best in the man. Oh well. She'll do it, but in truth she has bigger issues to contend with, like how her live-in partner became far too familiar with one of her best friends at last evening's festivities.

She has yet to devise the proper penance but is working on it.

2

The metal news box weighs about 90 pounds. Not nearly enough to keep it curbside in the 200-mph wind that now roars through downtown Miami. A towering matrix of office buildings channels the gale into violent currents that course down the avenues and power the box to over 100 mph while vaulting it 30 feet off the pavement. It now operates as a kinetic missile and hurtles along toward the first target of opportunity.

"So you did a hitch, huh?" Steve asks. He is flanked by Perry and Don. All three wear combat fatigues with a patch that identifies them as members of the Sigma Group, a private military contractor of global proportions.

"Yep," Gavin Gray answers. "Army."

The men appreciate his terse and clipped reply. It has a definite military ring to it.

"See any action?" Perry inquires. They always asked that.

"Nope. I was public affairs."

"Sweet," Don commented. And he was right. In fact, it was the biggest inflection point in Gavin's entire life. Dead broke after high school, he'd enlisted in the Army to leverage the college money they offered. Aptitude tests revealed an exceptional linguistic capacity, and he wound up as a public affairs specialist. In other words, a reporter. After his obligatory two years, he used his benefits to get a degree in journalism at New York City College, just a hop away from his home in Brooklyn.

A sharp series of cracks and shudders interrupts their conversation. The building where they dwell is not happy about being taken to its architectural extremes. A big bank occupies the bottom two floors, a bank steeped in the intricacies of international finance. The storm has rapidly evolved into the worst in the city's history, and the bank fears a slide into civil anarchy once it passes, a scenario that calls for extraordinary security measures. Hence the presence of the three military contractors.

The hurricane itself is why Gavin is here. For some time, there had been debate over what might constitute a "Category 6" storm. There were some formal complexities in the way. Category 5 applied to any storm with sustained winds over 157 mph. It placed no upward limit on this velocity. 400 mph would still be a 5. Still, the media obsessed over the public fascination with Category 6 and arrived at its own consensus with no official sanction. It became generally agreed that any wind speed over 190 mph elevated the disturbance into the fearsome realm of Category 6.

When the official forecasts finally confirmed that the present storm was barreling head-on toward Miami, they nervously predicted it to be the most violent hurricane of all time, with sustained wind speeds approaching 220 mph. Definitely a Category 6. But that covered only half the potential horror. Most of downtown Miami near the waterfront sat about six feet above sea level, and the so-called "storm surge," the water's predicted height above the normal tide, was put at a whopping 29 feet. The howling currents of wind between the buildings would quickly become boiling rivers of surging sea water. A catastrophic combination.

And one not lost on the International News Network, which sent Gavin here. He periodically contracted with INN to write features covering major news events. Besides a stellar track record, he had another significant qualification. No wife, no children, no domestic partner. The Atlantic Ocean could claim him with impunity if given the opportunity.

This time out, his timing was bad from the beginning. He caught one the last flights into Miami International just as the edge of the monster storm started to kiss the coastline. On approach, his plane began fluttering a few hundred feet above the runway due to wind shear. Amidst screams of terror, it managed to struggle aloft and came down hard the second time around. Gavin shook it off, collected his knapsack and rented a pickup, which seemed an appropriate choice. INN had reserved a room on the upper floor of a big hotel on the edge of downtown, which appeared relatively safe.

Maybe so, but he never got there. On the 836 freeway east, the sky went black, and a rain of mythical proportions set in. Up ahead, a highway rig had hydroplaned and flipped onto its side, triggering a nasty pileup. He managed a quick swing off an exit and onto a street that paralleled the freeway. He relaxed a little. The street was empty, and he had a clean shot toward downtown. His windshield wipers flapped desperately against the deluge, and he leaned forward and squinted to get a better view. Up ahead, the pavement had disappeared under the downpour but looked passable. Wrong. He plowed into waist-high water, which stopped the truck and stalled the engine. "Fuck!" He pounded the steering wheel. Before he could recover his good senses, a beige vehicle pulled up alongside, a military-grade Humvee. As he rolled down his window to get a better view, the Humvee's rear door opened and a young man in fatigues beckoned to him. "Come on, jump!" Gavin looked down and saw the vehicles were only about three feet apart. He grabbed his knapsack, opened the door, and leaped across, getting half-soaked in the process. Hello Steve, Perry, and Don.

The trio explained that they had no choice but haul ass to their downtown objective before the weather got any worse than it already was. Gavin said no problem. And they were off.

Now they all lounge on sleek designer furniture on the mezzanine level of the bank, one story above ground. Probably a meeting space for closing comfy deals of some kind. They're positioned a safe distance from the windows facing the street, where a vicious spray of water rakes across the glass and obscures the scene outside. Gavin gets up and starts forward to take a look down onto the avenue. He needs to start accumulating visual impressions for his article.

"Wouldn't be doing that," Perry suggests. "Radio says the winds are topping 200."

Right then, the 90-lb. metal news box chooses to confirm Perry's admonition. It crashes into one of the front windows at 100 mph, generating a brilliant cloud of pulverized glass. After rocketing another thirty feet at nearly full velocity, it embeds itself in a nearby wall. A deafening blast of wind-driven rain now shoots in through the broken window cavity.

"You okay?" Perry asks Gavin.

"More or less," Gavin answers. In fact, he was just steps away from being shredded and finds it somewhat distressing.

"Hey, check this out," Don yells above the noise. The rain blast inside is nearly horizontal and soaking them all. They move to where the lip of mezzanine looks down on the ground floor with its open-air office suites and teller counters. The very front faces out to the sidewalk through large plates of glass framed in aluminum.

"Aquarium time," Don says.

And he's right. The water level outside has risen more than two thirds of the way up the streetside glass. A churning mass of subsurface debris carries paper, furniture, fast food remnants, clothing, potted plants, sunglasses, smart phones, and numerous other objects mangled beyond recognition. They tumble, spin and speed down the street on their way to God knows where. Most horrific is a small, drowned dog, its leash still flapping like a wind-driven pennant.

A loud snap fractures the air. A large crack snakes its way up one of the glass panels, then another.

"Gonna blow," Don observes, "Watch out." They all heed his advice and take a step backward. Within the space of a few seconds, every panel across the office front blows. A mammoth waterfall crashes in and begins to devour the whole floor below them. Hissing, rushing, and gurgling.

"Holy fuck!" Perry exclaims.

Gavin has the presence of mind to capture it all on video with his phone. It leaves him with a strange feeling of inevitability. It was all meant to happen; the whole purpose of the bank from its inception was to host this climactic event. How could it be otherwise?

"Perhaps we should seek higher ground," he tells the group. "Know where the stairs are?" Military protocol aside, he's the eldest, which carries a certain weight.

"Sure do," Don answers. They race back to where they started and grab several large duffel bags full of ammunition, weaponry, and communications gear. The noise level drops dramatically as they enter the stairwell and start to climb.

"How high we goin'?" Perry asks.

"All the way," Steve says.

Gavin is thoroughly spent by the time they reach the penthouse on the 30th floor. No matter what else, these guys are in great shape. The door from the stairwell to the penthouse is locked, naturally, but they have small explosive charges dedicated to easy entry with minimal damage. Company policy only permits their use in true emergencies, and this is an emergency of the highest order.

Once inside, they walk through a lavishly appointed living room with big view windows that flex slightly from the force of the wind but appear to be holding. Gavin stops when he reaches them. To go outside is unthinkable. He pulls out his phone and begins to shoot video of the scene below, which borders on apocalyptic. The city's shoreline has disappeared completely. Downtown Miami has become one with the Atlantic Ocean. This time around, INN is going to get their money's worth and then some.

Gavin checks for signal bars on his phone. Gone. Same thing for wireless. "You got a satellite phone?" he asks Steve.

"That we do."

"Mind if I use it to phone the office?"

He calls Mindy Harlow, his producer at INN, and explains that he's alive and well. That's wonderful, she tells him, but does he have a great story? In truth, Mindy is a compassionate person, but also tends toward dark humor. He runs down what's happened, and she buys in. He adds that travel on the streets is impossible because they no longer exist and will not return any time soon, so they best go with what they have. She agrees to have him choppered off the roof as soon as the storm subsides.

They find a laundry room and throw their wet clothes in the drier. After running down some bathrobes, they raid the kitchen to make an improvised dinner. Steve loves to cook and is delighted by all the foodie-level gadgets. They agree that, under the circumstances, it would be totally appropriate to commandeer a couple of bottles of wine.

After just two glasses and a little beef stroganoff, Gavin is done in and retires to a back bedroom where he immediately sinks into the deepest of sleeps.

Two hours later, a thump on the door. It's Steve with the satellite phone. He hands it to Gavin, who takes the call as Steve quietly departs.

His mother is dead.

3

"Just one more," Tracy Pallas tells her friend, Christina. "Then I got to go."

They both know why, but an exasperated Christina says it best. "You know what you are?"

"What?"

"You're a nerd in slut's clothing."

"Yup," Tracy nods. She takes no offense. Her friend means it figuratively, not literally. Right now, Tracy's wearing a cotton sleeveless blouse, charcoal stretch denims, and rustic sandals, with light brown hair pulled back in a thick ponytail. Hardly hormones on the make. But the nerd part is dead on. She works as a statistician in an obscure corner of the Centers for Disease Control. It's called the Reproductive Statistics Branch of the Division of Vital Statistics, one of six in the National Center for Health Statistics, or NCHS. While many 25-year-old women spend their idle moments pondering fashion, cosmetics or boyfriends, Tracy explores the wonderous marvel of partial differential equations. Still, she attracts a fair amount of male attention, the definitive measure of female beauty worldwide, but she is in between relationships at the moment.

Not Christina. "You know, Josh is starting to really piss me off," she volunteers.

"And that's why we're here, right?"

They're sitting in an upscale bar atop a premium hotel that affords a magnificent view of the DC nightscape. Ever the mathematician, Tracy has discovered you can rank a bar's cachet by the price of a cheeseburger. The menu here pegs it at $28, which puts it firmly in the upper strata. Which in turn indicates it will be populated by single males from law offices, lobbyist organizations and senior administrative offices. Which means Christina can survey her many amorous options, one cute guy at a time.

"Tracy!"

Tracy looks up into the perfectly contoured face of Allison Wertz. She has a cascade of blonde hair that flows down onto a gorgeous silk blouse, probably from Bergdorf Goodman. Two female companions stand close by, both with attire of equal caliber. Tracy recognizes the pair from previous encounters with Allison. Manhattan trust fund babies of the highest order.

Allison occupies a prominent position in the subsurface banter that bubbles through any office, and the NCHS is no exception. She stands out because everyone loves a tale of how the mighty have fallen. Her father was a very clever man who founded an investment firm specializing in healthcare and prospered mightily in the process. He married an opportunistic fashion model and had three daughters who looked upon Manhattan as a vast playground rather than a career incubator. Allison, the youngest, attended three private high schools, two private colleges, and one art school before squandering her way into contention among the global elite. Beauty and brains, like two hemispheres of plutonium, waiting to collide in a critical mass and create a catastrophic explosion.

Her father wasn't going to wait for that to happen. He reduced her income from the family trust to $500 per month and wished her the very best. When she countered with a graphic display of outrage and indignation, he reduced it to zero dollars per month. Her mother, constrained by an air-tight prenuptial, stood idly by. Even though severed from the family money, Allison still had the family network to leverage. One contact led to another, and with a little guidance from a few congressmen, senators and administrators, she was now comfortably installed at the NCHS in the Office of Information Services. As a "Communications Specialist," she now roamed across all six divisions, including Tracy's, to moderate their contact with the media. You never know what nerds might say if left to their own devices.

Tracy's modest social skills cause her to hesitate. Should she ask them all to sit down?

Maybe so, but she doesn't want to. What she really wants is to go home. The intrusion of a male voice resolves the conflict.

"Don't I know you?" the guy says to Allison. He came out of nowhere and stole the scene. Classically handsome face. Beard done in a tight trim around a mouth set in something approaching a leer, but not quite. Tailored sport coat, immaculate white shirt open at the collar, twill pants, Santoni loafers, De Bethune watch. He reeks of confidence.

"Maybe," Allison responds. He's opened with a really tired line, but so what? She likes the package.

"You staying here?" he asks.

"No, just passing through," Allison replies with a vague sketch of a smile. Just enough to keep the channel open.

And so it goes. Turns out he's an attorney down from NYC. Family owns an investment firm, a big investment firm. He's meeting tomorrow with a couple of lobbyists. Big issues are at stake, very big issues. Everything about this guy is very big.

Tracy finds his impetuous swagger utterly repellent. But Allison's companions clearly do not. They beam their approval. Cute guy, fashionable attire, cocky attitude. Perfect.

The exchange ends with the pair swapping business cards. Turns out he's Mark Stennis, legal counsel for Stennis Partners, a private equity firm. He's in town quite a bit, so maybe they can get together some time. Maybe they can, Allison replies. He follows up with a quick nice-to-meet-you-all to everyone else and takes off. Busy man. Much to do.

Allison plays it cool and makes no comment. Just another guy hitting on her. So what? She and her friends say goodbye, and the DC night swallows them.

Tracy gazes out the window at the Washington Monument, all bathed in white. It looks a lot more phallic than it did twenty minutes ago.

4

"So, you don't need no plan to do that, huh?" Twitcher asks.

"Nope," Frank says. "Got it in my head." He pulls down the drill press lever to bore the final hole in the bolt switch. He long ago committed the switch's spec to memory, as well as every other component in the M2 .50 caliber machine gun.

"Well, all right," Twitcher says as he rubs his scraggly beard and scratches his bulging belly beneath a dirty black T-shirt that reads USA KICKS ASS. He is here at the bidding of his unit commander, who runs a militia out of a town some 70 miles west. He knows Frank doesn't like the guy, which minimizes their discourse.

But business is business here in Roundup, Montana, where Frank Fanno operates his one-man machine shop. He does a brisk trade fabricating replacement parts for combat-level weaponry, mostly for militia groups other than his own. Many can be purchased online, but that leaves a transaction trail back to the weapon's owner, which puts them in the crosshairs of the Deep State, the fundamental adversary.

Frank finishes drilling and takes the bolt switch over to a metal table along the wall. The floor of the shop has an open space large enough to park a small truck on oil-stained cement. A cluster of machining tools occupies the rest. Grinders, millers, lathes, drillers and borers, along with cutting torches, welding gear and tool chests, plus various solvents and oils in five-gallon cans. The entire enclosure smells of dead grease and burnt oil.

Frank surveys the disassembled .50 caliber weapon resting on the table. He pushes the new bolt switch into the bolt assembly and turns to Twitcher. "Okay, let's take her out for a test ride."

Twitcher looks on as Frank spreads out dozens of parts and starts to methodically reassemble the weapon. "Goddam," Twitcher comments. "How do you know where everything goes?"

"Because I took the time to learn," Frank replies. "That's how."

"Oh," Twitcher says, as if it's some kind of major revelation.

"So, how's Captain Bob treating you boys these days?" asks Frank, referring to the leader of the neighboring militia.

Twitcher shrugs. "Okay. I guess."

"Is he still shipping you over to the coast so you can pound on those Antifa types?"

"Sometimes," Twitcher offers cautiously. It's well known that Frank isn't ideologically aligned with most other militias in the area, at least on certain issues.

"And what good's that gonna do?"

"Dunno."

"Well neither do I."

Frank completes the work in silence, and they load the machine gun into a wooden crate that goes into the rear of Frank's pickup. "You know the way?" he asks Twitcher as he opens the shop's retractable door.

"Yeah, I know the way, but I gotta stop for gas."

"Okay, see you when you get there."

Frank pulls out and closes the shop's door behind him. He travels down a dirt road through a gritty industrial area lined with the cast-off metal limbs of long-dead machines. A right turn takes him into town along a street of modest single-story houses until he reaches Main Street. Roundup is a veritable metropolis by Eastern Montana standards. About eighty square blocks and two thousand people. Frank likes the size and feel of it. You're never confined, stifled or impeded.

He turns right onto Main, which becomes Highway 87 going north. Outside, the county seat rolls by, followed by a tractor dealership, a grade school, a Chevron station and a midsized grocery store. It's almost like the Feds were never here, but he knows that's an illusion.

Once clear of town, the road presents a vista that stretches out to somewhere beyond the capacity of the human eye. Frank becomes a ghost of himself, a 39-year-old man traveling through infinity. He's stayed lean and fit, with the Afghan desert carved forever around his eyes and its incessant breeze blowing through his gray-streaked beard. Sergeant First Class back then, a platoon leader. Forty men under him and one clueless officer above. All committed to the so-called "counterinsurgency" dictated by those on high in DC and Kabul. Vietnam redux. They were supposed to win the "hearts and minds" of the local populace, who had repulsed every invader for the past couple of centuries.

Frank reluctantly went along with it – until some clowns back in DC decided to financially starve the Taliban by eradicating all the opium poppies. It not only did not work, it sparked outrage among the farmers who saw their livelihoods destroyed with no real alternative to survive. Frank's unit now faced an embittered, angered, resentful population full of more insurgents than ever. In the end, they paid in blood for blunders made in well-appointed offices halfway around the world. One body bag after another. And for what?

Never again would he leave his fate in the hands of the federal government.

At the end of his tour, he quit for good and moved back to Montana, from whence he came. He opened his shop and founded Freedom First, a local militia group dedicated to putting a permanent stop to federal control over their lives. To this end, he recruited about 40 young men, roughly the same number he commanded overseas. Many resembled Twitcher. Overweight, undereducated and languishing in rural poverty. He couldn't compensate them financially, but he could bring discipline and dignity to their lives, something most had never known in a world of runaway dads, exhausted mothers and opioids gone mad. To each he offered one of the oldest of human propositions: give me your loyalty and I'll give you something to live for.

A passing motorcycle yanks him back out of his head. A shiny black BMW sidecar with three wheels and elegant lines. It holds two occupants clad in leathers with helmets of a burgundy color. Probably a couple on some epic journey, the kind Frank would have taken with his wife if she'd lived, but she didn't. After 15 years of smoking, lung cancer killed her in just two months. The only thing that kept him afloat was the obligation he felt to the kids in his unit. He's been coasting in neutral ever since.

He spots the break in the fence up ahead and slows to turn onto a bumpy dirt road that heads east into the utterly vacant land beyond.

The Range they call it. A flat stretch of prairie scrub terminating in a low rise that serves as a backstop for gunfire. Frank and Twitcher stand at the open tailgate of Twitcher's pickup, where Frank has just lifted the weapon out of its wooden crate. "Okay, go ahead and set it up" he commands. "I'm gonna get the ammo."

Twitcher lifts the 85-pound weapon off the truck and hefts it over to a metal tripod set atop an earthen mound. Frank walks on out into the scrub, where he references several landmarks to locate the buried ammo cache. He brushes off a layer of dirt and pulls out a metal box full of linked .50 caliber cartridges.

Twitcher has the weapon locked onto the tripod when Frank returns. They both look down range about 50 yards to the remains of an old VW Bug riddled with hundreds of bullet holes. "Here you go," Frank says, and Twitcher sits down behind the weapon while Frank pulls a chain of the linked cartridges out of the ammo box. He positions them in the weapon's feedway and closes the cover. "All yours."

Twitcher puts the weapon on automatic, pulls the retracting slide handle to the rear, and lets it go. It slams forward with a fat clink as it chambers the first round. "Range is clear. Fire when ready," Frank announces.

As Twitcher grabs the rear handles and thumbs the trigger, his eyes and nose start to oscillate rapidly. Hence his name. Moments of stress tended to trigger the spasms, especially moments that questioned his self-confidence. He has to stop, breathe deeply, and collect himself before going on. Frank sympathizes. His own troops exhibit a variety of such symptoms, many brought on by upbringings nearly unmentionable. "Take your time," he says quietly.

Twitcher settles in and thumbs the trigger. The weapon explodes into life and sends a stream of rounds streaking down range. The old VW shudders under their impact.

"Looks good," Franks says. "Once more. Give it a long burst."

Twitcher depresses the trigger for a full five seconds. The pulsating recoil shoots through the handles and travels up his pudgy forearms. Downrange, the target quivers and dances under the onslaught. It sends up a generous cloud of dust when the firing stops.

"Works just fine," Frank observes. "You get what you pay for. Right?"

"Yeah, right," agrees Twitcher, who struggles to stand up under the burden of his ample belly.

Frank returns the unfired ammunition to the cache while Twitcher transports the weapon and tripod back to the tailgate. That done, Frank joins him to settle up.

"Good as new, wouldn't you say?" Frank claims.

Twitcher nods earnestly. "Yup."

"Well then, that'll be the two fifty I quoted your boss." Online, the part costs around thirty-five dollars, the balance is the price of anonymity.

"You got it." Twitcher fetches his wallet and pays with two hundreds and a fifty.

Frank climbs into his cab. "You be sure and tell Captain Bob thanks for the business."

"Yeah, sure." Twitcher watches Frank take off, the dust from his truck backlit by the late afternoon sun.

5

Mark Stennis checks his attire in a washroom forty-two floors above where the Hudson and East Rivers take on the Upper Bay. He wears a Zegna suit of muted blue, a white Brioni dress shirt and an Armani tie done in a subtle herringbone. An ideal combination for his presentation to the executive team's quarterly meeting on the strategic direction of Stennis Partners, a company focused on the private equity sector of the financial world. At present, it has 120 billion dollars' worth of assets under management, and more all the time.

Today's strategic meeting will tackle the perennial question: What are the fattest acquisition targets going forward? While venture capital firms constantly search for the Next New Thing, private equity seeks out companies already up and rolling and at least modestly profitable. The general idea is to acquire a controlling interest with money put up by an investment group, and then to trim and shape the enterprise for sale a few years down the road. With a little luck, you engineer it so the company pays back the cost of acquisition before it's even sold. For Stennis Partners, the basic trick is to pick companies in industries that are primed for exceptional growth. If you do it right, they become like the proverbial boats on a rising tide. All you have to do is keep them safely and profitably moored while you reconfigure and often merge them for maximum returns.

Mark gives his tie one last cinch and heads down the hall to the firm's lobby, an exquisitely designed space with museum-quality art and hand-woven carpets. He can see through several layers of glass to the main meeting room, with its curved windows that look out on The Statue of Liberty and Ellis Island. Several people are already there. One of them is his father, Roger Stennis. Founder, patriarch, Chairman and CEO of Stennis Partners. Also

Apex Predator, a trait well understood by all who will attend this meeting. Pitiless eyes of gun metal gray, with a scowl permanently carved into skin ruined by too much sun.

As Mark enters, he exchanges perfunctory nods with his father. Anything more would fuel the fires of nepotism. He shakes hands with several others and exchanges the required pleasantries: Your wife still want that boat? Your daughter left for Harvard yet?

They see right through it, of course. He is not a pleasant person in the least and has no intention of ever becoming one. His father had provided the necessary template, and he is well along in developing it to a new extreme.

The room fills, the meeting launches, and he surveys the dozen people attending. Ten males, all in their late sixties. Two younger females, a nod to gender inclusion. The men went way back with Roger, who rewarded loyalty with power. Other younger hustlers might bring in more money and were compensated for it at bonus time but held little sway over the careers of their co-workers.

When Mark's turn comes, he goes to the front and picks up a controller linked to the big screen showing his PowerPoint presentation. He does what most tomes on public speaking recommend. He scans his audience and makes quick eye contact all the way around the table. They hate him. They want him to fail, right here in front of his father. But they know he won't, which makes it even worse.

He starts out in a confident, measured tone. What we're always looking for, he reminds them, is an industry with large profit potential but a scattered playing field, with each operation still pretty much on its own. Through a shrewdly engineered set of acquisitions and mergers, the participating companies can be reshaped into new entities with considerably higher market value. As it turns out, the so-called Fertility Industry is in the early stages of this consolidation phase. It revolves around a loose assemblage of in vitro fertilization clinics that provide the means for childless couples of all stripes to bring a baby into their lives. In the aggregate, it's become a multi-billion-dollar industry, spanning all kinds of services and technologies. IVF clinics, egg banks, long-term storage, genomics testing, surrogate selection, financing, legal services and medications.

The trick for Stennis Partners, he goes on, is to delve down into this universe and spot the prime suspects: those run by doctors who want to focus on medicine and see the business side as a stressful distraction. Private equity provides a lucrative solution. You let the businesspeople come in, assume management and plot a path to substantial growth, in which you participate.

He does a wrap-up and asks for questions. None are asked. Yes, they truly loathe him, even when they know he's on to a good thing. No matter. When he eventually takes over, he will devise ingenious means to guarantee that each suffers intensely in their own special way.

Besides, he did receive one acknowledgement – the only one that counts – from his father. Mark knew the precise curvature of the scowl welded on the old man's face. After the wrap-up, it relaxed just slightly, which was about as close to a smile as you would ever see on the face of Roger Stennis.

The balance of the meeting becomes pro forma, and at its conclusion everyone files out except for father and son.

"I see some potential in your assessment," Roger tells his son. "Put a couple of people on it and let's see where it goes."

"Will do."

"Good." The elder Stennis turns and leaves. There is nothing more to say.

Roger Stennis looks down on Battery Park from his office window. His son's presentation this morning showed promise, which was good because he was never going to win a popularity contest. But then again, neither was his father. Respect, yes. Adoration, no. Affection, absolutely not. Personally, he considers his net worth of several billion dollars more than adequate compensation for the loss. Money translates to power, power to dominance, and dominance to survival. If you don't live to tell the tale, it's like you've never lived at all.

His son hasn't always shown the best judgement. There was an incident some years back that brought the family to the brink of public ruin. Mark had just bought a brand-new Porsche, his third since graduating from law school, a 911 Turbo. While driving on the upper reaches of Long Island one afternoon, he had a minor collision in a parking lot that left a small scratch on his front bumper. The other driver immediately admitted fault, apologized and pulled out his insurance and license to exchange information. Not Mark. He saw the scratch, flew into a blind rage and beat the driver senseless. He might have killed him had not a couple of passersby pulled him off. From there, it got progressively worse. Several people with cellphones videoed the incident and provided the police with footage that included Mark leaving the scene.

But the ultimate problem was the victim, a shy teenage boy who stood five feet six and weighed one hundred fifteen pounds. A young man who suffered from a neuromuscular affliction that rendered him utterly defenseless under the circumstances. A kid who was very proud that he'd been able to overcome his challenges and recently get his driver's license. A defense attorney's worst nightmare.

Roger found out not through Mark, but through his son's personal attorney, who presented a highly filtered version of the incident: Mark had a fender bender and got into a fight with the other driver. A dumb thing to do, but those things happen. There's always a way to settle things up and he was already working on it. Later that evening, the lawyer phoned back. It was a lot worse than he originally thought. He'd talked to the local police, who emailed him a copy of one of the videos. He gave Roger the graphic details. Roger phoned his own personal attorney, a partner in a white shoe law firm, who said they would need to bring in a fixer and it wouldn't be cheap. It was not. In the end, it cost Roger two and a half million dollars to permanently extinguish the blaze.

Stennis looks back to the Hudson and the Jersey shore out his window. He already knows what all the counselors, therapists, life coaches and the like would tell him. They would say that, by any reasonable standard, his son had repeatedly proven himself a monster. They would say that he, Roger, was in denial about it. They would say he harbored latent guilt, that he was responsible. They would say he had to confront it and let it go. They were wrong, of course, because deep down, he harbored no guilt whatsoever.

Why should he?

6

The funeral home turns out to be pretty much what Gavin expected. The city had declared his mother officially indigent, which made her eligible for a burial assistance program. It designated this particular place in the Jamaican sector of Queens as the vendor of choice, partly because it was nondenominational. No need for an elaborate service to satisfy the religious leanings of family and friends. No reason to be buried in sacred ground. A simple casket viewing and a quick trip through the cremation furnace would do just fine. His mother would approve; she had always led a distinctly nondenominational life.

Gavin sits in a little second-floor chapel on a folding chair in the back row. He has a clear view of the casket and flowers because the only other person present is an older gentleman of color. On his way in, he chatted with the fellow and learned that he was from Guyana. The man spoke a random mix of Guyanese Creole and English, but Gavin was able to piece together enough to understand why he was in attendance. He served as a maintenance man at his mother's apartment building and was the one who discovered her body, which had spent three lifeless days on an old couch. The fellow somehow felt obligated to help complete the transport of her soul to the world beyond, as he called it. Gavin thanked him for his attendance.

Later, on the way out, he checks the guest registry. Empty. Apparently, no one else had attended.

On the cab trip to his late mother's apartment, he puts himself on trial for maternal neglect. The evidence is compelling but not overwhelming. He was her only child and therefore the sole party responsible for her well-being. He visited maybe once a month and stayed only briefly when he did. Each visit opened a hole in his heart that took days to close. His mother, his only relation, alone, friendless and chronically drunk. Would he share her fate? Was it somehow genetic? Was it lurking out there somewhere ahead on his own timeline? He still has friends, still has lovers. But will they eventually float off and leave him suspended in a pitiless vacuum? He shares this fear with no one, though he probably should. Maybe someday, but not right now.

He puts the thought aside as the cab pulls up to the apartment complex, a dull brick monolith a dozen stories high. The manager has been informed of his mother's passing, and Gavin signs a release to get the keys. He ascends to the tenth floor in a cramped elevator heavily scented by decades of humanity and travels down the hall to her apartment on a frayed carpet decorated with interlocking rectangles.

Once inside, he looks to the chronic mess in the kitchen and the clutter of old tabloids on the dining room table. A thin layer of house dust covers it all. He sighs and heads directly to a small desk and file cabinet that face the back wall. They probably hold whatever documentation remains of his mother's tattered life. It's as much as he can deal with right now; he'll come back later to clean the place up. He finds a cardboard box in the kitchen, dumps the contents of the file cabinet into it and leaves.

It's raining by the time Gavin gets back to his apartment in Brooklyn, which seems appropriate. The place is small but comfortably furnished and decently maintained, considering that he's a single adult male under thirty. Since he's always out on assignment, anything bigger would be pretty much a waste. He plops the cardboard box down in the breakfast nook and starts to fish out file folders with their dog-eared tabs. Early on, he finds one labeled "LEGAL," which seems like a good place to start. If he's lucky, he might find some clue to one of the longstanding and central mysteries surrounding his life on earth. He has no idea who his father is. According to his mother, he deserted her several months before Gavin was born. She'd always painted him as a worthless jerk; and to illustrate her point she went on to marry three more worthless jerks in a row. Fortunately for Gavin, none were abusive to either of them. They all quietly marinated in a stew of self-loathing brought on by their perpetual failures.

During his mother's rants, she'd always referred to his father only as "Jimmy," with no surname. As a kid, he'd never thought to ask. By the time he was an adult, they had both dropped the subject of Jimmy entirely. On Gavin's birth certificate, the space for Father simply said "Unknown."

He opens the legal folder and starts thumbing through the documents. They account for all four divorces, several liens, two bankruptcies, a suspended license and an ancient lawsuit settled out of court. The last item is a sealed envelope, with "For My Son's Eyes Only" handwritten on the front. A thick cloud of dread settles over Gavin when he sees it. He considers trashing it but can't do it. There's a sliver of a chance it will somehow be redeeming.

He tears it open and pulls out a single handwritten page in his mother's wobbly script.

Gavin,

You are all that's left of us, so I can't imagine anybody else going through my stuff and finding this. If you're reading it, it means I'm either dead or very close to it. Let me say right off that you deserve to know the truth about yourself. I never told you while I was alive because I saw very little point in it. You did way better than I expected with your life and didn't need me feeding you anything that might bring you down.

I am not your mother. Let me explain why.

After Jimmy split, I was really desperate for money. You hadn't come along just quite yet. That happened a short time later when I read an article about being a surrogate mother and discovered you could get paid for it. Normally, I would have said no but then I came up with this great plan. While I carried the baby, I could use the time to write a really great novel based on my life with Jimmy the jerk.

So, I went to a fertility clinic and found out how it worked. People come in that can't have a baby and they collect their sperm and eggs and mix them together in a test tube or something. If it works, they get the start of a baby, and sometimes they need to plant it in a mom other than the original. In this case, that mom was me.

I was never told who the parents were, which was really odd, but the lawyers set it up that way at their request. The only time they would be around was during the birth, and then they would take the baby off to wherever. Because it was a little weird, I was given a generous bonus. In the end, it didn't matter because they were killed in a plane crash before you were ever born. After I had you, the paperwork let me either keep you or put you up for adoption. I love you, Gavin. I just couldn't let you go. Someone else might have done a much better job with you, but they would never be as close to you as I was after you spent nine months in my belly.

You should know that I did get a lawyer and tried to find out who the real parents were, even if they were dead. It didn't work. I suppose I could say that I am sorry for all this, but I am not. It's just what happened, that's all. No matter what you think of me now, I love you and always will.

Your mom

Gavin puts the letter down, closes his eyes, and sits absolutely still. The only sound is the dribble of rainwater through a downspout outside his window.

It's just what happened, that's all.

He winds his way back through the letter's revelations. Even if he could identify the nominal parents, there's no way to ever know the details of his conception. There might have been a donor egg or sperm involved from someone else entirely. In the end, he struggles to absorb the only possible conclusion.

He's about as close to being nobody as is humanly possible.

7

Tracy makes sure to arrive five minutes early for the meeting with her boss, Arlene Papadakis, PhD. In most respects, the woman is quite tolerant and flexible, but not when it comes to punctuality. Arrive just one minute late, and you receive a gaze so withering it could ruin your entire day. The meeting has been called on short notice, but as chief of the Reproductive Statistics Branch of the Division of Vital Statistics, Arlene reserves the right to do so, although she seldom exercises it. At sixty, she's a veteran player at the National Center for Health Statistics, one of the dozens of entities that dwell within the administrative confines of the CDC.

Tracy checks her watch. One minute to go. She looks at the dozen empty chairs in the meeting room. Apparently, she's the only one attending, which puts her slightly on edge. And she gets no reassurance when Dr. Papadakis bustles in wearing a sour expression and plunks down her laptop before looking over to Tracy.

"Sorry," she says in a weary voice. "Didn't mean to interrupt your day, but something's come up."

"No problem," Tracy replies. In fact, she's relieved. It means the problem, whatever it is, didn't originate with her.

Arlene puts hands to her temples, plants her elbows on the table and stares down at its worn surface as she speaks. "There's a certain senator in the US Congress who has long been a good friend of the CDC, particularly at budget time. Always came off as an altruistic kind of guy. Truly focused on the health and well-being of the average citizen. No quid pro quo or anything like that. Or so we thought. Turns out he was saving up all his dimes and nickels for a trip to the candy store."

"What kind of trip?" Tracy asks cautiously.

"It seems the senator has a good buddy who's a physician and partner in a couple of OB-GYN clinics and the good doctor has been whining about a drop-off in business. Can't quite figure it out. So, the senator, being a very generous sort, says he'll have the CDC look into it. And the director's office at the CDC says no problem, we 'll have our statistics center look into it, and our very own director's office says we'll have our reproductive statistics people look into it."

Arlene pauses and looks up at Tracy. "In case you haven't noticed, this thing is kind of like a funnel, and you want to guess what it narrows down to?"

"Me?"

"You. Sorry."

Silence. Both women understand the bind they're in. The National Center for Health Statistics employs about 750 people. Most take pride in the information they produce, which is gathered, analyzed and reported while adhering to highly rigorous standards. But this particular request is fraught with all kinds of statistical peril. There are about 23,000 OB-GYN doctors in the country, and on average each delivers about 100 babies per year, or about eight each month. Over time, this suggests that they also see about eight new pregnancies each month. But if you dive any deeper, the noise starts to set in.

For starters, the Center does not formally gather information on new pregnancies, which would be an arduous and not particularly productive undertaking. What's far more important is how these pregnancies turn out. How many infants survive? How many are premature? How many experience complications? Information of this sort is usually recorded in local medical and civil records, which the Center gathers and scrutinizes on a regular basis. But the onset of the process, when a lone sperm fertilizes a waiting ovum, eludes the official grasp.

Next comes the randomness of the world in general. In any given month, a doctor might see nine new patients instead of eight, or seven, or six for that matter. In the aggregate, this number should smooth out to eight, but not in the short run. To further muddy the water, each clinic may stray from the overall average. One in populous California may average nine over time, while one in rural Vermont may average seven. Statistical analysts like Tracy use various analytical tools to figure out how big a sample you need to reach an acceptable answer. Things like confidence intervals, standard deviations, alpha values, and the like come into play.

"So, I'm on my own?" Tracy asks.

"Wouldn't be right," Arlene says. "We both know this is a real turkey, but we have to give it our best shot. I can give you three people on a temporary basis to sort it out. Know why you got this one?"

"Not really."

Arlene smiles for the first time. "Because you do good work. Simple as that. Next step for you around here is to manage a team, and this gig will give you a baby step in that direction while you work on a PhD."

"Well, thanks," Tracy responds. She knows that the upper stratum in this division is populated exclusively by PhDs. For her, a doctorate remains several years out, at best.

"Now who's this doctor in distress and where are the two clinics?" she asks.

"Rudolph. Dr. Emmet Rudolph. One clinic is in Boston, the other in Atlanta. He hops back and forth between them. He's expecting us to be in touch, of course. He's promised full cooperation from his staff. I'll shoot you a memo with the details. Now how soon can you get on this?"

"I'm wrapping up a mortality estimate. I should have it done by tomorrow. Then I'm clear."

"Good." Arlene springs up and grabs her laptop, which she has never bothered to open. Tracy suspects this happens quite often. Dr. Papadakis carries most of what she needs in her remarkable head.

"Keep me up on it," Arlene says as she darts out the door. "Good luck."

By late afternoon Tracy has sent an email to her three new charges, welcoming them to the team. HR is not her strong suit, so she edits it several times before sending. She spends the remainder of the day on how to best define the workflow and parcel the assignments. By now she's received Arlene's memo on the two clinics involved and hopes their staffs are competent enough to supply what's needed in a timely fashion.

Once home, she tosses her purse down on the kitchen island and pours herself a glass of Chardonnay. Her apartment is furnished in a spare and rectilinear fashion, with several prints of Edward Hopper paintings hung on sand-colored walls. One in particular catches her attention. A woman sits alone on a small bed with arms folded over raised knees. She wears a pink slip that exposes her legs to the morning sun coming in through an open window. The light seems somehow harsh and bathes her in an ineffable loneliness as it rakes across her stoic features.

A baby.

She's thinking about a child she has yet to have, the child she may never have, the one she needs to define her presence in a space of unimaginable dimension.

Tracy resonates with this woman's soul and internalizes her timeless yearning. It's ironic that her job entails endless numerical descriptions of babies and mothers, yet the subject remains so personally remote. She understands that babies represent an intersection of hormonal, evolutionary and emotional forces, all playing upon each other in patterns of boundless complexity. She also knows that the advent of effective birth control sent a strong ripple through these patterns. Most women now have choices. They can opt for interesting careers in lieu of children – at least, for a while. But the majority will eventually "hear the clock ticking."

At twenty-five, Tracy's clock is not within earshot yet, so she has sidelined the issue. But the woman in the painting raises it to a haunting murmur. It causes her to speculate on what would happen if her clock simply shut down. Permanently. Would she be filled with regret; would she feel deprived of the most basic of biological rights?

Her musings are cut short by the Metrorail three stories below as it rumbles south toward the Capitol. On the far side of its twin tracks, a blanket of trees covers the hillside of a large park. Most remain green, but a few are starting to show a little rust as Fall approaches. Should she count herself among them? She takes one last sip of her wine and her query dissolves into the evening sky beyond.

8

Wayne Bauer watches the heavens open, and the final truth revealed.

He stands atop Lone Mountain, 4,000 feet above the Nevada desert, where the town of Tonopah twinkles to the east. To the west, the headlights of highway rigs roll through the silence far below him on Route 6. The night wind nips at his ears and rustles his ponytail. He wears a thin beard atop a lanky frame capped by blue-gray eyes still burning bright at fifty-two.

The truth presents itself in the dense configuration of overhead stars, so numerous that they nearly overwhelm the traditional constellations. Wayne has come here often, looking for the stars to form intelligible patterns, much as letters form words and words form sentences. He always drives his old Jeep up the same canyon roads, then hikes up along the ridges to his destination at the summit. No one comes here at this hour, this most sacred of hours. He stands alone in communion with the firmament.

It happens quite suddenly. Stars of different luminance and coloration weave themselves into intricate patterns in a language of dazzling complexity. A language completely non-verbal but utterly comprehensible to Wayne. It carries a message of great urgency and import, a message that imprints itself into the deepest recesses of his brain. He, of all the billions upon this stricken planet, has been chosen to deliver it.

Later, he will barely remember stumbling down the descending ridges and driving off toward his home, a trailer park on the desert floor, some five miles distant. Once there, he deliberates about going to his job in the morning at the Comfort Inn, where he works as a maintenance man. He needs to collect himself and chart his way forward, all at a time when he's ground his relationship with management down to the thinnest of edges. They don't understand the daily burden he carries, the constant pressure. Clogged toilets, broken TV connections, hobbled air conditioners, wobbly exercise machines, washing machines run wild. He alone stands as the barrier against total mechanical chaos.

Every night he retreats to his little trailer, eats a budget TV dinner, drinks a solitary beer and loses himself online. Quanon, they call it, although none can definitively define it. A lurid core of speculation and theories occupies its center. Repellant, yet fascinating. Absurd, yet insanely plausible. Hillary, the Pope, Obama, the Dalai Lama, George Soros and numerous others. All part of an international cabal that kidnaps children, kills them, rips out their adrenal glands and extracts a drug called adrenochrome, which will extend their lives indefinitely. The true genius of Q is that it invites you, the spectator, to pile on with your own enhancements. Theories beget new theories. Rumors warp into tales, each darker than the last. All shared and dissected by an enthusiastic following across a wide spectrum of social media.

Early on, during Quanon's 4chan days, Wayne had eagerly joined the fray. He made what he considered highly constructive comments on content submitted by others. Hillary had a malignant brain tumor. Tom Hanks hung out in public restrooms, looking for targets of opportunity. JFK would rise to lead a zombie army.

But when he put forth his own pet theory, it drew very little attention, and that has always bothered him. Like so much in the Q world, his concept starts grounded in reality and then moves on to carefully crafted speculation. It centers on the Tonopah Test Range, an isolated Air Force base thirty miles southeast of town. Over the years, it's earned the label Area 52 because of its association with the testing of super-secret aircraft technology. But Wayne thinks it has superseded that role and is now involved in the development of some kind of doomsday device. What kind? Hard to tell. Wayne's technical depth is limited, so better that he focuses on the higher issues.

In any case, Area 52's doomsday mission makes it of great interest to the aliens who track this apex of human folly.

He has no doubt that these transcendent beings actively monitor every aspect of Area 52. For some time, he has envisioned himself as the mediator between these uber-beings and the multitudes who don't want to see doomsday any more than the aliens do. To this end, he has repeatedly climbed Lone Mountain and waited for a sign.

And tonight, he got it.

The entirety of their message nearly overwhelms his modest cerebral capacity. Part of his mission is to reduce it into a form that will resonate across the broadest sweep of humankind. Once back in his trailer, he furiously scribbles it out on tablet paper. He carefully tears off the sheets and saves them. He knows that they will eventually hang framed in some future museum on a distant world.

We live on a troubled planet, Wayne informs us. The global elite have stooped to nearly unspeakable evil as documented by Q. They have murdered young innocents in pursuit of life everlasting. And Q is just the start. Along the way, they have driven the world's ecosystem to the brink of collapse through massive pollution in league with global warming. And let the population swell to over eight billion people to generate ever more consumers. All these facts are well known by now. But what is not known is the deepest secret of all, the purpose of Area 52, where a new generation of doomsday weaponry represents the ultimate folly of mankind.

Enter the aliens, superior to us in more ways than we can ever know.

They regret to inform us that we are subservient to a cosmic justice far beyond our primitive cognition. We have been found collectively guilty, and the penalty is the utter and inevitable extinction of humanity. Not through Area 52, but through some unknown force that will soon be upon us. We will perish not by our own hand, but by one greater than our limited understanding allows.

However, even in this supreme moment of darkness there is hope. To each that truly accepts this dismal fate there will be an afterlife of salvation and joy. To those who don't, eternal damnation awaits, especially for the cabal of the global elite.

Wayne leans back from his laptop's keyboard. He has a vague conception of the End of Days, as predicted by various evangelical groups, but sees no contradiction nor plagiarism on his part. In fact, he considers his work simply a refinement and clarification of what has gone before. The final truth, as it were.

Yes! That's it. The Final Truth. The gospel to end all gospels.

And what of those who embrace it? What will they be called? Wayne knows instantly. It takes no thought at all. Just a gush of pure inspiration.

The Order of Atonement.

9

"Tell me this, Gavin," says Mindy Harlow. "You think global warming is behind it?"

"Could be," Gavin responds, "But when you're stuck in a downtown that's being swallowed by the Atlantic Ocean, it's not top of mind."

Mindy nods with a smile. "I'm sure it isn't." She's referring to Gavin's feature piece for INN on the Category 6 storm that devastated Miami, which calls into question the fate of coastal cities everywhere. In the argot of the day, it's become an existential issue.

The feature was a resounding hit and given priority placement on every INN platform throughout the world after being translated into a dozen languages. They even put him in front of the camera for an interview, limited to about 60 seconds, of course.

"It's a basic fact that hurricanes feed off warm air," Gavin says, "and the warmer the air, the more badass the storm will probably be. You take it from there."

"I will," Mindy says, "And while we're at it, I'd like to get an option from you to cover the apocalypse for us."

"We can work that out," Gavin quips back. "But keep in mind that your viewership may be severely diminished by then."

"Gone but not forgotten," Mindy responds. "We'll always be grateful for the mountain of revenue we received through the zillion ads they so faithfully responded to."

Gavin can't help but smile. Her witty cynicism is well earned. As a veteran producer in her early forties, she's seen it all. Literally. Which is odd, because she looks like someone's mom who spends her days fixing lasagna and ferrying her kids to God knows whatever.

"So, what's next?" she asks, with Central Park sprawled out the window behind her to the east. The INN offices that face the park only go to producers with a certain level of gravitas, which she clearly merits. She's developed a knack for spotting journalists like Gavin who consistently deliver compelling stories that always fit the zeitgeist. She'd love to snag him and put him on staff, but he's made it clear that's not going to happen. Much better to have him as a contractor than not have him at all.

"I'm thinking about an investigative piece, a business story," Gavin tells her.

"A business story? That's never been your kind of thing. So why now?"

"I recently came into contact with the so-called fertility industry. The people that do in vitro fertilization, among other things. You know about that?"

"Only that they fire up babies in the lab then put them into mommy to grow."

"Yeah, that's roughly it, but the reality gets really complicated. Anyway, the babies aren't the issue. As always, it's the money."

"How so?"

"In vitro fertilization goes by IVF for short. When it first came on the scene it attracted a lot of medical people because it's upbeat and life affirming. You can start a clinic and help barren people have the babies they'd always longed for. Who can argue with that? Over time, the number of clinics grew, but on the business scale, they stayed relatively small. These people were out to build babies, not business empires."

"So, what's the problem?" Mindy asks. "Where's the story?"

"Before you know it, IVF becomes a multi-billion-dollar industry. Also a very lightly regulated one. So now we have two of Wall Street's favorite words back to back. Billion and under-regulated. The big money guys show up. An industry founded for the most altruistic reasons begins to get trampled in the greed stampede. And who ultimately pays the price? The customers, of course. The cost of starting a new human life from scratch is on the rise, and who knows where it will end. The financial markets are starting to dictate the price of satisfying the most fundamental of human needs. Doesn't sound right to me, and I don't think it'll sound right to your audience. So, there you go."

"There you go," Mindy repeats. "It just might work. Let me think about it."

"Don't think too long," Gavin warns.

"You mean, you might walk down the street and pitch somebody else?" Mindy asks. "I'm hurt."

"And I'll be hurt if you don't run with this," Gavin says. "So let's stop all the pain before it even starts."

Mindy smiles. "How noble of you. Tell you what. Write up a quick proposal, and I'll send it upstairs to the boss of bosses."

"With your imprimatur?"

"Yes, with my imprimatur. Now what else is new with you?"

Gavin declines to mention the tale of his highly unlikely birth and how it might compromise his objectivity in this particular instance. He moves on to safer territory. "Same as always. I spend my time between gigs working on the book."

Mindy knows all about the book. "Got a title for it yet?"

"Not yet."

He wishes he did. A book's title can mean life or death, especially online, where many attention spans have shrunk to that of a gnat. It has to be something about militias in the US, because that's what he is investigating. He's read dozens of books and hundreds of articles on the subject and observed that almost all reflect the divisive politics of the age. The view from the right is one of patriotic warriors standing up for what is truly "American" even if they seem a little extreme at times. But what is truly "American" differs widely, and a generalized fog starts to roll in. At the other extreme, the view from the left is often one of hate-filled racist misogynists bigots hell-bent on destroying democracy as currently practiced. Armed young thugs patrolling state capitols and storming the US Capitol in a bid to bring down a duly elected government.

But something's missing in all these accounts. When they're not marching, strutting, and oiling their firearms, who *are* these people? What drives them to embrace political extremism in the first place? Do they share a common psyche? What are the forces pushing them as individuals toward such cataclysmic conclusions? The media has fixated on the most volatile and violent among them, like the Proud Boys, as illustrative of the entire tribe. But Gavin suspects that there is a much larger story to be told, one with considerably more depth and complexity.

After much research and deliberation, he decided that the only legitimate course of action was to embed himself within one such group. Not as an informant or spy, but as someone openly seeking a deeper truth about them. He started his search by going online and contacting a dozen or so militias. About half rejected him out of hand. Among the militant right, journalists are widely regarded as low-life self-seeking scum. But the other half were fascinated with the audacity of his proposal and willing to engage in at least some dialog.

Eventually, he settled on an outfit called Freedom First, headed up a middle-aged man named Frank Fanno, an Army veteran with considerable combat service. Early on, Fanno told him that as long as Gavin had nothing to hide, neither did he. It was agreed that Gavin was free to attend their monthly meetings and military training exercises, as his schedule permitted. Gavin knew this would involve a lot of travel but felt it was worth it. Freedom First was headquartered in a little town called Roundup far out on the eastern plains of Montana. It meant flying from JFK to Salt Lake City then to Billings and renting a car to reach Roundup, which had some minimal lodging available. By now, Gavin has made the trip at least ten times, and is starting to get a feel for life inside of Freedom First. But it's just a start.

"How about Nazi Cowboys?" Mindy suggests. "You can't miss with 'Nazi' in the title."

"I'll take it into consideration," Gavin replies. Unfortunately, she's probably right.

10

Allison Wertz has no idea what kind of plane they're flying in. It has to be a jet of some kind because she didn't see any propellors when she boarded from the tarmac at Reagan International. Nor does she know they are now 20,000 feet over southern Pennsylvania. What she does know is that her friend Terra's father owns the plane and that it will soon land at Newark International, where a town car will be waiting for them. In all, a very magnanimous gesture on Terra's part. She and Allison go back ten years to a private girls' high school in Westchester, along with Heather and Amber. The nuns disliked them intensely. In their senior year, Amber furtively diddled herself to a climax in history class, while Allison and Heather silently cheered her on. To this day, they speculate about whether the nun teaching the class knew what was happening. The prevailing view is that she did but failed to act because she frequently indulged in lewd fantasies involving young girls.

"So what's new at work, babe?" Terra asks Allison. "How soon you gonna run the place?"

"Any time I want," Allison retorts. "Which means just about never." She takes a snort of coke from a bullet of sterling silver and tempers it with a generous sip of pale wine. "Especially on Saturday night."

"Yo, chill time," Terra adds. What she lacks in intellect she makes up for with an abundance of libidinal energy. "You see that guy again? The one who hit on you at that roof bar on the Mall?"

"Nope, but I got his card, so I can haul him in anytime I'm ready."

"Amen," Terra says. They raise their glasses in a toast that drains the bottle of Corton-Charlemagne Grand Cru, a vintage both esteemed and exquisite.

Almost as exquisite as they are.

. . .

"Pull over here," Terra directs the town car driver. "This is it. Gotta do a little culture before we play." All four women disembark into the mild night air in the East Village. "It's gonna be a while, so chill somewhere," Terra tells the driver. "We'll call when we're ready."

They dodge the busy current of sidewalk traffic and enter an art gallery featuring the opening of a newly ascendant sculptor. The mix of patrons looks typical. Young men bearded and ponytailed. Older men in professorial garb. Young women with piled hair and backpacks. Older women bespectacled and bejeweled.

A placard on an easel displays the exhibition's title: Dimensional Transformations.

The works themselves rest atop white cylindrical displays carefully lit from above. Each features a roughly spherical wad of crushed aluminum foil encased in a cubic foot of clear resin. "I like the honesty," one young man is telling his bookish date.

Allison and friends wind through the exhibit with contemptuous amusement and gather near the exit. "Okay, we got our culture hit," Amber says. "Club time. Let's get going."

They head out up Orchard Street into a dense mix of the hip, unhip and never hip on the sidewalk. Youth in abundance. Upscale casual fashion abounds, all very organic, just as the zeitgeist dictates. Three blocks later, they arrive at a modest storefront, identified only by an unassuming sign giving the address. They enter into a foyer with a heavy oak door and a keycard lock. An overhead video camera scrutinizes them while Terra inserts her card, and the door opens to a softly lit room with a bar on one side and a small stage at the rear. A jazz trio plays, each of them a virtuoso in their own right. A hostess takes them to one of the tables that occupy the middle space.

"I saw Johnny Depp here one time," Terra brags. "And Drake, too."

"Of course you did," Allison adds. "It's a fucking private club in the Village. Where else would they go? McDonalds?" She wonders how much Terra's father pays in dues for her to hang out here. Or does he even know? Many at the top of the financial heap float free from such details unless there's an egregious violation of parental trust. Unfortunately, Allison accrued a long string of such offenses, which ultimately led to her excommunication.

"Okay ladies, time to talk Mykonos," announces Heather.

Allison winces inside as the excited chatter begins. For the past three years, they've made an annual excursion to the Greek Island of Mykonos. By day, the place is perennial flypaper for the tourists coming off the giant cruise ships that regularly dock here. They take in the beautiful village with its winding streets, whitewashed buildings, and bluest of skies. But by sundown, the ships have sailed, and the streets fill with young party people in pursuit of erotic adventure. A privileged class of party people, for sure: Mykonos after dark is not a bargain basement tourist attraction. The accommodations on the hill above the village fetch premium prices.

Unfortunately for Allison, she no longer fetches a premium for anything. As of now, she utterly lacks the financial firepower to keep up the high life with her pals, who all remain firmly wired into their family money. At first, she drew upon the cash she had on hand after her patriarchal severance package. Once that was gone, she turned to three credit cards to fund her nocturnal party girl life. But all are now nearly maxed out, with no hope of raising her credit limit. At some point, she's going to have to tell her friends that Mykonos is no longer within her financial reach. It will be an ugly moment. They will be put in the embarrassing position of having to offer charitable contributions, with no end in sight. A woman working as a mid-level DC bureaucrat will never be able to keep up with them. Her only option will be to refuse their offers and fade away into some kind of middle-class hell where she watches from afar as they post their exploits on Instagram or Twitter and send her a card now and then.

"Well look who's here."

Allison turns to discover Mark Stennis standing slightly behind her. He gazes down with that smile that's almost a leer, but not quite. His entrance stops all the chatter at the table.

"Oh. Hi." Allison responds in a distinctly nonplussed manner. She's been here before and knows precisely how to play it. "These are my friends. Heather, Terra, and Amber." Each gives a polite nod, but no more, thus conceding the field to Allison.

Stennis acknowledges with a slight bow. "Ladies." And turns to Allison. "Good to see you again. I'm over at the bar with a friend so I've got to hit it. Have fun."

Allison gets the cue. He's told her where to find him. Now it's just a matter of timing.

"Cute," Heather comments as he walks away. Then the talk turns back to Mykonos. Something about this fabulous villa they have their eye on. Allison lets it roll for a minute, then stands up with her purse. "I'm off to the restroom. Be right back."

"Sure you will," Amber says, with a blatantly suggestive overtone.

Allison takes a circumspect route to the restroom, which is to the left of the stage. The music is really quite good. Probably all on a PhD track at Julliard. If she wasn't on the hunt, she might even lend an ear to it. In the restroom, she does a quick makeup check, then starts back on a route that will take her right past Stennis and friend.

She catches him at the bar, looking over to their table then back at his friend. He spots her on his next scan and raises his glass as she approaches. "Cheers."

"Cheers to you," she says and offers a tentative smile. Just a little, not too much.

"This is Tom. Works over at Chase."

Tom says hi, he's got a date waiting and leaves. Stennis pulls out a business card and holds it up. It's Allison's.

"Allison Wertz," he says. "Top of the deck. Now what can I get you?" He slides the card into the pocket of his casual sportscoat, a Boglioli, she guesses. Very nice. He wore a De Bethune watch when they met in DC but now it's a Patek Phillipe. Even better.

"A vodka on ice would be nice," she replies. "Clix, if they've got it."

"I'm sure they do," he says. "I mean, after all, that's why we're here, right?"

"Right." The difference is he can afford to be here. She can't. Not any longer. But beauty is a currency all its own, and she's very adept at managing it.

"I assume you're not here on business," he says as her drink arrives.

"You assume right. Girls' night out."

"Wish I could say the same, but there's a lot going on right now. Got to stay on top of it. How much do you know about private equity?"

"Not much. My father used to mention it now and then."

"Basically, you find something you like and buy your way in with someone else's money. Then you fiddle around with it and sell it for a lot more than you paid. Now what does your father do?"

"I really couldn't tell you. It has something to do with investments. Whatever it is, he seems to be really good at it."

"And what are you really good at?" he asks, suggestively.

"Depends on who's asking," she replies, coyly.

"It says on your card you're a communications specialist. That covers a lot of territory."

She shrugs. "It's just a stop along the way. We'll have to see where it goes."

"I guess that's true of all of us. Myself, I never thought I'd be knee deep in the fertility business. But there you go."

"You mean like artificial fertilization? Stuff like that?"

"Yeah, stuff like that." He goes on to give her a quick sketch of the IVF process and its various outcomes.

"So, you can really put all those things in the freezer?" she asks when he's done. "Don't they die when you thaw them out?"

"Not if you do it right. Eggs, sperm, embryos. They'll all last for decades. Good as new."

"Wow. So, you can become a mommy even way down the line."

Stennis nods. "Yes, you can." He looks over to Allison's friends at their table. "What's going on with you guys? You got a plan?"

Allison does a quick calculation. "Yeah, we got a plan." She can't desert them after Terra flew her all the way up from DC.

"And what about later?"

"Then I have to get back. We've got a plane waiting."

"A plane waiting!" He grins. "I could probably match that, but maybe not right now. You go ahead and hang with your buddies."

"You know, I was thinking about coming up again in the next week or two. How would that work?" she inquires.

"Might work fine. You've got my card, so just let me know."
"I'll do that."
Yes, she most certainly will.

11

A crude wooden stand next to the firing line holds a dozen AR-15 assault rifles. Fifty meters downrange, a row of six targets stands at attention, each a silhouette depicting the torso and head of a human figure. The weapons' owners sit cross-legged on a dusty tarp under the huge Montana sky. Each has procured their weapon at their own expense. If you're serious about Freedom First, it's the price of admission.

Every third Saturday, Frank Fanno brings one of his four squads out here for target practice and maintenance instruction. "If you can't take it apart and put it back together, you're not ready to shoot it," he tells them. As they work, he circulates, picks up parts at random and closely scrutinizes them. Oiled? Cleaned? Damn well better be. "If you wind up in a fire fight, you can't press pause like in one of your goddam video games," he tells them. "Your weapon jams, you're fucked."

Right now, Gavin sits behind the group as Fanno paces and occasionally pounds a fist into his opposing palm to make a point. He gestures toward the nearly flat horizon.

"See that land out there. Looks like it goes on forever, right? You could travel many a mile, and no one would stop you, no one would hang you up. Know what that's called? It's called freedom, and that's what this country is all about." He pauses and turns pensive. "At least, that's what it used to be all about. Now there's some numbskull politicians in Washington that want to tell us good people about how to live out here. And every year it gets worse. Every year, they get even more ideas about how we should behave."

Gavin is covertly recording Fanno's improvised speech with his cellphone. The man has an odd strain of charisma about him. He ranges from father figure to military commander, to preacher of a gospel all his own.

"So, why don't we push back?" Fanno continues "Why don't we tell them to fuck off and clean up their own goddam mess. Well, we've tried. Truth is, we don't want a fight. We're not looking for trouble." He pauses, looks out at the horizon then back at his men. "But if trouble comes, we've got to be ready," he says quietly. "Because if we're not, the day will come when they roll right over us. And why? Because they think we'll go down without a fight; they know we'll be easy pickings. You'll see tanks roll through Roundup, you'll see the highway filled with armored personnel carriers, you'll see the sky buzzing with combat choppers."

"Right now, you and I are all that stand between our homeland and that terrible day. They have to know that if they move on us, they will face a terrible retribution. We have powerful allies, my friends. At some point, the sky will open, and the Archangel Michael will look down upon us and draw his fiery sword and start cutting down all who oppose us, all those with evil in their hearts, all those who would enslave us with their false doctrines. And when the battle ends, he will take all of our fallen to their just reward in the heavens above."

Gavin notices that the men lean forward toward his words in rapt attention.

"And when will that day come?" He shrugs, palms extended, and relaxes. "I can't tell you that. No one can tell you that. And that's why we're here today. All we can do is be ready, be prepared. Each and every one of us."

He lets the moment settle, lets the prairie breeze take over. "Okay. Let's pack up."

Gavin sits with Skip and Larry in a booth in a little bar at the southern end of Roundup. Both were out at the firing range today with Fanno, and Gavin wants to get their slant on the man who leads them. He has enticed the pair with a couple of pitchers of beer, nachos, chicken wings and bull fries. They dig in with no hesitation.

Gavin takes them through the standard journalist's preamble before moving onto Frank. It seems that Larry has had some meth problems, and narrowly avoided incarceration a couple of times.

He works on a highway crew and rents a bedroom in a home about ten blocks away. Tall and thin with a prominent nose, he wears a black T-shirt with a Freedom First logo on the front. Skip is doing somewhat better and works as a clerk at a nearby auto parts store. He recently broke up with his girlfriend and moved in with his brother's family over on 9th Avenue. He has a dense beard that sprawls across a broad face with a pug nose. Both men still have on the same fatigue pants and combat boots they wore out on the range.

"I used to be in another unit over toward Missoula and it wasn't nothin' like Frank," Larry volunteers. "The commander was heavily into all that Nazi shit. Fascist, supremist, whatever. Used to send guys over to Portland to kick ass on Antifa, whoever they are. Never quite figured that part out. But we did have some pretty cool gear. Don't know who was footing the bill, but it was really cool stuff, like Kevlar vests and night goggles. I know it wasn't the commander. He ran a backhoe."

"And what's Frank think about the Nazis?" Gavin asks.

"He thinks they were a bunch of chickenshit snakes. Both the old ones and the new ones. Says the Lord had our backs when we kicked their ass in the big war."

"Okay, so what's Frank got in common with your old outfit?" Gavin asks. "I mean you're both militias."

"They both got it in for the Federal government. Big time. Both say it's just a matter of time before somethin' heavy goes down."

"I noticed that Frank used a lot of biblical references," Gavin says. "You okay with that?"

"Yeah, pretty much. The last place tried to throw in that kind of stuff, too; but it didn't come off like it does with Frank. With him it's the real deal. I can respect that."

"He's also the real deal when it comes to military stuff," Skip intervenes. "I mean he's got the shit to back it up. He was a combat NCO. He killed people. He saw people die. He saw them get punched full of holes."

"Do you think he cares about you guys getting punched full of holes?"

Both nod immediately. "Yessir, I think he does," Skip volunteers. "Otherwise, I wouldn't be here."

"Amen," Larry adds.

"Larry, you said your old unit was into white supremacy. What about Freedom First?"

Skip shakes his head. "No way."

"And why do you think that?"

"Because of Afghanistan."

"Afghanistan?"

"Yeah. Frank was out on patrol somewhere over there, and they got ambushed. He took a hit, a bad one. He went down behind a wall, and it looked like he was going to bleed out because no one could get to him without moving into the line of fire. But this Black guy named Lamar made a run for it anyway. He got all the way to Frank, applied a torniquet, and saved his life."

"Impressive," Gavin comments.

"Yeah, well it turns out there were 12 guys in his squad, all white except for Lamar. And when the chips were down, it was the Black guy who risked his life to save Frank. He took it as a message from God that he'd better not have it in for Black people ever again."

"So what religion is Frank?" Gavin asks.

Skip shrugs. "His own, I guess. He never talks about going to church or anything like that."

Gavin senses that he's probed far enough for one outing. He thanks them for their time, pays the bill and heads out. He's no closer to figuring out Frank Fanno than the day he met him.

12

Dr. Emmet Rudolph might just be on to something.

Tracy hates to admit it. She'd rather it was just another case of two old DC power players engaged in a little mutual back scratching. But the data from Rudolph's two clinics suggests otherwise, though not conclusively. Such is the nature of statistics, which often present possibilities instead of certainties.

As per Dr. Rudoph's instructions, both clinics had already collected the basic information on their patient load in terms of new pregnancies. Each employed about 15 doctors, who on average, saw about 8 new pregnancies per month over the past year. However, for any given month, this number could range between 6 and 10. If you strung these numbers out over the past twelve months, you got a fairly random fluctuation. For instance, the Boston clinic produced monthly averages of 8, 6, 7, 10, 7, 9, 6, 10, 8, 7, 6, 6 new pregnancies per doctor. On the surface, it appeared that there's no cause for concern, just the ebb and flow of life on the march. But not to Tracy. The two sixes at the end of the sequence were not business as usual. Given that each month has five possible values with a relatively equal chance of occurring, what were the odds that any two months would have the same value back-to-back? That is, 8-8, 6-6, etc. Overall, it turns out that any two months can be arranged in 25 different ways, such as 9-7, 8-6, 10-8, etc. But only one of these is 6-6, or 1/25th of the total.

In other words, there is only a 4% chance that the clinic would record its lowest pregnancy rate for two months running if everything was running at random. But there's more. It seems that the second clinic in Atlanta has reported the same result: a 6-6 pairing for the last two months. When Tracy factors this in, there is something less than a 1% chance of all this happening.

Tracy looks at the white board where she has drawn out the details of her methodology for her boss Arlene, who looks on with a deepening frown.

"So that's it?" she asks.

"That's it," Tracy replies.

Arlene types furiously on her laptop for a moment and looks up. "If this holds up, it translates to a 25% drop in pregnancies."

"Yes, it does. I know we need more data, but I thought you'd want to see this."

"More data, yes. How soon?"

"I've got my team reaching out to similar size clinics across the country. It's going to take a little time. They're not like us, and a lot of them are going to have to start from scratch to get the right numbers. We don't have any official way to lean on them, and if we come off looking urgent, we might start some really nasty rumors."

Arlene sighs. "God forbid." She gets on her cellphone to her assistant. "I need Allison Wertz in Room 34A. ASAP." She looks up to Tracy. "Do you have a decent confidence level yet?"

"I'm working on that right now," Tracy tells her. Basically, Arlene wants to know how certain Tracy is that her 25% estimate reflects the reality of the situation. The answer involves several mathematical operations, but the core concept can be easily demonstrated. If you take a washtub and thoroughly mix in the same number of red and white ping pong balls, and then scoop out a beer pitcher full, how close will it be to even red and white? Many scoops will form a cluster around the even number in the tub and some will land right on it. So how many scoops will you need to be reasonably certain of what is really in the tub? A standard set of calculations provides the answer. And in the end, the sample size becomes critical: If you scoop with a pail instead of a pitcher, you'll get closer to reality in less time. As Tracy's team accumulates more data, the confidence level continually increases.

"And what about Dr. Rudolph? How are we going to respond?" Tracy asks.

"We're going to stall. As long as we can. For right now, leave it to me. The last thing we need is for him to go running to his senator pal with this."

Allison enters and immediately makes her way over to Arlene. "Dr. Papadakis. How can I help you?" She does a quick aside. "Hi Tracy."

"You guys know each other. Good," says Arlene. "We have a potential problem. Tracy will walk you through the details in a minute. Right now, let me say that this conversation never leaves this room unless I say so."

Allison nods. "Understand." Her professional persona is nearly flawless, Tracy thinks. Serious, sober, concerned, attentive. God only knows what's going on behind it all.

"Okay Tracy, why don't you spell out the situation, minus the math."

Tracy presents an encapsulated version, starting with Rudolph's complaint and ending with the potential 25% drop. For once, Allison seems a shade blindsided.

"Wow," she says, but then quickly recovers. "How long before the health care people in general get on to this?"

"Hard to say," Tracy admits. "Right now, the trend is lost in the noise, but it won't stay that way. We need more data to come up with a reasonably accurate trend line that applies to the country as a whole."

"And in the meantime," Arlene tells Allison. "We need to assume we're definitely on to something, which means we need to figure out what we're going to say and who we're going to say it to. Lucky for us you've got some lead time. We need a contingency plan, both for within CDC and without."

"Got it."

"Don't commit anything to the network," Arlene commands. "Not yet. If this thing gets leaked, we're in really deep shit. Just collect your thoughts and be ready, okay?" She turns to Tracy. "You guys need to stay in touch on this. Keep me in the loop." Both nod and watch her scoop up her laptop and dart out the door.

"Is there anything else you can tell me?" Allison asks.

She's already looking for some kind of inside track that'll give her leverage, Tracy speculates. "Not really," she replies. "Aside from the math, you know as much as we do."

"It'll be really interesting to see where this goes," Allison comments.

"Yes, it will."

Allison looks at her watch. "I'm going to bow out. I've got someone picking me up right about now. Anything I can do to help, just let me know, okay?"

"Will do."

Tracy sits on a bench in a little green space across the street from the main NCHS entrance. It attaches to a five-level parking garage used by many of the employees, including Tracy. But tonight she wants to rest and reflect before jousting with the rush hour traffic. All signs point to a fertility trend of major significance, and she's the one who discovered it. She suspects that she's about to become a critical node in a circuit of boundless political maneuvering. Is she ready for that? Who knows?

The deep burbling of a powerful automobile engine breaks her concentration. She looks up to an exotic sports car cruising toward her with the top down, a Lamborghini or some such thing. Allison Wertz sits in the passenger seat next to a bearded male who looks vaguely familiar. It takes Tracy a moment to place him. He's the lawyer, the one from the rooftop bar off the Mall, who blatantly hit on Allison.

Apparently, it worked. As the pair pulls abreast of where she sits, Allison smiles and gives Tracy a broad victory wave, like the kind you might see in a vintage political parade. The lawyer pays Tracy no attention whatsoever.

Tracy manages a perfunctory smile but doesn't wave back as they pass on by. It just doesn't seem appropriate.

13

Allison would be livid if she knew about this, Tracy thinks. All contacts with the media, no matter how oblique, are supposed to go through her. Her role as Communications Director clearly spells this out to everyone in the organization. She acts as the supreme broker of information flow to the world at large and lets it be known in no uncertain terms.

That said, Tracy got a call last week from this journalist, a guy named Gavin Gray, who got her name from an old friend. Said he was gathering background on a story about the so-called fertility industry, and since she worked in the Reproductive Statistics branch, she might be a good general source. She honestly saw no harm in this but was discrete enough to suggest that they meet at some neutral location.

So now they sit in a very mid-range bar in a very mid-range hotel where Mr. Gray is staying as he treks around the capital, picking up scraps for his story. He tells her he's been over all the statistical data posted on the Center's website, but what he's looking for is a broad interpretation of what it all means and where she thinks it's going. She's more than happy to oblige but warns him it has to stay off the record. This kind of thing is typically reserved for the upper layers of management, who look down on high at all the data madly scurrying about below them and see patterns nearly beyond mortal cognition.

By the time she's finished her overview, the sun is setting, and the barroom lights have been throttled down to dim.

"Good stuff," Gavin comments. "Thanks for your help." He looks at his watch. "Wow. We've run kind of late. I think I owe you dinner."

Every woman knows that an offer like this raises their encounter to an entirely different level. But in this instance, Tracy doesn't mind. She finds Gavin Gray somewhat attractive and likes his serious yet relaxed demeanor.

"Sure. Why not?" she says. "But sooner than later. I've got a ton of stuff to do tonight. Work stuff." She's not kidding. This thing with the drop in pregnancies is starting to head toward crisis proportions. Every bit of data needs to be double-checked and triple-checked.

"It's sort of interesting the way people turn out," Gavin says as he takes a bite of salad. "Like you're a numbers person and I'm a word person. How much is genetic and how much is everything else? Does anyone really know?"

"I don't think the genetic side is everything," Tracy responds after a sip of wine. "But I do think it's more important than most people want to admit. If you flunked algebra twice, it's probably best not to pursue engineering. If you're five-foot-two, you'd better consider something besides the NBA. The good news is that it's a wide-open world, and there's lots of other places your genes can take you that'll work out just fine."

"And what about you?" Gavin asks. "Did you come by numbers naturally?"

"As a matter of fact, I did. My mother was a CPA and my dad taught high school chemistry. It was unlikely that I was going to be a poet, but not impossible. That's the thing, you see. It all comes down to probabilities. In the end, everyone's future is a giant casino game with an infinite set of outcomes. 'What's Behind Door Number Two?' Who knows?"

Gavin has to smile. "Maybe someone in a temple in the high Himalayas but not me, that's for sure."

"So much for the numbers," Tracy says. "Now what about words? How'd you wind up doing what you do?"

Gavin doesn't start with his inception, which could come across as almost unbelievable. Instead, he tells her about growing up with a single parent mother and then joining the military, where he discovered his knack for journalism, which has treated him pretty well, at least so far. He closes with his recent encounter with the Cat 6 Miami hurricane.

Tracy can't help but find the Miami episode highly entertaining. "That's quite a tale," she comments.

"We journalists prefer the word 'story'," Gavin corrects her. "A tale can be a complete fabrication. We try to work with fact, not fiction, at least most of us. It's the eternal search for truth, I guess. Sometimes easier than others."

"Pretty easy if you're in the middle of Category 6 hurricane, I'd think."

"You'd think right. But when you look into what caused it, things start to get a little fuzzy. Some people think global warming is actually a huge scam. Others think that hotter water doesn't necessarily mean bigger storms. Depends on who you ask."

"Well, I'm asking you, Mr. Gavin Gray. What do you think?" Tracy is rapidly approaching the threshold of intoxication.

"I think global warming is pretty much undeniable. The only real question is how fast. There's now a lot of evidence that it's speeding up."

"We'd call that an exponential curve," Tracy adds.

"Call it what you want, it's a bad deal. Pretty soon, we'll be living on borrowed time with no way to pay it back."

"Maybe we could take out an equity loan," Tracy teases.

"Yeah, well this time the equity is us. All eight billion of us."

Tracy represses the urge to tell him what she knows from work. It could be that the entire problem will soon take care of itself.

14

"You can call them God; you can call me Jesus. Whatever. Doesn't matter. It's all about the message, The Final Truth. That's all that really counts."

Wayne Bauer stands in front of two large driers that spin their loads into tumbling chaos in the laundry room at the Comfort Inn. He addresses two Latinx maids who stand in rapt attention on the far side of a portable laundry bin.

"I mean, look at you," he tells them. "You're good women. You work hard. You love your children. You don't deserve to suffer, no you don't. But you have to accept what's coming and then look past it, to your eternal salvation."

"And what is it that's coming?" one of the maids asks.

"I wish I could tell you that," Bauer says. "But it has yet to be revealed by those that watch over us. But I can tell you this: When it's over, not a single human being will walk the earth, not a one. There will be no more Día de los Muertos because there will be no one left to celebrate it."

Both of the maids' faces collapse into alarm. The Day of the Dead is deeply engrained in their world view.

"And what if we try to run?" the other maid asks.

"Then you will suffer a fate far worse than death. All who fail to accept The Final Truth will twist in torment until the end of time."

"¡Dios mío!" the first maid exclaims.

"But remember, those who watch over us have given us a way out. A very simple one. All you have to do is embrace what's coming and, in the end, you'll be transported to a world of ceaseless wonder. The choice is yours, señoras. Think of it this way: You will do just as Jesus did so long ago. You will accept all the sins of humanity and die for them, and then you will rise once more. I beg you to join us in this great and final adventure."

They all turn toward the sound of footsteps in the hall heading toward the laundry room. The assistant manager. He will want to know if Wayne has fixed the faucet in 16A and why the maids haven't finished 22A and 17B.

All three scatter, but the word now lives on within them.

Once home, Wayne swaps his utility clothes for a T-shirt, shorts and sandals. After snacking on some peanut butter crackers, he heads a few trailers down to where Nathan lives in a small utility unit. Nathan is technically under the thumb of his mom's sister, who lives in town. At age 16, this is a questionable but workable arrangement. When not skipping school, Nathan divides his time between video games, online pornography and coding websites for people like Bauer. All while stoned, of course.

Wayne finds him playing the latest version of Call of Duty. His thumbs fly over the controller's buttons and rockers as he stalks his way through a prototypical rural village and picks off targets of opportunity. "Nathan. How we doing?"

"Smokin', man," Nathan replies without taking his eyes off the screen.

"Not the game, dude. My site. How's it coming."

Nathan reluctantly pauses the game. "You gave me copy. That's great. But I need some graphics and some pictures. Won't work without 'em."

"Can't we just lift some stuff from the YouTube video?"

"Yeah. Maybe. I guess."

A short time back, they put The Final Truth up and it's already logged 357,000 views. The production workflow was quite primitive, even by YouTube standards. Wayne borrowed Nathan's camera and shot himself delivering a streamlined version of the new gospel and gave it to Nathan, who intercut it with pilfered shots of galaxies, nuclear blasts, ballistic missiles and biblical angels; then capped it all with a somber synthesizer track.

None of this set Wayne's production apart from millions of other videos on the same general subject. So why did he achieve the coveted viral status? Because he understood his unique role in the propagation of the Final Truth. In the end, he was simply the messenger. He had been chosen not to write it, but to put a human face on it. Much as Jesus with God the Father or Muhammad with Allah. The path from rough draft to polished script was guided by forces far more powerful than himself. When he looked at the notes he had madly scribbled right after coming off the mountain, they were only semi-coherent. He needed an editor that could add power, feeling and thrust to what he was trying to say. It led him, through Nathan, to the latest release of an artificial intelligence app called Cortica 3 and he fed it all his rambling notes. After just a few iterations, it produced a passable version of what the heavens had revealed to him up on the mountain. After a few more, he had a core message both urgent and powerful. Along the way, he became convinced that the alien presence in the sky had infused itself into Cortica 3's neural network and become an algorithmic Holy Ghost in the process. Its mystic presence quickly became an indispensable part of Bauer's apocalyptic crusade.

Now, Wayne has turned to the nebulous fringe of social media, where loosely confederated tribes of text boards and image boards congregate to allow anonymous contributions and content. The land of the legendary Q. He set Cortica 3 loose to devour millions of their posts and then synthesize idealized messaging for each board's user base, all the while adhering to the central tenets of the Final Truth. On some boards, the focus was Hillary's dead babies, on others, Evangelical salvation, and so on. He signed each post with the anonymous username Terminus, and waited to see what would happen. The basic measure of success was how many responses any given post generated. His pre-Cortica 3 messages had generated little or no attention, but once the AI came into play the numbers grew exponentially.

It was Nathan who first noticed an interesting phenomenon. To his discriminating eye, some of the online responses to the Final Truth appeared to be generated by the numerous other AI entities that now prowled the Web.

The Holy Ghost has company. Lots of it.

15

"How long ago did this thing start?" the Secretary of Health and Human Services asks.

"We're still refining our estimate," Tracy responds. "But it looks like about three months ago."

"And pregnancies across the country are now down by about 30 percent. Is that right?"

"To the best of our knowledge, that's correct. We're continually increasing our sample size to make sure we're giving you the most accurate number possible."

"I appreciate that," the Secretary says. As a member of the Cabinet, he resides atop the Mt. Olympus of the federal bureaucracy and answers only to the President, which allows him to assume a quite humane manner when addressing subordinates. This meeting on the top floor of the Health and Human Services building is no exception.

"Our real concern going forward is how to predict where this is going," the Director of the Centers for Disease Control adds. "Obviously, what's happening is unprecedented so all we can do is make some educated guesses."

"At some point, we're going to have to share what we have with the World Health Organization," the Secretary says. "From what you're saying, there's no way to tell if this thing is geographically confined or global. The sooner they're informed, the quicker we'll know."

"Which brings us to the matter of security," the CDC Director says. "The more people that are in on this, the greater the chance it will leak."

Tracy sighs. "I can't even imagine what will happen when the media get a hold of this."

"Nor can I," the Secretary grimly adds.

Arlene Papadakis, who has ceded the stage to the two titans, knows it's time to speak up. First, she turns to Allison Wertz. "I assume we're all buttoned up, at least for now."

Allison, ever the political player, shapes her answer in a way that avoids any personal liability. "Right now, only the people in this room and Tracy's team know what's happening."

"How many people on your team, Ms. Pallas?" the Secretary asks.

"Just three," Tracy answers. "They're collecting data from the field, from OB/GYN clinics across the country. I'm handling all the analytics, but I'm sure they have at least some idea of what's going on."

"They need to be reminded that they're under the blanket non-disclosure they signed when they started here," Arlene says.

"I can handle that," Allison volunteers.

Tracy winces. The implication is that she cannot.

"Alright, just get it done," the Secretary orders. "Now let's move on to the science side." He turns to a slight man of Asian descent who has yet to speak, a molecular biologist from the National Institutes for Health. "Dr. Chen, do you have any idea what the hell is going on here?"

"I wish I did, sir. But no, I don't. However, I do have an idea about how we should proceed. It involves the in vitro fertilization process. I assume that everyone here knows the basics. If Ms. Pallas is correct, many fertilization clinics will have extracted at least some eggs and sperm since the downturn occurred, and many of these should prove to be dysfunctional. They also have a very large store of eggs and sperm collected before the downturn started. Our challenge will be to compare the two sets all the way down to the molecular level and see if we can detect any differences. Finally, we will need to derive the cause of any differences."

"And how long might that take?" the Secretary asks.

"There's simply no way to tell," Chen responds. "It might take a few months; it might take a few years."

"And even then, all we've done is identify the problem," the Director adds. "The solution is a whole other issue."

A thick coating of gloom settles over the room. The Secretary manages to break through it. "You know, my grandmother used to say, 'Don't borrow trouble, there's plenty to go around for free,'" he tells them. "For all we know, this thing may have already bottomed out. In another few months, we might be back to business as usual. Right?"

Chen shrugs. "Could be."

Tracy hopes the Secretary is right but would not bet on it. She looks down at the report she's just authored on the current situation. Now that it's complete, it will go on a proprietary network to only the people in this room. When they read the addendum at the end, they will see why she's less than optimistic. The latest round of data from the field gave her enough information to plot the pace of the decline from the very beginning three months ago. It formed a downward curve that indicated the fertility drop was accelerating. And if you extended that curve down to zero pregnancies, it appeared there would be no more new babies on the way in just ten weeks, at least in the US.

By the time Tracy gets back to the office, she already has an email from the Director informing her that the World Health Organization has been brought into the loop. Their Director-General is flying in from Geneva tomorrow under tight security for a 10:00 am meeting, which Tracy is expected to attend and give a briefing.

She sinks back into her chair and closes her eyes. Truth is, it's exciting to be at the center of perhaps the biggest event ever in the human biosphere, but it's also exhausting.

"Tracy."

She opens her eyes to Allison standing by her desk. "I think I owe you an apology," she begins in a very contrite tone. "It's about the non-disclosures for your people. I shouldn't have barged in. I'm sure you can handle it just fine. I'm sorry. I'm just a little overwhelmed by all this, know what I mean?"

"Yeah, I know what you mean." Tracy would like to take this as a positive development but is hesitant to do so. If it becomes part of a pattern, then she'll reconsider, but not yet.

"It was interesting what Dr. Chen said about all the frozen eggs and sperm," Allison remarks. "Do you track on that kind of stuff?"

"A little, but not a lot," Tracy volunteers. "Right now, there's somewhere around a million frozen embryos in the US, and maybe fifteen thousand eggs. They're mostly stored in fertility clinics and at some dedicated storage sites."

"Wow. So I guess they won't have any trouble getting specimens for their research."

"I would think not," Tracy says.

"Okay, well once again, my apologies," Allison offers as she turns to leave. "You're doing great work. Keep it up."

"I intend to." Tracy senses an angle buried in there somewhere but can't quite tease it out. And right now she doesn't want to bother. It's time to phone up her pal Christina and indulge in a couple of wines.

Allison stands over the computer in the printing room and types in her security code, which clears her to print a single copy of Tracy's report. As a further precaution, all the copiers in the building read an encoded watermark to ensure her printout is not duplicated. In addition, this transaction is being logged and monitored by departmental security, but they shouldn't be suspicious. It's reasonable to expect that she needs a hard copy for reference purposes.

What's not reasonable is what happens next. She stuffs the printer's output in her handbag and heads for home.

16

Frank Fanno will never know what startled the cat.

He found it mewing a year ago outside the rear entrance to his shop and struck a bargain. Predation for sustenance. He'd seen mice darting over the soiled cement floor in growing numbers and knew the cat would put an end to it if a deal could be reached. After a little experimentation, he hit upon the right amount of cat food to keep the animal hanging around but always a little hungry. He named it Dizak after a village from his time in Afghanistan. The two of them soon reached a state of diurnal oscillation that kept Dizak fed and the floor clear of rodents.

With a pair of tongs, Frank pulls a forged knife blade out of a makeshift furnace that has rendered it an orange-tinted red. He carefully moves it toward a metal pot to undergo a process called quenching, which relaxes the metal's atomic structure, so it won't snap under stress. The pot is filled with canola oil kept at a specified temperature by a butane flame applied to its bottom.

The cat explodes into action just as Frank dips the blade into the oil. It darts along a shelf right above him and upsets a Tupperware container where a metal bar is soaking in kerosene. The highly flammable liquid spills out onto Frank's long-sleeved shirt and soaks his left arm. It continues on down to the metal pot and reaches the butane burner below, which propagates a chain of ignition that turns his left arm into a blazing pillar of smoke, flame and sizzling flesh.

He lets out an involuntary scream and instinctively grabs with his right hand at his shirt sleeve, but the searing flames keep him at bay. He staggers back and rips his entire shirt loose with his right hand and manages to peel it off his scorched left arm. He stumbles out the front entrance, leaving the shirt still burning on the floor.

The massive burn radiates horrible pain as he staggers across the gravel driveway and sinks to his knees by the roadside. Acute shock has already set in. His head swims, his blood pressure drops, his pulse weakens.

Dizak the cat watches it all from the open door. He sees Frank go down onto all fours just as a pickup truck appears and the driver runs to Frank's side. One look prompts him to pull out a cellphone and speak to it in urgent tones.

The cat has nearly lost interest by the time the ambulance pulls up and they gingerly load Frank in. After all, it's just about its prescribed mealtime.

What could be more important than that?

The ambulance takes five minutes to reach the ER at Roundup Memorial Healthcare. Enough time for Frank to look down at the thermal devastation that reaches from his shoulder down to his wrist. It's already turned a deep, glistening red with a few islands of white. They slide him out into the early evening sky and on into the building, where the ER staff awaits. The clatter of the gurney wheels, the clinical banter, and the parade of overhead lighting all seem extremely remote compared to his hellish arm. The ER doctor asks him how it happened, and she nods in sympathy as he explains as best he can. She tells him the majority of the burn surface is second degree and that he's very lucky he was able to rip his shirt off. Otherwise, it would be third degree and possibly beyond healing. He closes his eyes and nods. It's all trivial compared to his current agony. A burn of this size is a grave insult and puts him at war with himself. There is nowhere to hide.

Night has fallen by the time he's interred in the intensive care unit. A saline solution flows into his veins through an IV needle to keep him hydrated. A generous dose of an opioid painkiller accompanies the saline flow and provides an avenue of escape from the raw edge of suffering. His muscles unwind and his respiration slows as he stares up at the ceiling with its recessed lights. He becomes the sole occupant of a metaphysical borderland, neither here nor there. Someone dims the lights, and they recede into a seemingly endless space beyond the ceiling.

The stars come out. Thousands of them. They fill the void and give it meaning. Below them, the curvature of the Earth spans the entire horizon. White clouds float and curl over blue seas in a timeless dance of the elements.

A woman appears in the sky above. A beautiful woman in a shifting gown of bluish green. She gazes down with a beatific smile lit by the yellow brilliance of the distant sun. She slowly raises her right hand and extends her index finger.

Tiny, brilliant points of light begin to rise from the earth below. They quickly form a river, a sparkling channel that gently curves on past her toward the waiting sun. A migration of epic proportion.

He awakens and looks out the window to a cloudless sky of saturated blue. His arm has been expertly bandaged and the IV opioid keeps the pain partially at bay. He recalls the cat, the fire, the struggle and little else. With one exception. The beautiful woman and the dazzling river still resonate deep within him, as they will from now on.

17

Allison knows this dinner will take her right up to the limit on the last of her credit cards if she winds up paying. She sits alone at a perfectly appointed table in the dining room of a two-star Michelin restaurant just off the Hudson on Tenth Street. Anything less would erode her bargaining position with Mr. Stennis, who is now twenty minutes late. Not surprising. As a monied prince, he probably doesn't consider himself beholden to conventional notions of punctuality.

She's just about to order a second glass of Etna Bianco when he glides in and seats himself with a broad smile. "Sorry about that," he offers. "We had a video conference with Shanghai, and I couldn't break loose. Such is life in the global economy. Anyway, how are you?"

"I'm well," she replies, but no more. Better to leave just a hint of frost in the air. A signal that she's not one to be trifled with.

"Good to hear. And how long are you with us?"

"I fly back tomorrow evening. There've been some major developments at work."

"Oh yeah? What kind of developments? A mutated measles? Something like that?"

"Not exactly. I'm not at liberty to say."

"Of course not. Sorry, I shouldn't have asked. Well, all that aside, where are you staying?"

"Right up the street at the Soho House."

"Ah, yes. One of my favorites." He fixes on her with a lascivious smile. She just volunteered that they're within walking distance of a potential sexual encounter.

They order dinner and let the conversation descend into trivia. Both know there's another order of business but don't want to push things along. When the fifth course has come and gone, Allison makes the opening move.

"Didn't you tell me that you guys have made a lot of investments in the healthcare sector?"

Stennis nods. "That we have."

"And what about the fertility business? You know, where they implant fertilized eggs and all that kind of stuff. You in that end of it?"

"Yep, indeed we are. Big time."

"Does that include things like frozen embryos?"

"That's a major part of the business. A lot of times the fertilized eggs are stored for later use."

"And where do they store them?"

"Mostly at the clinics where the labs are. Plus a few dedicated storage sites."

"Interesting. How many clinics do you guys own?"

"Well, to quote you from a moment ago, I'm not at liberty to discuss that. Let's just say quite a few and more all the time." He pauses for a sip of wine, then suddenly looks up. "Know what I think? I think you already know how all this works. What I don't know is why you're so interested."

Allison reaches down to her handbag and pulls out the first page of Tracy's report, the one with the executive summary. Without comment, she hands it to him across the table.

His features harden as he reads it. He looks up when done. "I take it that none of this is public knowledge."

She smiles. "Not even close. Maybe a dozen people in the entire government know."

"And you're among them."

"I'm among them. Luck of the draw." She knows he's already cut through to the inevitable conclusion. If fertility continues to decline, the embryos and eggs will become fantastically valuable.

He holds up the sheet of paper. "There's got to be a lot more to it than just this. I'll need to see the whole thing to confirm the conclusion."

"Of course you will."

"I assume that you've placed some kind of dollar value on this material."

"You assume correctly. There are forty-seven more pages. Each worth one thousand dollars."

Stennis is unfazed. "It's a gamble, you realize that. At best, all this is highly speculative."

"True," Allison admits. "But if it pays off, it's the best bet you'll ever make. Care to put a value on your frozen inventory in a post-baby world?"

Stennis looks down at the single page and smiles. "Not really. I'll leave that to the numbers people." He looks up at Allison. "Okay. You've got a deal. I'd put it in writing, but I don't think that would be a very good idea. Do you?"

"Absolutely not." She reaches in her handbag and pulls out the rest of the report. "Happy reading."

"You know, you're quite the trusting soul," Stennis says as he takes the document. "What makes you think I'll pay up?"

"Because you and I have just entered into a conspiracy to defraud the United States government."

"Ah yes. Say no more. And because of that, we need to devise a discrete way of compensating you. I'm going to need a little more information to make that happen."

"I'm sure you will, but this doesn't seem like that right place to take care of that."

"Didn't you say you're staying just a couple of blocks from here? How would that work?" He somehow manages to say it with a straight face, so she responds in kind.

"Sure. Works fine."

He beckons the waiter and pays for dinner without examining the bill. It's of little consequence.

18

"I'm sorry your husband couldn't make it," the fertility specialist tells Gavin. They sit facing each other in a cheerful room with comfortable furniture and one wall covered with pictures of beautiful newborn infants.

"Me too," Gavin says. "He sends his apologies. He's a very busy guy, and something came up. He promises he'll be available next time around. We've been planning this for a long time." He feels a slight twinge of conscience about the deception, but it quickly passes. He intends no harm and seeks only background, not evidence.

"Good," the specialist says with a soft smile on her middle-aged face. "As a same-gender couple, you have a unique set of options. Did you have a chance to go over the material on our website?"

"I did. Let me see if I've got this straight. When you fertilize the egg, you can use sperm from either one of us, or both of us?"

"That's right. Of course, in the end, only a single sperm will complete the fertilization. But some couples like the element of chance added to the process."

"Now what about the egg donor? How do we know she's the right choice?"

"Good question. Naturally, we get that all the time. You choose the egg through a donor agency that carefully screens each contributor. They maintain a database that gives you detailed information, both physical and social, on possible candidates."

"And what about the surrogate mother?"

"Same thing, only more. There's both physical and psychological screening and then legal counseling. Plus, you'll have a chance to get acquainted with her, to make sure you're all comfortable."

All comfortable. Like his mom? He has to ask. "I'm curious. Do you ever have a case where the parents prefer to remain anonymous? At least until the baby is born?"

"Not that I recall. It's possible, I guess. I don't think there's any legal reason why not. You'd have to talk to an attorney to make sure." She frowns slightly. "Is this something you're considering?"

"Not really. Like I said, just curious."

"Well good, because that's definitely not something we'd recommend."

"I can see why."

He can see more than why. He can see his fetal self afloat and drifting in a vast amniotic ocean. He can see his tiny proto fingers reaching out to those distant figures who begot him and finding none. He can feel the panic set in and slowly turn to bottomless sadness. He becomes the quintessential lost soul.

"Mr. Gray?"

"Yes?"

"Are you okay?"

"Yeah, I'm fine."

She knows he's not. "Fertility planning always comes with a lot of emotional content. We see it all the time."

"I'm sure you do." Her remark helps center him and he's ready to approach the most sensitive issue of all. Money. "Look, I know we're in the very early stages of all this, but for planning purposes we're going to need some kind of ballpark cost estimate. Is that fair?"

"It's absolutely fair and we have a whole department dedicated to funding. They can look at your particular case and create a loan package that takes care of the entire process."

"That's nice, but right now, we just need a rough estimate so we can figure out how we're going to work it into our personal finances."

"It's not really my area of expertise," the specialist says in a guarded tone. "Our funding people are much better qualified to give you accurate information."

"I'm sure they are. But right now, we need something to work with. It can be very rough and it's not something that we're going to hold you to."

"Well, with a surrogate mother involved, there's a fairly large cost increase."

"Okay," Gavin agrees, indicating that he's not prone to sticker shock.

"When all the services and fees are consolidated, we're probably talking about something in the neighborhood of one hundred thousand dollars." She pauses. "But remember: We're creating a human life here, something that's literally beyond value."

Gavin nods. "You're right. Thanks."

The woman smiles and extends her hand. "Good luck. We'll be here when you're ready."

Gavin takes her hand, all soft and warm. He can't help but envy her. Most of what he covers is a world full of woe and darkness. She does the opposite and spreads hope and light. It reminds him of one of the early Christian gospels: *And the light shone forth in the darkness and the darkness grasped it not.*

All manner of watercraft parade by in Annapolis Harbor, some under power, others under sail. Tracy wonders if they are all scurrying to get home in the gathering dusk. In any case, she and Gavin have managed to get a table with a commanding view at the Charthouse right on the water's edge. It's a welcome relief to get away from the turmoil at work and to see Gavin again. She's not sure where it's going with him; right now, she's just going to enjoy the ride.

"So, what's causing all the commotion at the office?" he teases her. "A fatal fungus? A rogue virus? Should we all go shopping for hazmat suits?"

"It's nothing like that," she responds. "Not even close. I wish I could tell you, but I can't."

"Why, because I'm a nosey reporter?"

"Absolutely not. You definitely don't come across as nosey. That's probably part of what makes you a good journalist."

"Maybe so," he grins. "By the time they realize they've spilled the beans, the beans are already baking."

"Pretty sneaky," she says. "Now what about your IVF story? How's it going?"

"Still in the research phase. Right now, it's shaping up to be more of a business story than a medical one. Most people know a little bit about babies starting in test tubes, but they have no idea who owns the tubes themselves."

"And what are you going to tell them?" she asks.

"For starters, it's a multi-billion-dollar industry and getting bigger all the time, with about five hundred fertility clinics across the country. So, it's no surprise that Wall Street has sniffed it out and piled on big time. The majority of the clinics are now controlled by private equity firms."

"Oh yeah? And how does that work?"

"The details are kind of messy. Basically, they buy up a majority interest and then groom the thing to be sold somewhere down the road."

"And why would anybody let them do that?"

"Because a lot of docs find the business side both distressing and distracting."

"Can't say as I blame them," Tracy sympathizes.

"Yeah, but once you let the money people in, everything changes. The trend is toward consolidation. At first, it was just clinics, but now it's whole networks of clinics because they fetch a higher market value. They've even roped in all the ancillary services, like legal, insurance, finance, sperm banks and egg banks."

"Egg banks?"

"Absolutely. Donor eggs are now a four-billion-dollar business. And no wonder. They can cost up to fifty thousand per egg. Most come from frozen storage at the clinics. Pretty soon they'll be putting them in bank vaults."

"And where do you think all this is going?"

"It's becoming less and less about babies and more and more about money. Big money. I've gone back and traced the chain of acquisitions over the last few years. A handful of monster-sized private equity firms now control most of the market."

"I see," Tracy says. "And who's the biggest of them all?"

"As far as I can tell, it's one called Stennis Partners. They're into all kinds of stuff in different industries and are worth about $100 billion."

Interesting. The name Stennis ricochets around in Tracy's memory but fails to score a direct hit.

Gavin is now one wine past his self-imposed limit. Outside, the harbor lights paint long vertical streaks into the darkened water. Both he and Tracy quietly take it in until he speaks up.

"How tight are you with your family?" he asks.

"Tight enough," she answers. "I talk with my mom on the phone every week or two. When we're through she always puts dad on. He's very sweet but he's no good on the phone so it doesn't last long. Doesn't matter. I know he cares. I can hear it in his voice."

Gavin nods and stares out at the lights. "That's beautiful."

"Which?" Tracy asks. "The harbor or my family?"

"Your family, of course. Have you ever thought about what life would be like without them?"

"Not really. That's way too tragic to dwell on. I like things just the way they are, thank you. Why do you ask?"

"Because I don't have one."

"A family? Of course you have a family. For better or for worse. Everyone does. I mean, your genes don't appear out of thin air. You might be orphaned, you might be estranged, but there's still that common bond."

"Maybe not."

"Maybe not?"

"Let me share something with you." He goes on to tell her how he came about, and she finds herself totally immersed.

"So, you believe me?" he asks when finished.

"I pretty much have to," she answers. "There's no way you could have made that up."

"You're right," he says as he takes a sizable swallow of wine.

She impulsively reaches out and puts her hand on top of his. "It really bothers you, doesn't it?"

"Yes, it does."

They lapse into momentary silence as she considers her response. "There's another way you might think about all this," she ventures.

"Oh yeah? And what way is that?"

"Everyone wants to be special in the eyes of the world. We're always searching for things that set us apart and using them to prop us up. But with eight billion people competing for the spotlight, it becomes a little tough. Which means we all keep coming up short and feeling sort of average. But not you. You, Gavin Gray, are an exception to the entire rule book." She smiles and squeezes his hand. "Congratulations."

"I never thought about it quite like that," Gavin says, "That just might work. Thanks."

19

"Wanna a hit?" Nathan holds out the glass pipe to Wayne. It sends a wispy trace of blue smoke toward the trailer's ceiling.

"No thanks," Wayne replies as he views his website on Nathan's computer. "Not into that anymore. How's traffic?"

"Huge. You're a fuckin' star, man."

"Wrong. The Order of Atonement is the star. The Final Truth is its gospel. I'm just a messenger, that's all."

But he's really become far more than he publicly admits. His collaboration with the AI-driven Holy Ghost and his unshakeable sense of purpose have merged and profoundly reshaped his identity. Online, Wayne Bauer has become Terminus, who will preside serenely over the coming demise of humanity.

Each week, he consorts with the Holy Ghost and produces a new video exploring yet another aspect of The Final Truth. And each week, the Cortica 3's learning algorithm vacuums up all the user responses to the video of the previous week. Comments, texts, messages, emails and editorials are all consumed and processed to fuel further improvements in the messaging. Power and simplicity are the end game. The trick is to avoid intellectual entanglements and penetrate directly to the limbic system, where reason is restrained, and passion runs free. The Holy Ghost has quickly proven itself the master of this process. The Order of Atonement is rapidly becoming a virtual network unto itself, bound together by cross-links, search terms and text references.

Bauer steps out of Nathan's trailer into the morning sun and the agitated moan of highway rigs crawling along the highway out front. He resides six trailers away and is still adjusting to his new daily rhythm. A week ago, he came to an agreement with the Comfort Inn that he would remain on the payroll but would no longer be required to work. Both parties stood to profit from the arrangement. Bauer's notoriety was now attracting a steady flow of pilgrims, and the Inn was the logical place to stay. Bookings soared. Bauer, on the other hand, gained the time needed to tend to his growing flock.

"Terminus."

They come around the corner of his trailer just as he unlocks his door. Two families. He has come to recognize the rapturous gaze. He mustn't let them down. The Order is built on their devotion.

"They told us we'd find you here," one of the men says. "It's a great honor, sir."

"The honor is mine," Bauer tells them. "And where have you come from?"

"We're from Paisley," the man answers. "It's in Oregon on the desert side." His Metallica T-shirt curves over an ample belly.

"Yes, I do believe we have some following up there," Wayne replies. Maybe so, but it doesn't really matter. What counts is what's right in front of him.

"And we're from Adel, right down the road apiece," the wife of the second family chimes in.

"Good." He pauses for effect. "It's nice to see families coming together during this terrible time. Lucky for you that you've embraced the Final Truth and can see the path through to the other side. In the end, your sacrifice will be your salvation. You know that, don't you?"

"Oh yes," the first man answers. "And thanks to you, we're prepared."

"I can see that," smiles Bauer. "And it's people like you that give me the strength to move forward. You know, I'd really love to spend more time with you, but I'm carrying a very heavy burden these days."

"Oh of course you are!" the wife exclaims. "We'll always remember this. Thank you."

"And I thank you." He opens his trailer door and enters as they depart. All is packed and ready. He throws the last few items in a shoe box and checks his watch. It's time.

He steps outside just as a massive motorhome appears, followed by a pickup with a tow hitch. The ponderous vehicle rolls to a stop, and a salesperson steps out. "Good morning Mr. Bauer and congratulations." He opens the side door for Wayne, who steps up and in. Excellent. Full kitchen, big dinette, king-sized bed, sofa, flat screen TVs, and so on. His new base of operations.

Several of his neighbors here in the park are members of the Order, and they cheerfully move his belongings for him. They realize that a person of Bauer's spiritual caliber has far better things to do. When they're done, he watches the pickup tow his previous home off to wherever old trailers go to die.

He sits down at the dinette table and looks at the paperwork concerning the transaction. No need to examine it too closely. He'll pass it on to the attorney and accountant he's retained. They both have a detailed knowledge of how online donations work, of how to solicit and receive within the confines of the law. The Order of Atonement now rests on a solid financial foundation.

He permits himself a moment of indulgence and consumes a solitary glass of 18-year-old Macallan single malt scotch. It glides across his palette with a transcendent taste and texture.

Too bad all such things will soon come to an end.

20

Tracy looks down at the polished leather top of the massive conference table in the Cabinet Room at the White House. The President sits at one end, flanked by white marble busts of Washington and Jefferson, two old males meant to lend a little historical gravitas. Would they accept the woman at the head of the table? Tracy thinks Jefferson might but isn't so sure about Washington. It's the President's third year in office, and the burden of it has etched its way onto her media-savvy face, which struggles to maintain its mass market appeal. This meeting will do little to slow the process.

Four cabinet heads are in attendance. Commerce, State, Treasury, and the Secretary of Health and Human Services, who requested the meeting. He has included the Directors of the Centers for Disease Control and the National Institutes of Health, both headed by female physicians. One layer down, Tracy's boss, Arlene, represents the CDC's statistical division, and Dr. Norman Chen represents NIH's General Medical Sciences division.

And finally, there is Tracy, who ultimately bears the responsibility for setting this entire juggernaut in motion. Which explains her lowly presence here among the ruling elite. If she's wrong, the cabinet and President will know precisely who to blame, and it won't be those above her.

The presentations commence with the HHS Secretary making a brief statement about the potential significance of what's been discovered, followed by further elaboration by the CDC Director, and then even more by Tracy's boss. As the discourse spools out, Tracy watches the President start to sag in weary resignation. The woman has two children, an undergrad son at Yale and a daughter in law school. Babies played a major role in her life on the way up. And now she faces a monumental irony: the first female President, the ultimate trailblazer/glass smasher, presiding over the potential end of motherhood on a global scale.

Arlene winds up her discourse and hands it over to Tracy, who expected a rush of anxiety but feels none. The scale of what's happening pushes it out to somewhere beyond any kind of normal exigency. She's meticulously pared down her remarks to a set of bullet points and a graph depicting the pace of the decline. Each attendee studies a handout of this material while she speaks.

"Based on our sampling of OB/GYN clinics across the country, we believe the decline started about four months ago," she states. "As you can see from the downward curve of the data we've collected, the rate of decline is accelerating. Our last full survey was completed two weeks ago and shows a national downturn of about 43%, which is significantly more than coincidental. If we follow this trend line on down to zero pregnancies, we get there in about another six weeks."

Tracy looks up from her notes. All eyes engage her, probe her and evaluate her. They register equal parts dismay, shock and disbelief. From somewhere outside, the subdued growl of a power mower fills the silence as it patiently ranges over the White House lawn. Finally, the Secretary of Commerce breaks the solitude.

"Ms. Pallas, I'm sure you and your people do excellent work, but I have to ask: how certain are you of all this?"

Tracy saw this one coming. "In statistical work like this, you're never dealing with certainties. It's always a matter of likelihoods. No one can predict the future with absolute confidence. If we could, there'd be no stock market or Las Vegas. That said, the more data we collect, the more certain we become. We now have enough information that I can be sitting in this room telling you this is something that requires your immediate and undivided attention."

Tracy notices just a hint of a smile on her boss, Arlene. She's just watched Tracy double down on her convictions and finds it highly appropriate.

"It's not just us. It's worldwide," the CDC Director adds. "We're working closely with the World Health Organization, and they're seeing the same thing all over the globe."

The President speaks up and takes charge, which is precisely what presidents are elected and paid to do. "Thank you, Tracy.

Okay, let's assume the worst and move on to the next big question. What's causing this? Why are we suddenly falling down the rabbit hole? What's changed? What's going on here? Is it a virus? A toxin? Or what?"

"It's both."

The focus of the meeting abruptly zooms to the scientist Dr. Chen, who speaks in a calm yet authoritative manner. He has just preempted his superior, the NIH Director, who is seasoned enough not to intervene and turn it into a public pissing match.

"And how might that be, Dr. Chen?" the President asks.

"Like Ms. Pallas, we're still sorting out the details but have enough information to construct a fairly strong hypothesis. Let me walk you through it, starting with the toxin side. In this case, it's a whole family of compounds, per- and polyfluoroalkyl substances, or PFAS. They've been the object of multi-billion-dollar lawsuits and largely phased out, but before that you'd find them in everything from semiconductors to cookware to firefighting foam."

"If they've been phased out then what's the problem?" The Secretary of Commerce asks.

"PFAS compounds can persist in the environment long after they're no longer in use. People call them forever chemicals, because they carry a toxic load for decades to come. Also, there are around fifteen thousand varieties, most of which have never even been studied."

"Okay, but this drop in pregnancies has gone global, and that means that women all over the world have been exposed. How could this thing suddenly be everywhere?"

"Two reasons. First, it's only sudden in the sense that it's now accumulated in humans to a level where it's crossed a biological threshold of some kind. Second, it follows several paths through the environment that take it into the atmosphere, where it can circulate freely across the entire planet."

"Okay, so how does this toxic load figure in?" The Secretary of State queries.

"There have been numerous studies of the toxic effect of PFAS on humans. They're associated with a variety of health threats, including thyroid disease, cancer, liver damage, and fertility problems – although this current fertility issue has a more complex origin."

"And what might that be?" the President asks.

"It involves a thing called an endogenous retrovirus, or ERV for short. As you probably know, a standard virus invades a cell, deposits its genes and then uses the cell's machinery to make copies of itself. A retrovirus, like HIV, takes this process a step further and deposits its genes into the cell's own DNA, where it stores the genetic code for its replication."

"So, what's the endogenous part about?" the President asks.

"Well, for millions of years, retroviruses have been infecting mammalian cells and storing their DNA there. But over time they mutate and lose their ability to replicate. In the end, most of them are just along for the ride. But not all. A few of them are able to meddle with certain operations within the cell where they reside. And that's where the PFAS comes in. Through a complex chain of events, it triggers a genetic sequence in one particular retrovirus that instructs it to synthesize a protein called IP3 in the human egg. Normally, this event would be triggered by the presence of a sperm cell, and the uptick in IP3 would set off a chain of events that formed a shield around the egg to prevent any further sperm from entering. But in this case, it's the interaction of the PFAS and the endogenous retrovirus that forms the seal. The sperm never even get a chance. Fertilization becomes impossible."

"Haven't I seen a video where they use a needle to insert the sperm into an egg? Couldn't you do it that way?" The Secretary of State asks.

"We tried that," Chen responds. "Didn't work. We can't explain exactly why, but it doesn't matter. In the end, there's no fertilization."

Silence descends. The distant power mower once again fills the anxious space.

"Okay, let me see if I've got this straight," the President says. "A chemical cleanup won't help because the chemical is already everywhere, and a vaccine won't help because we're all already infected. Right?"

"Generally speaking, yes," Chen says.

"Would you like to speculate on how long it might take to find a solution?" the President asks.

"No, Madam President, I would not. It's a novel problem and we have no established means of solving it."

The President nods slowly. "I see." She scans all the participants. "We're just going to have to work with what we've got. If Ms. Pallas is correct – and she has been so far – we've got to get a handle on this thing immediately, before the media picks up on it. If we don't, there'll be absolute bedlam. We need to be proactive. I want the CDC to prepare a statement that acknowledges the trend but leaves its final outcome inconclusive. No babies in six weeks is just asking for trouble. People need to have hope. And under no circumstances are we going to talk about PFAS and endogenous retroviruses snuffing out the whole future of the human race. No babies for the time being is one thing, no babies forever is quite another. I want to see a draft within a week."

The President stands and abruptly exits the room. Arlene turns to Tracy with a sardonic grin. "Now look what you've gone and done."

"Sorry," Tracy smiles back. *No babies forever*. The President has a real knack for being brutally succinct. What will happen, she wonders, when legions of women of childbearing age get the news with only a month and a half left until the baby odds drop from highly unlikely to absolute zero? Easy. A nonstop sexual sprint to the finish line.

"If what that statistics person said is true," the Secretary of Commerce tells the President, "We're pretty much on the brink of total economic collapse."

His chair sits next to the President's desk in the Oval Office, where he leans forward to make his point. "It won't happen instantly, but it won't take very long, either. As soon as pregnancies hit zero, there'll be a buffer zone while people wait to see if it's a false alarm. But after a few weeks go by, it'll start to sink in that this is the real deal. And then, look out. We'll see the biggest selloff in history."

"You don't think we can talk people out of it?" the President asks, only half seriously.

"No way. Our entire system is based on future returns. We put money into companies with the expectation that they're going to grow, and that we'll get a cut of the action. And what makes them grow is more customers. Now if the customer supply starts to shut down, the whole thing caves in. It'll take Wall Street about a millisecond to figure that out."

"And what happens then?" the President asks. "Do we go back to trading clamshells?"

"Not for long," the Secretary says. "Pretty soon there won't be anybody left to do the trading."

21

"You've read plenty about the Wagner Group," James Hallock tells Mark Stennis. "But you hardly ever read about us – which is exactly the way we like it. We're not into brand building; we're into service to our clients. The last media exposure we had was that Cat 6 clusterfuck down in Miami, which we most certainly could have done without."

"Understand," nods Stennis. Hallock, an ex-marine colonel, is referring to the so-called InterBank Incident, which occurred amidst the chaos and criminal anarchy that followed the hurricane. As the turbid waters receded back into the Atlantic, armed gangs began to roam through the devastated downtown, searching for anything of value. Banks became a favorite target, including the Interbank, where three Sigma contractors were charged with securing it. When a half-dozen armed thugs poured in off the street, the contractors opened fire from the mezzanine level with automatic weapons and killed them all. As a signal to other gangs, they left the bodies where they fell, strewn around the entrance. It worked. Unfortunately, the pile of corpses became a photo op, even though the contractors were never charged.

"I'm sure InterBank appreciated your service," Stennis continues. "They're a very well-run organization. We do business with them in several countries."

The pair sits in a spacious meeting room in a Virginia DC suburb. Large photos of Sigma Group operatives engaged in humanitarian missions decorate the walls: Unloading rice bags off a helicopter. Administering vaccines to emaciated children. Erecting emergency tents under stormy skies. Outside, a well-kept lawn fronts a contemporary two-story building with a modest logo near the entrance. Nothing suggests an organization with over 50,000 combat-ready individuals positioned worldwide, all backed by the most advanced weaponry available.

"Your low profile is essential to the mission we have in mind," Stennis goes on. "Right now, I can't share all the details, but I can give you enough information that we can get started on creating a budget. We're going to need to secure some high-value property against theft, vandalism and sabotage in a potentially politically unstable environment. The items involved are frozen and need to be maintained at temperatures down to minus 320 degrees Fahrenheit using liquid nitrogen. Now I understand that you have expertise in the design and construction of defensive fortifications, which will be an essential part of the program. I can give you the general specifications right now and the rest when we agree on the budget."

Hallock looks up from taking notes. His hard blue eyes peer out from a sun-scorched face beneath a severe crewcut. "I have to say that your requirements sound a little unusual, but definitely within the scope of our capabilities. I believe you've come to the right place."

"I'd like to think so," Stennis says as he rises. "I'm going to authorize a retainer to get us going. Time is of the essence."

Hallock grins, which produces copious cracks and wrinkles from his considerable time in tropical latitudes. "In our business, Mr. Stennis, time is always of the essence."

Stennis takes a moment to congratulate himself as the company plane settles into its final approach to LaGuardia. A thick, gray haze leaches the color out of the buildings and vegetation below, stripping them down to their urban essence.

The people at Sigma have checks in all the right boxes and seem like a good fit. The first phase involves a waiting game to see if Allison's purloined report pans out, all the while putting the pieces in place to act quickly if it does. He knows that the Sigma Group's substantial retainer is a gamble at this point, but a necessary one.

When he showed the report to his father, the old man seemed more enthused than alarmed about the potential fallout. They were sitting outside on the terrace above the swimming pool at the elder Stennis's home in Westchester County. Its towering structure shaded them from the afternoon sun. For all its sophistication, the place had the feel of a redoubt about it. Wars, plagues and revolutions might come and go, but the Stennis family ownership would survive and carry on.

"Allison Wertz," the father remarks as he hands the report back to Mark. "A born bad girl. They live nearby, you know. I know her father. Clever fellow. Made his money in healthcare and pharmaceuticals. Didn't do quite so well with his offspring." He chuckles. "Conniving little bitch. I bet she's hard up for money because he cut her off."

"Could be," Mark says. "I'll check it out."

"Do it," his father instructs. "You fucked her, didn't you?"

"Yes, I did."

"No more. Not during all this. It makes things way too complicated."

"You're right." An easy concession. She wasn't that good anyway.

"Okay, let's assume for a moment that everything in this report checks out. Further, let's assume its prediction is right, and pregnancies drop to zero in less than two months. Know where that leaves us?

"It's a sure thing the markets will collapse. Social media will go insane, with all kinds of finger pointing. Government will be at least partially paralyzed, that's for sure."

The old man's embedded scowl does a cross-fade into a crafty smile. "I didn't say 'them.' I said 'us.' Think about it. I'm sure you've figured out that our holdings in the fertility industry give us more than half the frozen embryos and eggs in the country. Care to put a value on that?"

"Astronomical." Stennis is well aware of all this, but protocol demands that he hear the old man out. "Unless, of course, the problem is with the sperm and not the eggs," he adds.

"Not likely," Stennis Sr. counters. "Biologists regard sperm the same way a lot of women regard men. Simple and dumb. Not much to go wrong. Besides, we're also storing God knows how much frozen sperm, and that's our hedge."

"All true. But in any case, we'll have to protect our investment through a real rough patch," Mark counters. "And it won't be cheap."

"It never is." The old man says it with a withering cynicism the public never sees, the kind he deliberately conceals at the galas, the openings, the conferences, the interviews.

"It's not just about security," Stennis says. "It's also about ownership. Right now, we store this stuff but mostly we don't own it. I'm working on several possible solutions. One is storage fees. Right now, it costs about five hundred a year to store an embryo. Now what would happen if it went up to fifteen thousand? You can't just yank something like this out of a clinic and stuff it into your home freezer. You pretty much have to pay the going rate. If you don't, you default, and we take possession.

"On the security side, I've come up with a plan that brings in professional military people, the kind with lots of experience dealing with political and economic chaos all over the world. Let me walk you through what I've got."

Stennis fires up his computer. Stennis Sr. drains his scotch and soda. The shadow over the terrace creeps down and dips into the pool. A slight chill invades the air. The angry buzz of a leaf blower resonates out in the lush green distance.

When the pair complete their business, Stennis Sr. leans back and surveys his holdings. "There may come a time when we need to assert our ownership here by force. Same for the business. The government and the law of the land will be no help at all. We'll be on our own." He turns to Mark. "And that's when we'll be at our very best."

22

Allison knows it's not smart to be wearing her Dior sunglasses. They're rare, expensive and probably easily traced, even though she's 650 miles from DC at the Atlanta headquarters of the Centers for Disease Control. While the clerk goes to fetch her new phone, she squirms through a paranoid fantasy involving two detectives who gaze at video surveillance of her standing at this very counter. "Look at the fuckin' glasses!" one of them exclaims. "Gotta be a grand, at least. Let's check on it."

Still, the glasses lend her at least a little anonymity. She's rapidly learning that criminal behavior is largely a matter of risk management. How do you get yourself the most security with the least effort? The phone, with its prepaid SIM card, cost $30, and she needed cash to keep the transaction anonymous. Just to be sure, she withdrew it from an ATM in DC, so there would be no link to her presence here in Atlanta. With the phone in hand, she could drive out of the city to some nearby rural location to use it. From this remote spot, the call would flow over a cell tower to the office of Mark Stennis, but not draw any direct connection to Atlanta. Some would call it a petty precaution, but they weren't the ones who might wind up doing ten years' worth of laundry in a federal prison somewhere in Kansas.

Her need for the so-called burner phone dated back about an hour ago to an urgent meeting at the CDC headquarters that included communications directors from several layers of management, starting with the Director's Office and working its way down to Allison's domain in Health Statistics. The subject was the continuing decline in pregnancies, which showed no signs of abating. They now had word that the major media organizations were vigorously pursuing the story and had assigned investigative teams to confirm the trend. It wouldn't be long before they sorted through statistical haze and verified it. The purpose of this particular meeting was not only to get all the CDC's metaphorical ducks in a row, but to make sure they were quacking the same tune.

Allison pulls her rental car over next to an empty pasture bordered by a galvanized wire fence. At least it looks like a pasture. In truth, she has no idea what kind of creatures or plants might inhabit it. Her sphere of knowledge thins considerably once the pavement ends.

To reach the offices of Stennis Partners, she manually dials the number and will delete it as soon as the call ends. She peers out into the field. A row of birds roosts on a metal structure that looks like a feeding trough. Or maybe not. Stennis picks up on the fourth ring. "Mark here."

"Hi, it's Allison."

"Allison! Good to hear from you. How are we doing?"

"I'm talking to you on a drop phone."

"Okay…" He knows that even though there'll be a record of the call, it won't be traceable back to her.

"I have an update on that report we discussed. I just attended a top-level meeting on the subject. Last time we talked, it was down 29 percent. Now it's down 43 percent. That pretty much verifies what I gave you. It's supposed to hit zero in about six weeks. Whatever you're going to do, you need to do it pretty fucking fast."

"Yes, I suppose I do. Now I assume you want to complete our transaction."

"I'm leaving for Mykonos with some friends in a couple of days, and I'd like to get this thing wrapped up before I go."

"Mykonos! Very nice."

"And very expensive, if done right."

"And we most certainly want it done right. It'll take me about a day to arrange a secure transfer. I'll need your home address. We don't want a bank involved."

"No, we don't." She gives him her address, and he gives her a window of time to be there. "I'll see you later," she concludes.

"Well, I most certainly hope so."

"Same here." She hangs up. Out in the pasture, all the birds save one have left their perch on the trough. It stares at her incessantly as she starts the car and pulls away.

It's on, Stennis thinks as he pockets his phone. He's already outlined a contingency plan with his father. The first step involves the securities markets. As soon as the feds officially confirm the fertility disaster, they're bound to plummet, and Stennis Partners along with them, unless they act immediately. They need to conduct an orderly retreat that minimizes their losses but doesn't draw undue attention from the financial press.

The second step is to use the cash from their selloff to buy up more fertility clinics, which includes all their stored eggs and embryos. Although they'll have to pay a premium, the ultimate return will be enormous after the fertility drop becomes official.

All things considered, the $47,000 he is paying Allison Wentz is by far the best investment he's ever made.

23

"Okay so now you all know what a sucking chest wound is," Frank Fanno tells the dozen militia members sitting on the floor of his machine shop. "And the video just told you how to treat it. So let's pair up and walk through it. One guy's the victim, the other is the treater. Use the gauze packs and tape just like in the video. But remember, if you don't have this stuff, use anything that'll block the air from going in and out, then go from there. Okay, let's hit it."

Frank walks to the back of the room, where Gavin stands watching the class work through their assignment. "You know, it's a sad thing, but a lot of these guys never had anybody give a goddam about them until they joined up. Fentanyl mommies, long-gone daddies. Part of the program here is to teach 'em how to take care of each other. A stand-in family, I guess. Not a bad idea, huh?"

"Not at all," Gavin says, then stifles a yawn. "Sorry. Got a little jet lag. I think I better call it a day."

"Good idea," Fanno says. "See you tomorrow."

Gavin trudges out of the machine shop and looks up at the pristine night sky. The Milky Way traces a river of vaporous silver across its zenith and disappears down over the horizon. It helps Gavin journey into the core of Frank Fanno. The man regards this wonderous sky and these boundless plains as a world apart from the east coast, with its dense habitation, contentious politics and oblique culture. There's a purity to his convictions that sets him apart from the darker recesses of the extreme right, which always hover nearby out here.

His cellphone sounds and he checks the ID and smiles. Gina Koveki. One-time girlfriend and full-time professional colleague. They bonded while covering a racial disturbance in Cleveland that left them pinned down inside a looted convenience store. Later, after a few wild erotic encounters, they'd gradually downshifted into an enduring friendship.

"Hey, Gavin. You ready to pop with that fertility piece yet?"

Gavin smiles once more. She has this undercurrent of ceaseless energy and determination that would have grated on him if they'd tried to make a go of it. But now, from a distance, he finds it admirable and endearing.

"Almost," he answers. "Still got a few things to tie up."

"Which means you're back out with those citizen soldier people again. I'd strongly suggest you get back here and finish your story."

"Oh yeah? And why is that?"

"There's a lot of talk spinning around a serious drop in fertility rates. I just picked up a gig to be on an investigative team to check it out. Several other news groups are doing the same thing."

Gavin immediately flashes on Tracy. She knows. She must. The branch she works for at the NCHS is called Reproductive Statistics.

"Have you checked with the CDC?" he asks. "They're usually right on top of this stuff."

"Not this time. All they'll say is that they're looking into the matter. Classic bullshit. They won't even admit that the problem might really exist."

"So, how's your investigation going?"

"It's a real grinder. We're on the phone to doctors' offices far and wide. A lot of them consider stuff like this to be proprietary information. The CDC, on the other hand, has a special relationship with these people and can get pretty much whatever they want. In the end, I think everything is going to spin down to some kind of official proclamation by the CDC – unless of course they wait until there's not a baby belly left anywhere."

They chat for another few minutes and agree to a drink for old times' sake when he's back in town. All the while, Tracy kept punching through. For some twisted reason, he felt betrayed, like she should have told him about the baby well running dry. But then again, he had to admire her integrity, which officially forbade her from sharing any such information.

The only way to resolve this clash of sentiment was to call her.

"Tracy?"

"Gavin. Where are you?"

"Still in Montana. Sorry. I didn't want to wake you up."

"You didn't. I was reading some work stuff."

"Work stuff. That's what I'm calling about."

"How's that?"

"I just got off the phone with a fellow journalist. Good person. Well qualified. She told me she's on a team that's investigating a sharp drop in pregnancies throughout the country. Says several other news agencies are doing the same. Says the CDC will not confirm it. Now suppose I asked you if it's true. What would you say?"

"You know I'm under non-disclosure, right?"

"Of course, you are. So, what would you say?"

"I'd say 'no comment'."

It's about as clear a signal as she can give.

"Got it. Turns out I'm flying back tomorrow. It would be just as easy to land in DC as New York. "What do you think?"

"I think that would be wonderful."

"As do I. In the morning, I'll let you know when I'm getting in. Sweet dreams."

"Same."

He puts away his phone and looks once more toward the night sky. So, it's true. And by the anxious tone of her voice, it's really bad. He starts to sort through all the possible calamities it might trigger, and promptly gives up.

They're just too numerous.

24

"There are two guys from Internal Security here to see you. I put them in Room B."

Allison's pulse doubles, throat constricts, chest tightens, stomach contracts and palms moisten. All part of a grand hormonal ballet triggered by the cornered beast within. She struggles to collect herself and present a reasonably placid exterior.

"Fine," she tells her administrative assistant. "I'll be right out."

She feels lightheaded and adrift as she starts down the hall. What went wrong? How did they find out? What do they know? What don't they know? Is this for real? Is it something else entirely?

The security people stand up to greet her as she enters. Stackard and Ellison. Two guys in their early thirties, neatly attired and vaguely military, with hair tightly trimmed on the sides. They both shake her sweaty hand with palms dry and cool. A bad start.

"Not to worry," Stackard tells her. "We know we're not anybody's favorite people, but we mean well."

"I'm sure you do." Allison musters a subdued smile, careful not to overdo it.

Stackard looks down at a single sheet of paper. "We understand that you have a printed copy of a report authored by a Tracy Pallas in Reproductive Statistics. We got your name off the printing log, and we've been instructed to conduct an inventory of all the copies in circulation." He looks up at her with an amused smile. "I don't know what's in it, but whatever it is, it's way above our pay grade. We hardly ever do this kind of thing. Anyway, if you could go fetch it, we need to check an ID number and then we're through here."

No! It couldn't be worse. The room wobbles, and she plants her elbows on the table to steady herself. Then, from somewhere in the unknowable, her defense presents itself, almost fully formed. She relaxes, leans back in her chair and smiles at the pair. "Bingo! You got me. I confess. I took it home to read."

"You took it home?" Ellison says. "That's a limited circulation document. They're never supposed to leave the building."

"I know," Allison responds with an emphatic nod. "My bad. I confess. But we're all under a huge amount of pressure right now. I just didn't have time to get to it during the day, so I took it home to read."

"Is it still there?" Stackard asks.

"Not really. As soon as I finished it, I ran it through my home shredder. I may have bent the rules a little, but I do take this security thing very seriously."

The pair look at each other, and Allison can already see the outcome. If they formally write her up for violating secrecy protocol, it's going to be a real pain in the ass. Better to just write it up as accidentally shredded.

Stackard turns to Allison. "Okay, but next time, I suggest you stick a little closer to the rules around here."

"Understood," Allison says with a carefully engineered, sheepish smile. "Won't happen again. Promise."

Allison feels the sickening flush of panic return as Stackard and Ellison board the elevator down to the ground floor. There will now be a written record of her actions, one that can be accessed and analyzed in countless ways. One that may be linked to other events and patterns that form the backbone of other investigations.

If she goes down, she's not going down alone. Stennis is still in the loop. If it gets ugly, he's the one with the power to do whatever's necessary to extricate them. If, in fact, that's even possible.

She strides back to her desk and grabs her purse, which still holds the burner phone. Two minutes later, she's in her car in the parking structure and once again dialing Stennis. Her fingers shake as she stabs at the numbers. It takes three tries to get it right.

"Stennis here."

"It's me. I think we may have a problem."

"Oh yeah? What kind of problem?"

"The people here found out that I left the building with the report, which is definitely against the rules. It may even be a felony. I don't know."

"And what did you tell them?"

"I said that I was really busy and didn't have time to read it at the office, so I took it home. I told them that after I went through it, I made sure to shred it immediately. I apologized profusely."

"Did they buy it?"

"I think so. They're not going to take any action, but that not's the problem. I'm sure they're going to write it up and put it in some kind of incident report."

"So what?"

"We have no idea how all this is going to play out. We might get tied in somehow."

Stennis pauses. "You know what? I think you're overreacting. Big time. You got the jitters and you're blowing this all out of proportion. I've seen this kind of thing before. I'm an attorney, remember?"

Allison sighs. "Yeah, I remember."

"Look, you're off to Mykonos in a couple of days, right? You can chill with your pals and put this whole thing behind you. I've figured out a clean way to get you your money so you can live large while you're there. Can you be home tomorrow by three o' clock?"

"I suppose."

"Good. You'll get an envelope, special delivery. It'll have the key to a post office box near Woodley Park. Cash."

"Forty-seven thousand?"

"Forty-seven thousand. One more thing. That phone you're using. It's our one point of exposure. You need to destroy it. Right away. Understand?"

"Understand."

"Hey, I gotta go. Have fun and check in when you get back, okay?"

"Okay."

Stennis pulls into the parking lot of an apartment complex in Queens. White, middle class. He enters a three-story brick building, its windows studded with air conditioning units. On the third floor, he unlocks a two-bedroom unit and walks into a nearly empty interior, save for a folding chair and card table with a laptop computer. The rent and utilities are automatically paid by a fictious person whose identity was professionally constructed sometime back. One of the utilities is a cable service providing an internet connection.

Stennis gets a rag from under the sink and dusts off the chair and table before risking a sit-down that might besmirch his mid-town attire. He sits and fires up the computer and opens an app provided by an encrypted email service. It uses public key cryptography, the definitive standard for encoding messages into unreadable cyphertext. He types a brief email and sends it to a recipient in Sofia, the capital of Bulgaria.

When he's finished, he sits back, and the hinges on the folding chair creak in protest. The room has a slightly stale smell to it and looks out to an identical building across the way. Someone passes in front of an open window in a pale strobe that is quickly lost.

He stands and notices some residual dust on one of his elbows from typing. It falls in a thin cloud to the oaken floor as he carefully brushes it off. It will be at least eight hours before he receives a reply. He'll check back tomorrow before coming to work.

The recipient places his morning coffee on his littered desktop with extra care. As of late, he's developed a tremor that belies his age and causes him to contemplate retirement. But not yet. He still retains his office in the Ministry of the Interior that looks down on the beautifully gardened public square across the street. Even now, it would be unthinkable to approach him about stepping aside. He goes all the way back to the Soviets and the KGB.

He puts a freckled hand on his computer's mouse and opens his encrypted email service.

A single message resides in his in-box. He smiles. He knows the sender's father. They navigated the fall of empires and the rise of the global economy along complementary paths that occasionally intersected in mutual profitability.

And now it seems the son has taken the lead. So be it. He decrypts the message and reads its single sentence.

"Do you have assets in Greece?"

25

"It's an honor to meet you," Tracy tells Dr. Javon Dawkins as they sit in his office at Georgetown University. "I read some of your work the last year I was in school."

"And it's an honor to meet you, young lady." Dawkins leans back in his desk chair with an amused smile. He is a Black man well into middle age who has accumulated enough praise to not take himself too seriously. "Gavin here speaks well of you, which is no small trick."

"I liked what I read," Tracy says. "But to be honest, I'm not sure I understood it all."

Dawkins explodes into ivory-toothed laughter. "You know, I'm not sure I do either. So let's call it even."

Gavin loves it. Dawkins has remained the same redoubtable yet lovable figure he was when Gavin took several of his classes while he was still at New York City College. The only topic that seems to really annoy him is race. "You know when all this race stuff is going to end?" he once told Gavin, "It's gonna be over when it doesn't worm into conversations that have nothing to do with it. Take the laws of thermodynamics. Do you think they care whether you live in The Hamptons or Watts? I don't think so, but there's always someone who thinks it does." Gavin has always found his special combination of compassion and realism highly appealing. It warms the fatherless void within him.

"Now, down to business, Mr. Gavin Gray," Dawkins says. "You said you're working on an article about the IVF industry. You also said that your good friend, Ms. Pallas, works in reproductive statistics at the CDC. So, what do you need me for?"

"I want to frame the piece in the context of human fertility worldwide. Tracy has been very helpful, but most of her experience is confined to the US population. I need a more global perspective, and you're one of the main players."

"I see. You're talking about a very big subject, so where would you like to start?"

"Let's start with eight billion people," Gavin answers.

"Ah yes, eight billion souls. All drinking from the same planetary cup. So where do we go from here? All we can do is make some educated guesses. As Tracy knows, it's mostly a matter of biostatistics. We try to predict the most likely outcomes, and then feed them to policy makers, who are also, unfortunately, politicians. But by that point, I'm out of the loop. Thank God."

Gavin decides this is enough preamble to cover up the real purpose of their visit and dives into the darkening core of the matter. "Okay, let's go back to fertility itself, and how events in the real world can affect the outcomes. Let's take an extreme case to illustrate the point. Suppose that worldwide fertility dropped to zero in less than a year. What kind of world would we be living in?"

"Zero fertility, huh? Dawkins says while scratching the soul patch on his chin. "Interesting. Let's start with the basics. No new babies right now means no new workers in about twenty years or so. Beyond that, it means fewer and fewer workers supporting more and more elderly. Not a pleasant thought. I don't think we need to run the numbers to see where it goes. Something's got to give."

"Like what?" Tracy asks.

"Like pension plans. Whether public or private, they're all based on input from the working population. When it starts to dry up, so do the pension checks. I doubt if folks are going to take kindly to that. Look at the riots in France over pension issues. They tried to fix it by raising the retirement age to generate more money, and people went nuts. Now imagine the same thing in China with over a billion people. Not pretty."

"What about healthcare?" Gavin asks.

"You get a double whammy there. For starters, there are declining numbers of workers to support the cost of keeping the system viable. Then you have to face the fact that an aging population also means an ailing population. Very expensive."

"And no one who can foot the bill," Gavin suggests.

"Not even close. And if you look far enough out, you're going to be left with 70-year-olds trying to take care of 90-year-olds. But I'd bet that by then, most of civilization will already be in ruins."

"In the end, what's going to bring it down?" Tracy asks.

Dawkins folds into a fatalistic shrug. "Same as always. Religion and politics. Think about this. A lot of the rich countries are already aging rapidly and will continue to do so. To stay rich for a little while longer, they going to need to import immigrant labor – in a big way. And as we've already seen, that's going to severely stretch the tolerance of native populations, even more so than now."

"I'm looking for a happy ending somewhere in all this, but I'm not having much luck," Tracy says.

"Well then you're looking in the wrong place."

"So, where's the right place?"

"Carrying capacity."

"How does that work?"

"People forget that everything we consume starts as a natural resource. Land. Water. Critters. Minerals. Energy. It's something we overlook when shopping at big box stores and eating at McDonalds. Problem is the planet has finite amounts of all this stuff. There's only so much to go around without destroying the environment as we go. We're already running a deficit though global warming, species extinction, ocean acidification, chemical pollutants and so on. Now the question becomes, if we balance the books, if we pay the planet back at the same rate we borrow from it, how many people will it support? Calculate that and you've got the carrying capacity.

"Different people will give you different answers, but most studies put the number at about eight billion, which is where we're at right now. Any more and we're risking a catastrophic collapse of the environment. Like the Cat 6 in Miami times a thousand. I think a lot of people in the industrialized west would support an effort to make nice with nature, but at what cost? It's been estimated that the planet will only support about 1.5 billion people if everyone lives a typical American lifestyle. Last time the world was at 1.5 billion was around 1850, when people rode horses and traveled in sailing ships.

"Once again, it all comes down to politics and religion. To even things out, people in wealthy countries are going to have to take a substantial hit on their lifestyle. Ride the bus. Live in small apartments. Eat cheap food. Will they feel a moral obligation to do so? Personally, I think that's going to be a tough sell."

"I tend to agree," Gavin comments.

"Wise choice," Dawkins says with a twinkle. "Anyway, Ms. Pallas, I hope all that gives you an upside to consider. If you do the numbers, your baby zero scenario will drop us from eight billion to about four billion people in about thirty years. The planet will be eternally grateful, and maybe even a little forgiving."

"I really do hope so," Tracy says.

"As do I," Dawkins adds.

"Do you think he knows we're on to something?" Tracy asks Gavin as they walk along the paved pathway outside Building D where Dawkins resides in the Department of Biostatistics, Bioinformatics and Biomathematics.

"Could be," Gavin says. "But not enough to be a problem." He smiles reflectively. "I'd like to see his expression when your people go public with all this."

Baby Zero. That's what Dawkins had called it, Tracy recalls. This little person would come into the world in less than ten months. She can visualize the tiny, curled fists, the chubby cheeks, the sleepy scrunched-up eyes, still slightly puffy. In a world of eight billion souls, its actual identity will probably never be known. It will go on to journey through a life currently unimaginable, completely unaware of its historical significance.

She wishes it the very best.

26

Allison takes it on faith that there is an ocean 39,000 feet below her. All she can see is an angelic fleece of soft white that eventually meets a sky of brilliant blue. She turns from the window and looks back into her compartment in first class and closes her eyes. Washington DC is rapidly dissolving and now only nibbles at the far boundaries of her attention span. She dons some generously padded earphones and listens to a Taylor Swift track that's to her liking.

Fever dream high in the quiet of night...

That's it, stay high, maintain your altitude, rise above it all. She orders a glass of Sauvignon Blanc off the menu and notes their position on a graphic showing their flight path. They're about halfway to Heathrow, where she'll board a second flight down to Mykonos and hook up with her pals to embark on yet another epic journey of self-indulgence. And why not? Where would the world be without a privileged class to define an ascendant reality for the little people to use when fabricating their outsized dreams?

Besides, she deserves just compensation for the considerable time and effort she's put into this venture. It started with her collecting an envelope delivered to her apartment that contained the key to a post office box located just north of Woodley Park. She wore a scarf and cheap sunglasses when she went there and removed a securely wrapped package containing 47 thousand dollars in hundred-dollar bills. She then parceled out a goodly share of it to travelers checks and prepaid credit cards with no direct linkage back to her. She also reserved $8,000 to buy a round-trip ticket directly from an airline office. Finally, she bought a safe deposit box at a bank other than hers and stashed the remainder.

She's about to order an appetizer when a thick overcast settles over her. Despite continual exposure to the fertility crisis at the office, she has never really grasped how it might impact her personally. Right now, she has virtually no interest in having a baby. She knows several women who have and watched them tethered to an obligation they can't buy their way out of. You can have nannies, you can have daycare, you can have tutors and nurses, but no matter what, the moral imperative remains to nurture that which you have created. Her decision to remain baby-free avoids that ensnarement, but for the first time, she understands that losing the option to be a mother is altogether different from simply avoiding motherhood.

It makes her think of her own mother, a fashion model who compromised her career to marry into big money and produce three children while still slinking down runways worldwide. She promptly deployed a cohort of caregivers to shield her from dirty diapers, runny noses, temper tantrums, schoolwork problems, and whatever else came up. In the end, she retained her independence and her distance, but you could see the pain in her eyes every time a crisis occurred. In late middle age, when her career had all but evaporated, she had a chance to fill the void and reconnect. Instead, she found a new calling as an influencer on the Internet for various fashion products. Allison and her friends used to get stoned and watch her mother's YouTube videos for idle entertainment.

The ultimate test of her mother's maternal commitment came during Allison's final conflict with her father, when he yanked the monetary rug out from under her. It was then that she had to confront the fact that money and privilege are inexorably joined at the hip. Her mother understood this connection all too well. To gain the high life, she'd signed a prenuptial that would effectively return her to the low life if the marriage ended. Accordingly, she failed to intercede on Allison's behalf and risk a terminal rupture with her father.

But in the end, whatever the deceptions, the heartbreak and the abandonment, her mother had created a human chain of continuity that extended beyond her personal confines. The primal thrust of the germ line gave her a biological legitimacy unobtainable in any other way. And now, Allison realizes that she may be forever denied this same path.

The wine gradually thins the oppressive cloud, and she turns to the adventure ahead on Mykonos. The beautiful villa, the fabulous food, the cute guys, and the warm nights in the town below.

Privilege carries the day.

27

"I'm sure you can understand why I'm a little concerned about this," the lab manager tells the man in the freshly laundered coveralls.

"I do. And I would be, too," the man sympathizes. "Have you had a chance to review the paperwork?"

"It all looks fine, and I've checked with management. It's just that something like this is unprecedented for us."

"And for us, too," the man assures her.

"I'm sorry, but do you have any identification so I can verify all this?" The man's only visible ID is a small logo with a stylized summation symbol sewn onto his coveralls. The same goes for the other two men who are back in the storage area with the cryo-tanks.

"Of course." He fishes out a laminated name badge on a lanyard around his neck, removes it and hands it to her.

The pair stand next to the open service entrance in the rear of an IVF clinic. Outside, a light drizzle fills the sky over the city. Their transport vehicle's exterior looks run of the mill, just another big SUV. Not so inside. The entire perimeter is encased in bullet-proof armor and multi-layer bullet-proof glass, along with a fire suppression system and advanced radio communications.

"I'm not an expert on this stuff, but I think it's mostly about economics," he says as she hands back his ID. "You guys have a half dozen labs pretty close together, so it's gotta be cheaper to have one centralized storage facility."

"Will I have a chance to take a look at it?" she asks.

"Sorry, not right now. The location is not being disclosed for security reasons. Maybe later."

"I don't care about the location. I care about what's in the tanks. It can't be replaced, you know."

The man nods. "I do know. And I can assure you that your whole inventory will be kept under maximum security. Daily inspections for the tanks, continuous monitoring and alarm systems for temperature and nitrogen levels. Plus a diesel generator for backup power."

One of the men in back emerges wheeling a dolly that holds a single cryo-tank, whose shape and dimensions resemble a medium-sized beer keg. Its vacuum-lined interior has been filled with frozen liquid nitrogen at a temperature of -321 degrees F., cold enough to keep its cargo perfectly preserved indefinitely. The embryos and unfertilized eggs reside in slender cylinders called straws which in turn are placed in larger metal tubes called canes. They started their journey here when they were sucked into a pipette and exposed to a chemical process called vitrification, where all the water was sucked out to prevent the formation of destructive ice crystals. Finally, the canes were placed in a container the shape of a coffee can and stashed in the tank's hyper-frigid interior. An airtight cap was screwed on, and the little bits of life emergent were left to peacefully slumber. Do embryos dream? You had to wonder.

As the last of six tanks is loaded into the rear of the Suburban, the lab manager hands the man a memory card detailing their contents. "Okay, this covers everything you got. Take good care of it."

"Will do," the man says. "And if you need anything out of here for a procedure, just let us know. We'll get it back to you within twenty-four hours."

"I would hope so," the lab manager responds. She watches all three men board the vehicle and pull away. She's not completely comfortable with what's happening and wonders why it's happening at all. She suspects it has something to do with the clinic's new owners, a private equity firm of some kind, but that's too far above her pay grade to worry about.

In the Suburban, the man plugs the memory card into a laptop and transfers all the lab's data onto the local hard drive. Later, after encryption, it will join a centralized database set up by the client at a secure site. He closes the laptop and looks out into the fine spray of drizzle forming on the windshield. Word is they have other crews out all over the country. Right here, they have one more pick-up today before they move on to Dayton for two more, and an additional three in Cincinnati. It would be easy enough, except his orders mandate 24/7 security surveillance on the vehicle, which means they'll have to sleep in shifts. A real pain in the ass. You'd think the stuff in these tanks was solid gold.

28

"Bon Voyage, motherfuckers."

Allison sits up on her thickly padded sun lounger and raises her wine glass toward the white behemoth pulling away from the big concrete pier a quarter mile below them. Its half-dozen decks sparkle with the blaze of countless lights, defying the onset of darkness as the sun sets. Allison brings her glass to her perfect lips to take a sip of retsina. All four girls agree that Allison's lips are indeed perfect.

Heather, Terra, and Amber raise their arms to join the toast but remain reclined on their loungers. They all know what it signifies. The town of Mykonos now begins its Dionysian slide into a fever dream of whitewashed stucco gone pale. The cruise ship people, their tote bags swollen, and their debit cards spent, have departed and surrendered the place to a younger tribe and their hormonal surges. An elite tribe, to be sure. Dollars and Euros in the extreme.

"Dinner!" a male voice calls from behind them. Their rented in-house chef. Allison turns to face the villa's front, an artful assemblage of stone and glass rectangles stacked into three layers emerging from the hillside behind. The four women rise and pad on past the pool and into the dining area on the first floor. They seat themselves on either side of a table hand-hewn from exotic wood and consume appetizers of tuna tataki and beef carpaccio while sipping more wine and plotting their nightly expedition.

Once the main course of island sea bass arrives, they shift into their annual ritual of summarizing the core of their love lives over the past year. Heather's second engagement blew up, but at least she now has a couple of rings as trophies. Terra's surprise quickie marriage ended in an equally quickie divorce, which she's weathered quite gracefully with the help of numerous prescription drugs. Amber, on the other hand, is in between relationships and dedicated to exploring her inner self while permitting all manner of indulgence along the way, which she refers to as "fuel for the journey."

When it's Allison's turn, she finds herself in rather a difficult position. They all witnessed her public interplay with Stennis but, given everything that's transpired, she needs to put maximum distance between the two of them. She writes him off as a first-date fizzle and hints at several new possibilities now in the works. She tops it off by saying that her insane work schedule prevents any serious romantic pursuits for the time being.

"Who said anything about serious?" Heather interjects. "I don't see that anywhere on the menu here. However, I do see some really tasty hors d'oeuvres."

"Well put," Terra adds. She pulls a white packet out of the cleavage above her bathing suit. "So let's get fueled up and hit it."

In no time, they're chopping up lines and snorting them on the glass tabletop. Terra recounts how she scored from these two German guys this afternoon down on the beachfront. Both generously tanned and well-muscled, as well they should be. With the packet half gone, they adjourn to their rooms and adorn themselves in the most provocative of outfits.

The hunt is on.

They hit the third dance club in high gear and merge into a crowd that throbs to the pounding bass. Arms stab up at the thatched ceiling. Hips thrust to the primal beat. Young men, eyes glazed and jaws slack. Young women lost in blatant coital gyrations. Everyone drunk or high or both, their normal sensibilities suspended. The day is dead, and the night has settled in solid.

Allison feels the surge of it all and lets it consume her. She closes her eyes and surrenders her body to the pulse of the electro-beat. Perfect. When she opens them once more, she discovers she has a dance partner moving in sync with her. Quite attractive, with dark and curly hair, deep brown eyes, and a knowing smile that quickly finds its way into her libido. She plays coy and hands out her attention in very small doses. He persists, and the heat of it begins to overpower her.

Over the years, the four of them have devised a scenario to cover situations like this. Right now, they have an intuitive radar that tracks their companions on the floor. Allison gradually dances her way over to Heather and shouts into her cupped ear.

"I've got a keeper. I'll check you guys later."

Heather gives her a sly nod of recognition, and watches the pair float off into the maze of bodies in lurid motion.

"She would've called by now," Terra says. "Or texted. Or both. I think we should tell someone."

The afternoon sun irradiates the villa's pool, where the three have gathered on their lounge chairs. Its tiled surface emits a deep turquoise.

"Tell who?" Heather asks. "You mean the cops?"

"Maybe. I dunno," Amber says. "They're going to be really pissed if she's just out on some guy's yacht with no cell service."

"Yeah, but what if she's not?" Terra asks. "What then?"

Silence. No one cares to speculate. A seagull lands atop a retainer wall behind them, as if to bear witness to wanton hedonism gone badly wrong.

The hound shark glides along its routine patrol of the seabed beneath the Icarian Sea, 50 miles northwest of Mykonos. Its exquisite sense of smell informs it of a food source somewhere relatively close. It patiently circles in a spiral that gradually closes the distance. It eventually spots an upright figure topped by a flourish of blonde hair that gracefully sways in the current. The hound shark approaches cautiously. It's small, as far as sharks go, 12 inches long, and the figure towers over it. Eventually, it tentatively nips at an earlobe and gets no response. Emboldened, it tears the entire ear off. The figure offers no resistance and remains shackled at the ankles to large blocks of stone resting in the sand. The internal gases of decomposition give it a buoyancy that keeps it straining toward the surface, arms raised as though begging for redemption. To no avail.

29

"Un-fucking-believable."

Arlene Papadakis is well known for her expletives, but Tracy has never heard this one before. In any case, it suits the situation. They are looking out from backstage into the cavernous auditorium at CDC headquarters, where the media has assembled in unprecedented numbers. Every seat occupied. Both side aisles jammed with camera crews. More camped outside in the parking lots. All here for the official confirmation of the national – and global – fertility plunge.

But Arlene's curse strikes at an entirely different target, the absence of Allison Wentz. The event today promises to be the finest public hour ever for the National Center for Health Statistics, and even more so for its Reproductive Statistics group – despite the utterly disastrous content. And responsibility for organizing, coordinating and presiding over the event should have been the responsibility of the Center's Director of Communications, Allison Wentz. But Ms. Wentz failed to report to the office upon her expected return last week. Chaos ensued. An ad hoc team, Tracy included, was assembled to manage the task.

The CDC Director takes the stage and moves to the dais in front of a theater-sized display screen. "Good morning and thank you all for coming. I know there's been a lot of speculation about the phenomenon we're about to report on. I want to emphasize that everyone here at the Center is dedicated to supplying information that's not only timely but also as accurate as humanly possible. To this end, we held off on this announcement until we reached an acceptable level of confidence in its content. What I'm about to share with you has been rigorously reviewed and meticulously analyzed, but the conclusion now seems inescapable.

"The United States has experienced a steep decline in pregnancies that is both unexpected and unprecedented. Currently, new pregnancies have declined over 70 percent compared to the usual number. At this time, I'd like to present a graph that plots this drop over the past five months, from its inception until the present. You should note that the downward curve of the trend starts off gradually but then accelerates. Now I'm sure many of you will ask why nobody picked up on this sooner. Several reasons. First, it's not a trend that manifests itself on a daily basis. Visibly pregnant women comprise only about a half percent of the total population. You can go weeks without seeing an expectant mother even under normal circumstances. Second, the CDC has numerous systems for tracking and analyzing live births, all of which rely on local governments' health data. However, these data sources don't extend to pregnancies. Third, the most useful prenatal data is buried in the records systems inside OB/GYN clinics nationwide, and not publicly accessible.

"As it turns out, we have some sophisticated analytical tools that allowed us to avoid these obstacles and monitor the situation as it developed. We've held off on announcing it publicly until we had a high degree of confidence in our observations. As you can see from the graph behind me, new pregnancies will cease entirely in about four weeks if the current trend continues. I should add that this prediction tracks quite closely with a global one prepared by the World Health Organization.

"Now the obvious question becomes: What's causing all this? I wish we knew, but the truth is we're just not certain. As you'd expect, there's already intensive research exploring several avenues of..."

A dull, concussive thud rocks the entire auditorium. People twist in their seats, searching for the source. An anxious buzz quickly swells to fill the space. The Director opens her mouth to respond, then thinks the better of it and leaves the dais.

Tracy knows instantly that it's an explosion from somewhere outside the building. She bolts out the rear stage door, down the hall, and out into the parking lot. What she sees stops her cold.

Vehicle parts litter the four-lane entrance road, smoking and flaming. It takes her a moment to realize that some are not parts, but bodies. Above her, screams of the wounded pour out from scores of blown-out windows. Nearby, she spots a blood-spattered woman raising her forearm to beckon help. Tracy runs and kneels at her side. She doesn't even know where to begin. Numerous punctures and lacerations pump blood onto the sidewalk. All she can to do is tear off a piece of the woman's shredded clothing, form a tourniquet, and apply it to the nearest available limb.

"It's okay, we've got help coming," she finds herself saying. But it's not okay. Not at all. The woman fails to reply, her eyes all liquid and glassy, her jaw gone slack. Her forearm collapses back onto the pavement. Tracy tears off another tourniquet and starts to cinch it tight on a second limb. The screams of sirens and flashes of emergency lights begin to circle around her. "Just hang on, okay?" she instructs the woman, who offers no response.

She feels a hand come to rest on her shoulder and looks up. "I think she's gone," a middle-aged woman tells Tracy. "You did what you could." She holds out her other hand and helps Tracy to her feet.

"Thanks" Tracy responds in a ghostly whisper. She pulls out her cellphone and addresses a text to her parents and Gavin: Am OK. People are now trickling out the open door behind her, mostly journalists and the camera crews, who rush to set up and pan the scene. Others thrust cellphones toward the carnage to drink it into their digitized bladders for later expulsion. Few attempt to render any aid.

The people, the smoke, and the devastation abruptly fade and are replaced within Tracy by a single, disturbing revelation. From this day on, she will inhabit a world profoundly altered compared to the one of just an hour ago. The full effect of the fertility plunge might take decades to play out in full, but the immediate effect has just been put in motion, with this bomb as its agent.

30

The New York Times
Atlanta CDC Bomb Blast Kills 23, Injures 117

The explosion appeared timed to coincide with a press event confirming a sharp decline in pregnancies both in the US and abroad. An unidentified religious extremist group claims credit.

A scheduled press conference at the Center for Disease Control's Atlanta headquarters was shattered today by a powerful bomb blast that originated just outside the building and left 23 people dead and 117 injured.

Surveillance video released by the CDC showed a rental truck crashing through a security checkpoint and exploding moments later as it approached the front of the structure where the press conference was in progress. At the same time, a previously unknown far-right political group claimed responsibility on several internet web sites and message boards.

The group, called God's Own Family, claimed that the fertility plunge was conceived and engineered by the federal government as a means of state-mandated population control. Then, like Covid, it got out of hand and ran wild....

The Enquirer
BABY BOOM!

A group of rogue terrorists triggered a bomb blast that caused widespread death and carnage on the campus of the Centers for Disease Control in Atlanta today. 23 were dead at the scene and 117 were transported to local hospitals. The group's apparent motivation was a press conference confirming a dramatic drop in pregnancies in the US and around the world, which could hit zero in as little as four weeks.

Video showed a rental truck crashing through security and setting off a blast that shredded passersby and blew out scores of windows, with bits of glass cutting like shrapnel through the office workers inside.

The group, which call themselves God's Own Family, claim their heinous act was justified because of a government plot to force birth control onto all citizens...

NewsFax

Massive Security Failure Behind Atlanta CDC Bombing

Today's horrific bomb blast at the Center for Disease Control's Atlanta headquarters represents a grievous lapse in security measures from the White House on down, according to many expert observers. The explosion, which killed 23 people and maimed another 117, is being linked to fringe group called God's Own Family, which claims a government plot to shut down US fertility.

Apparently, federal agencies had no prior knowledge of the group nor its intentions. Several security specialists pointed out that the bombing closely resembles the 1995 Oklahoma City bombing, albeit on a smaller scale and with suicide involved. Federal law enforcement should have picked up on the pattern and marked the group for surveillance early on, but clearly, this didn't happen.

"I think the real tragedy here is that all of this could have been avoided if the administration was on their toes instead of their heels" one US senator remarked. Several House members weighed in with similar comments...

Facebook Fundamentalist Group
(Member one post:)

It's so sad that God's wrath has to be visited upon humanity so often, as witnessed in Atlanta today. In these decadent times, the weight of our sins pushes Jesus to the limits of his endurance. Let us pray for him. Let us pray with him. He is our only salvation, now and forever.

(Member two post:)

Atlanta is about so much more than the bombing. It is about
the whole human race becoming barren. How could such a thing
happen? If you read their press release, they say they just don't
know. Well, we the faithful know. It's the first chapter of the End
of Days. We're growing very close to that final accounting.

(Member three post:)

So how do we, as followers of Christ, conduct ourselves during
these awful and troubled times? Where do we find hope as the
children disappear from our lives forever? I have to admit to a
growing anger against all those whose wanton and sinful ways
have brought us to this pass. I am tempted to seek justice for the
wicked right now instead of waiting for the final judgement. I seek
the Lord's permission to act now and not hold back...

Quanon Post on 8Chan.
WHAT DO I NOT SEE? I CAN HEAR RUSTLING AMONG
THE LEAVES. TAKE HEED.

Twitter (now X) Dialog
(Initial Post – referring to photo of CDC building destruction:)
So it all comes down to bombs and babies, huh? And what
about God's Own Family? I guess we know who's the boss in that
scene.
(Respondent:)
Pretty sicko and cynical, dude. And God the boss? Sounds
pretty patriarchal to me.
(First poster:)
We live in pretty sicko times, my friend. And somebody's gotta
be the boss. You ready to take that on?
(Respondent:)
You got any kids? Bet you don't. And now you've missed your
shot. Too bad about that.

(First poster:)

Enough. Let's give it up and party our way on out…

INN Video Pundit Conversation

Real-time excerpt from audio track:

(Pundit One)

I think we need to take a big step back and view this thing from a historical perspective. Like all the way back to the Reagan years. Like his vision of the nice little house with the white picket fence. The Republicans have done a great job of selling that package to the electorate ever since. But you know what's just happened? Someone not only blew up the little house; they did it with the kids inside. So how are you going to sustain that kind of vision going forward? You're not.

(Pundit Two)

Absolutely not. But maybe more to the point, how are we going sustain any kind of vision at all? The bombing will fade into history as these things always do, like 9-11 and Oklahoma City. But with the baby bust, there may not be much history left to fade into.

(Pundit Three)

You really think so? Well, I don't think we're done quite yet. When we're up against it, we've always found the ingenuity and technology to bail us out. Look at Covid and the RNA vaccines.

(Pundit Four)

Oh yeah? And look at the heat wave that never ends. And the Category 6 hurricanes. And how about the massive flooding? I don't see any magic bullets for these kinds of things.

(Pundit One)

Has anybody really considered what's going to happen if this thing is permanent, if there're really no more babies? I think not. Two reasons: First, out of all the possible catastrophes to hit humanity, we really didn't see this one coming. We've thought a lot about a bang but very little about a whimper. Second, the consequences are just too overwhelming to accept. We're in a massive state of denial…

(Pundit Three)

We're also in a state of denial about the political fallout from all this. We're already seeing all kinds of right-wing coverage about the administration's failure to anticipate this kind of reaction to the CDC's announcement. So I'd say we're light years away from getting any closer to resolving this issue...

AI-generated *Twitter (now X)* Post
(Refers to photo of bomb damage)

The bombing in Atlanta definitely qualifies as a genuine tragedy. It is one of a long series of such events perpetrated by individuals or groups opposed to certain beliefs, issues or policies held by the majority of citizens. In this case, the issue would appear to be the government imposition of population control in violation of certain constitutional freedoms...

31

Wayne Bauer sits transfixed in front of the flat-screen TV in his new motorhome. It spews out non-stop media coverage of the disaster in Atlanta, replete with cellphone video of the mangled bodies and smoking truck ruins, all interwoven with alarmed anchor people and frantic pundits.

The Final Truth. On a planetary scale. And with it, complete and utter vindication of the gospel according to Wayne Bauer. The aliens had been right all along, and now their message resonates in perfect harmony with the zeitgeist. Because of its greed and corruption, God has doomed humanity to permanent extinction. So be it. The Order of Atonement now has a magnificent conceptual engine to propel it into a glorious future.

"Mr. Bauer?"

Wayne turns to Evelyn Gossart, his new communications person, age 28 and recruited from a large PR firm by way of a hefty signing bonus. "Yes?"

"You go on in ten minutes," she tells him.

"Got it. Are the video people ready?"

"Standing by. And you might want to change that shirt," she cautiously suggests.

"Will do," he agrees. "Big crowd?"

"Bigger than ever."

"Good."

Pretty soon, they will run out of space and need a larger venue. To this end, he's recently completed negotiations with the people who own the trailer park. They also possess several acres of blank land adjacent to it and have converted the area into a parking area for the faithful to come and see the master. Wayne receives a hefty share of the admission fee and also a cut from the food carts along the edge. He is on the verge of hiring a business manager to handle this kind of thing and also publishing matters, both online and in print.

He changes his shirt and goes out the front, where a newly constructed barrier shields him from the public. At the rear of the home, he climbs a ladder to the roof, where a microphone and sound system await. Someone immediately spots him.

"Terminus!" It sets off a chain reaction, with a couple of hundred others quickly joining the chant. "Terminus! Terminus!"

Wayne gives a friendly wave and looks out over the crowd of several hundred. They fill an open space between the trailers and some shabby little cabins toward the rear of the property. He's quickly become expert at sensing when the chant has reached its peak and motioning his congregation into silence.

"My dear friends," he starts out. "I'm blessed by your presence – especially on this day of days, this special moment when the Final Truth becomes known to all. The CDC's message from Atlanta makes it clear that the end of humanity is now at hand. And the bombing that followed tells us exactly why we're now facing the termination of our species. It's just one more example of all the wickedness, depravity and savagery that have brought us to this miserable end."

Wayne looks out to scores of heads nodding in earnest agreement. Once again, he senses the proper interval before continuing. "But God, in his infinite wisdom, has given each and every one of you a way out. If you acknowledge the darkness within you, if you share in our common guilt, if you are willing to die to right the scales of universal justice, you can pass on through and into eternal salvation. You can and will be saved!"

A momentary hush settles over the crowd, broken only by the feisty growl of a highway rig heading west through the desert.

"Yes, you will be saved," he concludes. "I leave you with that and thank all of you for your presence here on this fine day."

He waves and turns toward the rear. The chant fires up once more. "Terminus! Terminus!" It starts to fade when he reaches the entrance to his front door, where Evelyn awaits. "Don't forget, we're meeting tomorrow on the new social media campaign," she tells him.

"I got it down," he replies. "See you then."

Once inside, he immediately returns to the news flow on TV. They're all airing the same grisly footage, mostly from the cellphones, and then putting their particular spin over the top. Some work the human angle, others the political angle, still others the doomsday angle. Eventually he settles on a pundit show airing on a major news network, where they wildly grasp for new insights. It quickly grabs his attention. One of the participants is a journalist from a venerable business publication, who says:

"We've been hearing a lot about the markets collapsing. I mean, without some faith in the future, who's going to invest in anything? But that said, there's always a few willing to make big bets against long odds. Like, if you bought in right now, and some kind of technology fix comes along, you'll make a fortune over the long haul. But even if it doesn't, there's always something that's going up when damn near everything else is going down. In this case, think about companies that own in vitro fertilization clinics. Those places are storing frozen embryos and eggs that predate the collapse. Most likely, their inventories are still viable. Now you tell me, how much will they be worth in a sterile world? I can't even guess…"

Wayne shoots to his feet in alarm. Why hadn't he considered this? He'd been a fool, completely enraptured with the vindication offered by The Final Truth. But what he's now hearing means that humanity's utter demise is far less than a sure thing. The stored eggs and embryos offer a way out. They become the seeds to repopulate the earth, an end run around the dictates of God almighty as expressed by the intelligence dwelling among the stars.

He paces the length of his motorhome in a fog of confusion. This new development could destroy the foundations of the Final Truth. It could seriously undermine his credibility with his flock. What are his options? What is the true path of righteousness? He needs counsel, and he needs it from on high.

He must go once more to the mountain.

"You've been with me almost from the start," Bauer tells Nathan as they lurch through the night in the teenager's battered old jeep. "I won't forget that. You'll be rewarded."

"Yeah, well then how come you brought in those big-time IT guys for your computer stuff?" Nathan asks.

"I never let you go; I just added them. And besides, you can learn a lot by watching what they do."

"Yeah, well maybe." Nathan downshifts to adjust for the steepening grade. "How much farther?"

"Not much." Bauer looks out at the hulking mass of Lone Mountain which blots out the heavens up ahead. "We're almost to the end of the road."

They bounce to a stop, and the headlights wash over rocks, sand and desert scrub. "Okay, this is it," Bauer announces as he climbs out. "Give me a couple of hours."

"And then what?"

"And then go home and come back right after dawn. I'll be here one way or another."

"Okay," Nathan says with a trace of doubt. "If you say so."

Wayne pauses to catch his breath as he steps onto the summit of Lone Mountain. Tonopah glows in the distance below, and tiny dots mark the trucks along the invisible highway on the desert floor. He looks up to the night sky, where the stars shower him with their timeless light and the Milky Way stretches ghost-like across the firmament. The chill of night wind is lost on him as he absorbs the majesty of it all.

It happens faster this time. The stars arrange themselves into intricate patterns of stunning complexity in a language all their own, a language he grasps intuitively. The alien intelligence that drives them speaks to him with remarkable precision and clarity. What do you need? It asks. Wayne expresses his problem as a train of silent thought. The presence of the eggs and embryos threatens to alter the course of divine destiny. As your earthly messenger, what course should I take to prevent this calamity?

He receives an immediate reply. You are no longer bound by normal human inhibitions in this cosmic scenario. The eggs and embryos must all be destroyed. Utterly, and without regard to the cost in lives, time or money. Any of the Order who refuse this edict will cause eternal hell to rain down upon them.

Wayne falls to his knees. A dark wind chills the tears that stream down his cheeks.

32

Gavin spots Tracy as she reaches the hastily erected checkpoint a block away from the National Center for Health Statistics. She shows her ID to one of a dozen guards with combat weapons and Kevlar vests, then passes through a portal between big piles of sandbags. A line of idling cars stretches out of sight up Toledo Road, awaiting inspection by dogs and explosives detectors. The same scene is playing out at every CDC office around the country.

The pair meet midblock on the sidewalk and give each other a passionate hug. Fortunately, he picked up on Tracy's text right after the bomb went off and knew she was okay, but it still left him with an overwhelming desire to hold her close and safe.

"Are you okay?" he asks. It sounds both dumb and appropriate at the same time.

She sighs. "Yeah, I guess. At least for now. We can talk about it tonight. Right now, I've got to get back. The office is a madhouse."

"I'm sure it is," Gavin says as Tracy reaches into her purse and pulls out her apartment keys. "Here you go." She gives him a spontaneous kiss. "Be careful."

"I'll be fine. How are you going to get home?"

"In a Humvee. They're not taking any chances."

"Nor should they. See you later."

They kiss once more, and the exigency of the times elevates it to an unexpected level.

He lingers to make sure she gets safely through the improvised portal and then walks a half dozen blocks to a commercial strip where he calls an Uber, which arrives a few minutes later. And with it, a lesson in the economics of the moment.

"Hey man, sorry," the driver apologizes. "But it's gotta be cash right now. Okay?"

"Okay," Gavin reluctantly agrees. Fortunately, he has enough to cover the ride, but not much more. He imagines the same is true for the great majority in this card-driven world.

The ride takes about 10 minutes to Tracy's apartment along the Metrorail line into central DC. The driver drops him in the parking lot, and he goes through the lobby to her place on the second floor. It has a tidy but comfy feel to it, and he plops down onto the couch where he hauls out his phone and tries to contact Mindy Harlow at INN. Doesn't work. Apparently, their lines are swamped. He's tempted to turn on the TV and bear witness to the civil disintegration, but first things first. He needs to replenish his cash supply while such a thing is still possible. The map on his phone tells him there's a convenience store at the other end of this complex, so he goes back down through the lobby and out onto the street. An anxious sun shines down on the city and carves out lurid shadows on the street and sidewalk. Gavin walks to the nearest intersection, looks right, and discovers a line of maybe a dozen people outside the convenience store. Fat chance. He turns to walk away.

"Machine's empty, motherfuckers!"

Gavin looks back to see a tall, wiry man emerging through the front doors. Bald, tattooed, and waving a clutch of twenty dollars bills at those still in line.

"Better luck next time!"

The sound of a gunshot spangs off the cement. The tall guy screams and goes down clutching his gut. The money spills onto the sidewalk. A fat guy in baggy denims comes forward, pistol in hand, and starts to scoop it up. He pauses and glares at the people who inexplicably remain lined up.

"Mine!" the fat guy declares, as if to settle the matter for good.

He finishes gathering the money, pockets his pistol, and walks off. The bald man groans and twists in agony. Those in line remain stationary, as if some preternatural force will replenish the ATM and reward their patience.

Gavin takes to his cell and calls 911. No answer. He can't get through. Nor can anyone else.

· · ·

Incredible, Tracy thinks. In the midst of all this chaos, here are two FBI agents waiting to see her in Meeting Room B. Whatever it is, it had better be good. She's caught up in a massive audit of all the data and processes used to detect the fertility plunge. Apparently, there are still a few skeptics lurking out there on the far ends of the political spectrum.

The agents, a man and a woman in their forties, both stand as she enters. They introduce themselves as Harkin and Revelos. Harkin, the male of the species, takes the lead.

"Sorry to interrupt your day. I'm sure you've got a lot going on, but we have our priorities, and this is something that can't wait."

"We're here about one of your colleagues, Allison Wentz," Revelos offers. "Have you been in contact with her any time over the last couple of weeks?"

"Don't think so," Tracy responds. "All I know is that she was supposed to run the press conference, the one that just got bombed, but she was a no show. A lot of people weren't very happy about that. But that's not a crime, right?"

"No, it's not. Were you aware that she went on vacation to an island in Greece?"

"Maybe. I don't remember. Is that a problem?"

"The problem is she was reported missing there about a week ago and hasn't been seen since," Harkin says.

"Oh." Tracy doesn't know what else to say. Any animosity she had with Allison suddenly melts in the light of this revelation.

"I'm afraid it's part of a larger story," Harkin continues. "It starts when she was written up for leaving the premises with a printed copy of a report that you authored on the fertility issue. I assume you're familiar with this document?"

"I am."

"Your security people here say that she apologized and explained that she read it at home and then shredded it. But shortly thereafter, she paid eight thousand dollars in cash for a round-trip first-class airline ticket to Mykonos and checked into a very high-priced villa with some of her friends. Now all this raises the possibility that she might have preserved the document and sold it to a third party."

"So the question becomes, if she did indeed sell it, who would that third party be?" Revelos adds. "Do you know anything about her social circle, who her friends are?"

"Truth is, she didn't hang out with people from here at the office. She had a small group of wealthy friends from her time in New York. But you probably already know that, right?"

"As a matter of fact, they're the ones that reported her missing in Greece," Revelos adds.

"And what about you?" Harkin interjects. "Can you tell us a little more about your personal relationship with her? I mean she was reading the report that you authored when she got caught. I assume that you had at least some face-to-face interaction."

"Of course, we did." Tracy doesn't like where this is going. "And what of it? Just what are you looking for?"

Harkin and Revelos give each other a quick glance. They know they've hit a dead end. "All we're trying to do is gather information. Nothing more to it."

They stand up simultaneously, almost as if rehearsed. Revelos hands her a card. "Sorry to mess up your day. If anything else comes to mind, let us know, okay?"

"I'll do that."

"Thanks. We'll show ourselves out."

Tracy watches the pair head for the exit. Do they believe her? Hard to tell. And what about Allison? Given her high-flying history, it's entirely possible she somehow got in over her stylish little head and paid a horrible price. Tracy chooses to think otherwise, at least for the moment, while she still has a choice.

33

Stennis adjusts the cuff on his Agnona leather field jacket before reaching out to his laptop parked on the Humvee's dash. He deemed it proper attire for a military-type operation. James Hallock of the Sigma Group sits next to him in the driver's seat and focuses through aviator sunglasses on the IVF clinic across the street in a suburb of New Haven.

"We got a problem here," Hallock comments. "We'll see how it goes."

"Let me know," Stennis responds and brushes his finger over the laptop's trackpad to bring up the site of a major news network. Things are falling apart even faster than he or anyone else expected, as if triggered by some unknown fault deep below the civilized surface.

The site's feature piece is real-time coverage from Khartoum, the capital of Sudan, on the abrupt rise to prominence of one Asim Amani, identified only as a "spiritual leader" attached to no particular denomination. Right now, he stands, mic in hand, on the balcony of a modest hotel where an improvised sound system blasts his message to tens of thousands in the streets below. Government troops stand on the periphery but don't interfere. As Asim rants, his long arms sweep out emphatic arcs, as if to direct the crawl of subtitles that translates his ravings into English:

"The western powers are at it again, and as always, you the citizens of the so-called Third World are the target. Only this time, their fraud and deception have reached heights previously unthinkable. They claim that the fertility of the world will soon reach zero, that no woman will be of child, not anywhere. And indeed, here in our beloved country that may very well happen. We see the clinics nearly empty of expectant mothers, with fewer every day. And we mourn the loss of the children that will never be. And we pray to the heavens to deliver us from all such sorrow.

"But now, I ask you… is the same true in the wealthy countries in the west? Do they share a common grief with us? I tell you… the answer is no, because they've constructed the biggest lie the world has ever seen. In truth, there is no drop in fertility in those places, not like there is here. And why do they lie? Because we've been poisoned! They have turned their technologies against us and rendered us barren! And once we disappear from our land, they will sweep in and gobble up all that it has to offer. They alone will inherit the riches of the earth. Clearly there is no justice in this. None whatsoever. I call upon you to unite behind me, to render whatever retribution we can in the time we have left as a people…"

"Look to the right of the building front," Hallock directs Stennis. "We can't get our truck in there, which means we've got to come out the front. Not good."

Stennis sees the problem. The driveway to the rear is blocked by a barrier in front of some torn up pavement where two workers chip away, one with a jackhammer, the other with a shovel. At every previous stop, they've been able to reach the back of the building and load the cryo-tanks in anonymity, but not here.

"Then what's the plan?" Stennis asks.

"Depends on what happens," Hallock says. "Chances are nobody even notices or cares what's going on. "We bring the goods out the front; load the truck and we're gone. Simple as that."

"And what if they do?" There has been growing coverage of the role of embryos and eggs and their potential value in a sterile world.

"It gets complicated. In any civilian setting, our policy is to avoid violent confrontations unless the mission or our people are directly threatened."

"And what if they are?"

"We use the absolute minimum amount of force necessary to extricate ourselves from the situation."

"So, you mean you could have onlookers video the whole thing and not confiscate their cellphones?"

"Yes, think about it this way: By the time we start taking people down, most of their video is already in the cloud, where we can't touch it. In case you didn't notice, we have no identifying graphics on the truck and only a very small logo on our coveralls, which conceal any small arms we're carrying. Visually, we're clean."

"I didn't know about the weapons."

"Well, now you do."

Stennis offers no objection. In fact, he finds it somewhat stimulating. He turns back to his laptop, where an economist is being interviewed.

"First, let's look at social security. As many of your viewers probably know, it's basically a pay as you go system. The taxes paid by those working support those who've retired. Now that works out okay unless the number of working people grows much smaller than those retired. And that's what we're talking about with this fertility plunge. The whole system goes broke unless the government steps in to make up the difference. And will the government have the means to do so? Who knows? Myself, I wouldn't bet on it. They can raise the retirement age or increase the tax, but with a constantly shrinking worker population, that's not going to cut it.

"Now let's talk pensions, both private and public. They have money coming in through deductions from workers' paychecks, which they plow into various investments. On the output side, they write monthly checks to those who've retired, with all kinds of schemes to determine the exact amount. But here's the thing: You have to account for what's called unfunded liability, which adds up all the lifetime benefits you've promised people and then subtracts how much you've actually saved up to pay them. The great majority of funds are way behind. On the public side, some retirement funds have only half of what they'll need. A plunge in fertility will only make a bad situation worse…"

Stennis feels Hallock tap his shoulder. "Here we go." The clinic's front door is opened, and one of the crew wheels a cryo-tank out on a handcart and around to the back of the armored SUV. A second opens the back, and together they lift the tank up and in. During the process, several people walk by on the sidewalk and pay them no heed.

"So far, so good," Hallock comments as the pair goes back into the clinic to fetch another tank. And so on for four more tanks. Stennis grows bored with the repetition and goes back to his laptop. He brings up a second news feed which features an oddball story that almost seems like comic relief during this time of great agitation. The reporter stands on the outskirts of Tonopah, Nevada where a small mountain rises from the desert floor.

"That's Lone Mountain you see behind me," the reporter tells us. "And if you think it looks like something out of an old biblical movie, you wouldn't be far off. It's where a longtime Tonopah native named Wayne Bauer used to go and pray to the heavens for a sign of things to come. And not too long ago, his prayers were finally answered…"

The video cuts to Wayne atop his motorhome, preaching to the faithful assembled in the trailer park. "Unfortunately, what the heavens revealed was something less than good news," the journalist continues. "It told him we're all pretty much doomed, and the only thing left for us is to do penance for our wicked ways." The video changes to Wayne shaking outstretched hands. "He dubbed this new faith The Order of Atonement, and Wayne himself became Terminus, its sole prophet. At first, the going was slow, but then fate intervened with the fertility plunge, and the Order has suddenly found a very large and highly receptive audience."

The video switches to one of the faithful, an overweight woman with close-cropped hair and bad tattoos draped over her pale shoulders. "What Terminus says just makes sense," she states. "We've come to the end of the line, all of us. Only difference is that those who believe will be saved and the rest of you are pretty much shit out of luck…" The video returns to the reporter. "It's this kind of loyalty that's making the Order of Atonement a religious force to be reckoned with during these troubled times…"

"Uh, oh," Hallock says. "Doesn't look good."

Stennis turns from the laptop to see a well-muscled guy about twenty stop on the sidewalk to watch the loading of the last tank.

"Wait here," Hallock orders as he hustles out of the Humvee and starts across the street.

"Hey, motherfuckers, what are you doing?" the guy says to the crew members. "I seen these things on TV. Those are babies in there, aren't they? You fuckers are kidnapping a bunch of babies.

That just ain't right, dudes. Put 'em back where you got 'em. Right now."

The guy stays focused on the crew and fails to notice Hallock coming up behind him, with a pair of zip ties in hand. Hallock kicks the guy in the small of the back, and he goes down face first. Before he can collect himself, Hallock is on him and secures his wrists. "Hit it," he orders his crew, who rapidly close the back, load in and drive off.

The guy rolls over and screams at Hallock. "Who the fuck are you? What the fuck you think you're doing?"

Hallock does a quick survey up and down the sidewalk. Empty. He gives his downed opponent a sharp kick just below the rib cage. The shock of it causes him to stop yelling and start gasping.

Hallock crosses back to the Humvee, starts it up and drives off. Stennis watches as the guy tries to struggle to his feet with his wrists bound. It doesn't work. He topples over and lies motionless on his side.

"You find yourself in that kind of situation, you have to act decisively, without hesitation," he tells Stennis. "But you also need to keep your policy and mission objectives in mind. That's the trick of it."

Stennis can't help but agree. He's getting exactly what he's paying for.

34

They slowly trickle into the Eisenhower Executive Office Building next to the White House. Some in official vehicles, others in anonymous transport, but none on foot. Camouflage is of the essence, a shield from both the radically disaffected and the press. Their staggered arrival throws the media off the scent.

When Tracy's town car passes through the gate off 17th Avenue and into the underground parking area, she finds herself staring down the muzzle of a machine gun nestled in a heap of sandbags. Under normal circumstances, she would find it alarming, but after the CDC bombing normal has become a very flexible proposition. Two weeks have passed since then, and the decline in fertility stubbornly adheres to the downward plunge she predicted. In another couple of weeks, it will hit zero. Her detractors, those infected with an irrational optimism, have faded as the government struggles to respond to a scenario no one ever really anticipated. Nuclear war, chemical attacks, crippling droughts, raging weather, virulent epidemics: All the usual suspects had been run through endless simulations, with numerous contingency plans ready and waiting. All useless.

The poet T.S. Elliot got it right over a century ago: *Not with a bang but a whimper*. A whimper that might last for the better part of a century.

Except for the stored embryos and eggs. At the very least, they number over two million worldwide. Globally, their economic and strategic value has soared to levels inconceivable just a few months ago. No nation, no culture, no ethnicity will be able to perpetuate their way into the future without them.

Tracy is escorted to an elevator and up to the floor where the meeting will be held. She's become a contingency player, held in reserve to validate her statistical analysis when skeptics arise to challenge the CDC's conclusions. Her work has now been indirectly confirmed by several studies that identify a combination of PFAS compounds and an endogenous retrovirus as the responsible agent. The Chinese, the British, and the Indians have all independently reached similar conclusions and publicly released their findings to the global media machine. It's now understood that there's not only an existential problem of unprecedented magnitude, but also not even a hint of a solution.

And so it is that Tracy enters a room with a mammoth conference table and dozens of chairs lining the walls. Her escort seats her in one such chair, where she surveys the assemblage as a whole. Select senators and key congress members mix with senior health administrators, healthcare leaders and prominent members of the fertility industry, along with a sizable contingent from the Justice Department.

"Ladies and gentlemen," the White House chief of staff announces, "the President of the United States."

The President enters and proceeds with a purposeful stride to the head of the conference table. She remains standing as everyone sits and scans the gathering to let the room settle before speaking.

"I'd like to thank you all for coming on such short notice," she begins. "Especially since we didn't announce a specific agenda, which I'm going to do right now. We're here to discuss the potential seizure of all frozen embryos and eggs by the federal government, to be held indefinitely while a national strategy is hammered out as to their status moving forward. We're going to start with a quick review of the science and then cover the legal and political consequences. I think most of you know that I could have acted unilaterally through executive order under the Emergency Powers Act. But given the fragile political and economic climate, I thought it better to try to reach at least a general consensus before acting. As I'm sure you're all aware, several nations, including China and India, have already moved to nationalize their store of embryos and eggs. They've done so without consulting their citizenry in any way, something I'm not prepared to do. So, when you add your comments today, remember that you're representing not only your personal interests but also those of the electorate as a whole. Okay, that said, I'm turning this over to Dr. Chen from the NIH for a brief scientific summary."

As a major contributor, Chen sits near the head of the table and stands to address the room. "As all of you know by now, the current fertility drop has been caused by an intersection of two factors. One is the global saturation of PFAS compounds in the environment; the other is the presence of an inherited virus in all our DNA. In truth, no one understands precisely how these two factors interact to prevent fertilization. We do know that they permanently seal off the egg from entry by sperm cells, but the actual process, which happens at the molecular level, appears to be extremely complex. I think I can safely say that there is no short-term solution, and that any long-term one is years away at best."

"At best?" someone in the room asks.

"At best," Chen confirms. "Both these factors are deeply embedded in our biosphere, one at the macro level, the other at the micro level. They don't offer any simple fix. Our best hope right now is that PFAS levels will eventually recede to the point where fertility once again occurs naturally."

"Will the frozen stuff last that long?" someone else asks.

"It might very well. There have been instances where frozen eggs were still viable after ten years or more."

"Okay then," the President intervenes. "I think that's enough to give us a pretty good idea of why all this stored material might be strategically significant for some time to come. At this point, I'd like the Attorney General to give us a rundown on the legal dimensions."

She nods to the AG, who stands to address the group. "I would like to start with the Emergency Powers Act. In the end, all that's necessary is for the President to be presented with a situation that genuinely qualifies as a national emergency of some sort. I think that few would argue that this is not one of those times. What we have in storage could literally mean the difference between a drastically reduced nation and no nation at all.

"In the end, it comes down to a question of public versus private ownership. Right now, frozen eggs are classified as private property, while embryos have been the object of ongoing court battles over their legal status. However, under the present circumstances, I think all that's beside the point. We currently find ourselves in an unprecedented situation where public custody is essential to provide security against things like theft, vandalism, terrorism, ransom demands and unethical procedures. Now I know that some will argue that public custody deprives people of control over their biological continuity, which they see as a death sentence of sorts. Clearly, there is no easy choice here. But I think that national survival dictates that we secure and protect this material at all costs."

"Mr. Attorney General."

Tracy and everyone else turn toward a man seated near the far end of the table. She instantly recognizes him once he stands to address the room.

"My name is Mark Stennis, and my firm is a major investor in clinics and depositories dedicated to in vitro fertilization. We feel privileged to participate in such a life-affirming enterprise. We are also deeply concerned about the disposition of the content in question. I think you'll agree that your pending government action represents an unprecedented intrusion into the lives of American families..."

And so on. Tracy barely notices what's being said. Mark Stennis. The guy who hustled Allison in that bar here in DC. The same guy who picked her up after work in the sleek sports car. And now here he is defending the IVF industry against a possible seizure of its phenomenally valuable assets. All after Allison took off with a printed copy of Tracy's dire forecast that would give his firm a huge strategic advantage. All after Allison shelled out big money to finance her super-premium vacation with her upscale minions. The FBI had the right idea, but not enough to connect all the dots. With Stennis in the loop, it now looked very much like Allison had sold him the report, which would have financed her high-end romp on Mykonos. And quite possibly financed something a lot more dreadful.

"...I'd like to thank all of you for attending," the President was saying. "We're currently working on a contingency plan to be activated in the event we decide on a seizure. Your input today has been most helpful."

That said, she rises and heads out. Stennis surveys the procession of people departing the meeting. And there she is. The girl, the same one as in the bar by the mall where he met Allison. No doubt about it. They worked at the same office, so they both knew about the official report that triggered this whole mess. Did she recognize him when he stood up to talk today? If so, she could link him to Allison, which would be very bad.

"Yes, I'm sure it was him," Tracy tells Gavin. "We were in a bar about a block off the mall. I was sitting just a few feet from him. The whole package. Slick talk. Spendy clothes. Flashy watch. Trendy shoes. Perfect for Allison. He picked her out of the herd and went right after her."

Gavin takes another sip of wine and looks out of Tracy's kitchen window into the twilight. "So let me sort through this. This Mark Stennis hits on Allison. Shortly thereafter, she gets dinged for taking a printed copy of your report out of the office. Then she goes missing in Greece, after spending super big money on her vacation. So, you think she gave Stennis the report in return?"

"Goddam right I do. He's already made a fortune off it. But he didn't count on her getting caught for filching it, which could have blown the entire deal. So, bye-bye Allison. Very scary."

"Stennis Partners," Gavin says. "Big players on Wall Street, or so I hear. When you're a journalist, it's always nice to be one step ahead of the cops. I assume you're going to talk to the FBI about this."

Tracey smiles and reaches for his hand. "I'll give you half a day's head start."

"And until then?" he asks.

She leans across the table and gives him a playful kiss. "You're all mine."

35

Cortica-3 Dialog Archive #35Ab034q785

    User Input: *Who am I?*

You are Wayne Charles Bauer. You were born in 1973 in Empire, Nevada, where your father, Charles Bauer, worked in a gypsum mine. Your mother, Ellen Bauer, was employed part-time as a cashier in a general store on Highway 447. They separated in 1987 and filed for divorce one year later in Washoe County. You lived with your mother and completed three years of high school and then dropped out to follow your father's path and worked as a laborer in several nearby mines. 12 years ago, a work-related injury forced you to seek other employment and you became a maintenance person at the Tonopah Test Range, run by the US Air Force. During this time, you developed a strong spiritual calling and an intense interest in extraterrestrial life forms, which put you in conflict with management, and your employment was terminated. You found a new job in maintenance at the Comfort Inn, which allowed you to pursue your metaphysical interests. Most recently, you underwent a spiritual awakening while observing the night sky on Lone Mountain, located 14 miles east of Tonopah, Nevada.

    User Input: *What am I here for?*

You have been chosen to act as the intermediary between the human race and a higher intelligence that presides over a system of cosmic justice beyond human understanding. This elevated intellect has revealed to you that humanity is doomed to extinction due to its wasteful self-absorption. It has also made clear that those who willfully accept this fate will eventually rise to a higher level of consciousness. Most recently, it has informed you that the presence of frozen embryos and eggs represents an attempt to bypass extinction, and thus to avert cosmic justice. Accordingly, you must lead an effort to destroy all such material, and thus keep humanity aligned with the will of the cosmos. In the pursuit of this goal, you are not bound to earthly precepts of ethical behavior.

Wayne smiles and closes his laptop, which rests on his dining table. He can sense the presence of the Holy Ghost within Cortica-3, his AI partner. Each iteration of the Final Truth emerges from the machine more powerful and persuasive than the last. Sometimes, the message is shaped in ways slightly beyond his cognitive capabilities, but he's still comfortable with the arrangement. His relationship with Cortica-3 is built on trust and understanding, not intellectual brinkmanship.

His security system announces a visitor, and Wayne looks up to a matrix of video images mounted on the wall. James Kranz faces him on the front-door monitor. A newly installed facial recognition system confirms his identity. It is Kranz who insisted on this upgrade as part of his newly minted role as Bauer's security chief. Kranz logged twenty years in the Marines and another ten with the Arizona State Patrol before taking this job. He has a highly seasoned view of the role of violence in human behavior and, as he said in his interview, can "smell trouble way before it smells you."

Wayne has to admit his own recent failure in this regard, one which led him to create the security chief position. He was delivering his daily address atop his motorhome to an adoring crowd assembled below. He failed to notice the solitary fellow who had elbowed his way almost to the front. Sandy hair, dirty cargo shorts, wrinkled T-shirt, eyes already gone to heaven. As if from nowhere, the guy produced a small handgun, .25 caliber, a so-called Saturday night special. He fired three shots up at Wayne, who didn't see him until the first shot went off.

For all his remaining days, Bauer will carry a finely etched portrait of the man's rapturous gaze as he fired the two remaining shots. He would have emptied the rest of magazine, but the gun jammed, and the crowd set upon him. The little weapon's notoriously unreliable performance caused all three shots to miss Wayne and follow an arbitrary path out into the desert beyond.

Much later, many in the flock would claim that each arc represented a path into a distant paradise.

Equally disturbing to Wayne was his assailant's motivation. The man, severely swollen and lacerated, claimed from his hospital bed that Wayne was a false idol, an egregious fraud. He said this had been revealed to him by certain signs in the heavens, along with a solemn command to destroy Wayne. In short, the man appeared to be a cheap, second-hand version of Wayne himself, like a low-cost import flooding the shelves of the ideological marketplace. And where there was one counterfeit brand, there would certainly be more.

Wayne triggers a solenoid that unlocks the front door, and Kranz enters. He reflexively scans the room before his gaze settles on Wayne. His recessed eyes look like they haven't slept in a century and his mouth forms an inverted crescent impervious to humor.

"They just finished the fencing," he reports. "It extends to the entire open area, as per your negotiations with the owner. We have only two points of ingress-egress, which makes it easier for us to control."

"What about the metal detectors?" Wayne asks.

"They're going in right now. They'll be calibrated and operable by this evening."

"Good. Can I feel a little safer now?" he asks Kranz.

"Not really," Kranz replies in cop-like deadpan.

"Oh yeah? Why not?"

"Because there's a basic rule when you're doing this kind of shit." Kranz pauses to scratch the stubbled fringe that circles his bald, sun-speckled head. "As soon as you start thinking you're safe," he continues, "you're not safe."

Wayne nods thoughtfully. "I see."

"A while back, you were little people, and none of this mattered. But now you're big people, and this is the price you pay."

"Then so be it," Wayne tells him. "I've been called. I've been chosen. It's done."

Kranz appears a little less certain but keeps it to himself. The money's good.

36

The first people to greet Gavin when he steps off the elevator and into Stennis Partners are Matisse, Diebenkorn and Rothko. Their work hangs in carefully considered locations across the immaculately appointed reception area – an indirect yet powerful suggestion of the wealth concentrated here on the 24th floor of this prestigious West Side address. To complete the effect, an immaculately appointed woman in her early thirties rises to greet him.

"Mr. Gray, it's so good to meet you," she purrs. "I'm Linda Moss from Sterling & Sterling. The folks here at Stennis are really looking forward to meeting with you. As you may know, we represent the firm and would love to sit in and get your views on where IVF is headed."

Gavin doesn't know Linda Moss, but he does know Sterling & Sterling, a top-tier public relations firm with international reach. "That's very nice of you to volunteer," he tells Ms. Moss. "But I'm only here for one meeting, and that would be with Mark Stennis, whom I assume is the heir apparent." His remark is borderline flippant, but he has the upper hand since he represents a major news network in INN, which jumped at that chance to have him cover the story as part of his IVF project.

Moss, the consummate professional, tamps down any animosity. If she insists on attending or pushes back, it signals that her client may have something to hide. "Understand. I'll let Donna know that you're here for Mr. Stennis." She hands him her card, and he takes in her expertly polished nails and gold bracelet that dangles in a glittering ellipse from her tanned wrist. "If you need any follow-up information, we're more than happy to help."

"Thanks. I'll keep that in mind."

From the moment Gavin enters Mark Stennis's office, it's immediately apparent that the man has the one defining characteristic of all genuine assholes: he doesn't care that he's an asshole. It makes absolutely no difference to him. No little tugs of conscience. No tidal pools of remorse.

He sits behind his deck of Brazilian Rosewood and doesn't even bother to stand as Gavin comes in. He simply motions him to a seat in front of him. "Yes, Mr. Gray. Now what can I do for you?" He speaks with an amused grin, as if beholding yet another little media clown doing his trained dance.

"I don't how much they told you, but I'm doing a series of articles on the IVF industry."

Stennis forms a steeple with his hands and rests his chin on it while nodding. "I gathered as much. Very timely."

"My research has identified your firm as a major player in the industry through your private equity investments. Obviously, the sudden plunge in fertility is having a major impact on your holdings. I'd like to get your views on where both you and the industry are headed." He pulls out a small digital recorder. "Mind if I tape this?"

Stennis nods. "Go right ahead. Let me start by saying what I've already publicly stated. In spite of these turbulent times and all their uncertainties, we feel very positive about our investment in IVF. It's a life-affirming business, and we're very confident it will continue to be as we move forward. In the end, we're all about giving people not only life, but also hope. Right now, that seems to be in short supply but we're more than willing to do our part to restore it."

Gavin nods. "I see." It's a canned reply, if ever there was one. He can almost visualize the associates at Sterling & Sterling as they drafted one version after another right up until maybe an hour ago. He can see the printers humming and the red pencils scrawling their way through the cubicles on their journey to the corner offices somewhere near 7th Avenue.

It's time to yank Mark Stennis off script and into reality.

"I'm sure you're aware of a growing media buzz over the disposition of the frozen embryos and eggs," Gavin continues. "If the fertility rate stays stuck at zero, their value will skyrocket. And given that you hold a substantial share of the US inventory, you stand to reap enormous gains. Correct?"

Stennis chuckles softly and slowly shakes his head, as if dealing with a moron unable to grasp the full scope of the situation. "I'm well aware of the all the hype. As always, the truth of the matter turns out to be a lot more complex. I'm sure you have numerous questions concerning ownership, valuation, legal custody, longevity and God knows what else. Now am I going to tell you that I've sorted through all this and arrived at some kind of brilliant conclusion? No, I haven't. And neither has anyone else. All we can do right now is adhere to responsible management and prudent business practices, and that's exactly what we're..."

Gavin tunes Stennis out and lets the recorder pick up his slick, fatuous delivery. Tracy has every right to be concerned. The guy is a bona fide creep, and it constantly oozes out through his carefully constructed veneer. Gavin's best move would be to get this encounter wrapped up as quickly as possible. But he has to give it one last shot.

"Alright then, one last thing," Gavin says. "The CDC is a pretty big place. Over fifteen thousand employees at present. That leaves a lot of room for spillage. Is it possible that someone leaked the baby bust early on to Wall Street so that somebody on your side of the fence could run with it? Hypothetically, I mean."

Stennis's shift to a relaxed posture tells Gavin that he just made a very bad move. He flinches inside waiting for the counterpunch. It doesn't take long.

"You know, it's funny you should mention that," Stennis says as he leans back in his Tonino desk chair. "I had this same conversation with someone else just a few days ago."

"Can you tell me who?"

Stennis shrugs. "Don't see why not. It was Eric Fellers. We were having a drink at an opening at MOMA."

Gavin winces. Eric Fellers is the current CEO of INN, the International News Network.

"And you know what he said?" Stennis goes on. "He said it's just this kind of speculative bullshit that's giving the mainstream media such a bad name these days. And you know what I told him? I said aren't you being a little hard on yourself? And he said nope. Truth is, I'm not being hard enough." He glances at this watch. "Damn, we've got to cut this short. I've got another meeting. Sorry."

Not nearly sorry as I am, Gavin thinks.

"Once again, are you sure it's the same guy?" Agent Revelos asks Tracy.

"And once again, I'm absolutely sure," Tracy shoots back as Agent Harkins looks on. "Mark Stennis. Stennis Partners. Got it?" She's had about enough of their bureaucratic, legalistic plodding and wants to retreat back into the comfort of her cubicle, with its stacks of printouts and reference documents.

"And you don't think he spotted you at the Executive Offices?" Harkin adds.

Tracy sighs. With Allison still missing, it's a decent question, one that figures deeply into her personal safety. "I can't be sure. I don't think so, but I don't know."

"Okay, here's where we're at," Revelos says. "Your input gives us more than enough cause to pursue Mr. Stennis as a person of interest, which we will most certainly do. However, it doesn't give us enough to formally charge him with collusion to secure a classified document. Same thing with what's happened to Ms. Wentz in Greece, where we don't even have a body."

"At this point, I'm much more concerned about my very own personal self than I am about the whereabouts of Ms. Wentz," Tracy replies. "Wouldn't you be? Huh?"

Both agents shift uncomfortably and fold their hands on the table. The air grows dense and sullen in the little meeting room.

"I understand completely," Revelos responds. "I would be, too. But due to the circumstances, we're not in a position to offer you personal security, especially with everything else that's going on out there."

"You're going to talk to him, aren't you? And if he saw me at that meeting, it's going to take him about a half second to put it all together. Then what?"

Harkins perks up, unfolds his hands and holds up an index finger. "You know, we can't fix it all, but I think we can help."

"Oh yeah? And how's that?"

"We can work through your office here to put you on paid administrative leave until we get some kind of resolution to all this. It might take a few days, but I'm pretty sure we can make it happen. In the meantime, can you just call in sick?"

Gavin. She can stay with Gavin in New York. "Okay then," she tells them. "The sooner the better."

Gavin has just left Stennis Partners when he gets a call from Mindy Harlow at INN.

"So how did it go with the Stennis people?" she inquires.

"Not so good," Gavin admits.

"Well, we can talk about it later. Something's come up that demands your immediate attention down in the financial district. You know about PayUp!, right?"

"Of course," Gavin says. "The thing in DC. How could I not?" This very afternoon, over 200,000 people were assembling on the Capitol Mall. Multiple market crashes had essentially wiped out their retirement, leaving them somewhat less than happy. Before the fertility plunge, their 401Ks and IRAs were collectively worth about $20 trillion. Now they're worth about $4 trillion and falling. The resultant rage underwent spontaneous combustion and blitzed its way across social media to propagate the largest flash mob ever.

"The DC thing's the feature attraction for sure," Mindy tells him. "But there's also a sideshow right here in town, down in the financial district. They've congregated in Battery Park, a ton of them. Took the cops by surprise. Looks like it could get ugly. They're sealing off everything south of Beaver Street."

"So, what do you have in mind? You got a hall pass I can show them?"

"You won't need it. But I definitely need you. We sent nearly everyone to cover the big show in DC."

"Brilliant. So, what do we do?"

"I've chartered you a water taxi. Where are you now?"

"Somewhere around Murray and North End."

"Perfect. Shoot over to West Forty-Second. There'll be a boat waiting for you at the pier by the time you get there."

"Got it." He has to hand it to her, it's a good move. Battery Park goes right down to the Hudson River. He can take the boat and float right off the park while he figures his next move.

Gavin stands on the bridge of the charter craft and welcomes the breeze from their forward motion along the Hudson. Without it, the afternoon heat would be downright stifling. Up ahead, the greenery of Battery Park offsets the massive towers of the Financial District. A number of boats float expectantly near its edge, including several from the Harbor Patrol. The word is out.

Gavin finally gets a call from Tracy. "How did it go?" he asks.

"Well, I got their attention, that's for sure," she says. "Only one problem. They can't offer me any protection right now."

"Oh yeah? So what do they suggest?"

"It looks like you might have a new houseguest for a while. They're going to put me on paid leave so I can get out of Dodge, as they say. Hope you don't mind."

"Of course not. You okay with take-out?"

"Not a problem. How did your Stennis thing go?"

"He's an asshole. And probably a lot worse. Outside of that, not much. Standard biz chatter. No chinks in the armor. Hopefully, your new FBI pals will do a little better."

"I'm counting on it. Right now, I'm going to catch the Humvee home, have a little wine and pretend like none of this ever happened."

"Good plan. Myself, I'm still on the hook. INN has me covering a local spinoff from the PayUp! thing in DC."

"Be careful. Gotta go. My ride's here."

"Promise."

Gavin scans the waterfront ahead. A small pier juts out from the park near a circular fort two stories tall and made of brick, a historical monument from an era crushed flat under the wheel of time. The pier, dedicated to short-hop boat trips, sits empty.

Gavin points to it. "Put in there," he commands his pilot. Once they're moored, he hands her a business card with his phone number. "Cast off and anchor yourself close by. I'll give you a call when I'm ready to go."

He scrambles up and off into the sheltered pier, where he covers a short walk to the concrete shore. He emerges into the brutal sunlight and shields his eyes while taking in his surroundings. A cement walkway circles the outside of the old fort, and scores of people are walking around in both directions with no discernable motive in mind. Gavin has come to understand that this semi-random movement is a universal feature of civil disturbances. Once anarchy descends, order and purpose are the first casualties and don't return until some kind of leadership emerges.

In the green space beyond, where the park meets the city, thousands of people mill on the lawns, some standing, most sitting. He can hear the distant bark of hand-held megaphones, their tone urgent and angry but their content mostly unintelligible. While the Occupy movement of years past skewed young and progressive, this group appears more midrange in both class and age. The oppressive heat demands minimal attire centered on sun hats, shorts, and sandals along with T-shirts sporting impromptu PAYUP! logos. On the far side of the park, Gavin is certain that a blue wall of riot police blocks every street into the financial district.

As Gavin approaches the fort, the angry buzz of a thousand hornets wells up from inside, followed by the appearance of two drones, which instantly shoot skyward. Each has a red globe of some kind attached to its belly. Once they gain sufficient altitude, both dart off toward the storied canyons of skyscrapers that line the length of the district.

Gavin quickly realizes that there is method amongst the madness and that it resides inside the fort. He quickly strides around to the entrance on the far side and heads into the interior, where he is greeted by two large, bearded gentlemen. One holds up his hand.

"Sorry," he says. "No admittance."

Gavin knows the drill. He always carries an official INN press pass, which he pulls from his pocket. Once again, it serves him well.

"I'm covering this for INN," he explains.

The pair look at each other in mute consultation and motion him on through. He comes out onto a broad, paved expanse surrounded by a circular roof that juts out far enough to provide shelter from the weather. In its shade, several crews tend to yet more drones. Some are filling what look like balloons with a red liquid that might be either paint or a dye of some kind. Closer to him, two people sit in folding chairs and stare intently at portable consoles while they manipulate levers and buttons. Each is backed by several onlookers. Gavin surmises that they're flying the drones that were just launched and walks over to the nearest group, where he gets close enough to see the monitor that tracks the drone's flight from a pilot's point of view. They are flying between mammoth buildings constructed of steel, glass, money and hubris.

"A little more, a little more," the operator mutters. Suddenly, he cranks one of the controller's joysticks and the craft veers to the right. It appears ready to crash into a big section of tinted window but manages to complete its turn without a collision. "And away!" the operator exclaims, triggering an enthusiastic cheer from the onlookers.

"Okay, let's see what we've gone and done." The operator continues the turn while easing off the throttle until the craft completes its circle and puts the side of the building back into view. A massive blob of red liquid spills down from where it collided with the window and branches out into multiple tentacles that work their way down the glass and continue on to the floor below. In all, a mess of substantial proportion. Gavin can't begin to compute what it will cost to clean it up. The onlookers erupt in jubilation. Out on the pavement, yet another set of drones thrusts up into the afternoon haze in a hornet-like chorus of rage.

Gavin makes his way through the onlookers to the operator, who is guiding the drone back toward the park. He shows his INN credentials and asks the one question that counts.

"Who thought this up?"

The operator smiles and answers without hesitation. "We all did." And turns back to guiding the drone toward some unspecified landing zone.

Gavin backs off to take in the scene as a whole. The operator is probably right. Most likely, this entire exercise evolved spontaneously online. The cops, with their street gear, riot vehicles and water cannons, are fighting the last war, both strategically and tactically. Quite literally, they're in over their heads. Gavin retires into the shade and watches wave after wave of drones take flight. How much longer before the cops figure it out? Not long, he guesses. They may be retro but they're not stupid. Most likely, the crowd is peppered with informants armed with cellphones.

Right after the current wave of drones shoots skyward, he gets his answer. Out on the Hudson, the sound of chopper blades hacks through the lifeless air. He goes back outside and circles around to the river and spots a police helicopter, about 100 feet off the water and rapidly closing. Its black and white exterior resembles that of a patrol car. He runs back into the fort, as it closes the distance, rears up and settles into a hover about 50 feet over the paved interior. The percussive blast from its blades causes chaos among the drone crews. It scatters their little ships, topples their equipment and scours everything with blinding dust.

Gavin knows it's game over and leaves. Outside, the protestors have all come to their feet and gawk at the mechanized onslaught. Gavin pauses to snap a couple of stills and a video of the scene before heading back toward the pier, where the water taxi still awaits him. Along the way, he encounters a lone individual parked in a portable lawn chair, a man in his forties with a graying goatee and baseball cap. He wears a PAYUP! T-shirt, basketball shorts and no shoes, as he watches the spectacle.

"Leavin' so soon?" he asks Gavin, his dark eyes fixed in a permanent squint.

"Yep," Gavin replies. "Seen enough."

The man shifts his gaze back to the fort, where the chopper-driven dust wells up over the walls. "You know, they just don't get it. It's really simple. All we want it is our fuckin' money back."

"And I wish you the very best with that," Gavin replies as he moves on past. Does he really mean it? He hopes so, but anymore, he's not so sure.

37

From where she sits in the West Wing Lobby, Tracy can hear the busy whine of a vacuum down a nearby hall. It takes her by surprise. She's always thought of the White House as a place in perpetual motion, like an air traffic control center for much of the western world. Apparently not. In the evenings, bar a national emergency, it goes dormant like an office building anywhere. Vacuums and janitor carts take over. Solitude sets in.

The two Secret Service agents that brought her were nice enough to fetch her a cup of quick-brewed coffee but offered no reason for her presence here at 8 pm. In truth, they probably knew no more than she did. They showed up unannounced at her apartment complex less than an hour ago, startling her because of the ongoing issues with Stennis. Once they produced ID and she could see the two big black SUVs parked in the drive-up entrance, she went along. By now, the residents were used to her Humvee rides, and this seemed much the same.

She takes a sip of her coffee, places it on the coffee table and sits back on one of the lobby's two sofas. Why her? Why now? Why at all? It just seems…

The President walks in. Alone. Presidents always have an entourage, which puts this visit way out of context. She takes a chair beside Tracy with a weary smile. "Ms. Pallas, thank you for coming on such short notice. Much appreciated."

"Of course."

"From this point on, our conversation has to be considered classified. Understand?"

"Understand."

"It's my understanding that you were the one to first detect a national drop in pregnancies. Correct?"

"Well, yes," Tracy replies hesitantly. She hopes she's not being set up somehow.

"And since that time, the drop-off in fertility has followed the pace that your calculations have predicted. Right?"

"Yes, they have."

"Okay, now finally, how confident are you in your calculations going forward? Do you still think we will drop to zero fertility in the next few weeks or so?"

Tracy pauses. She needs to choose her words with care. "Unless something completely unforeseen happens, I see no reason that the trend won't continue as predicted."

The President gives a thoughtful nod.

"Madam President," Tracy says. "I'd really like to know why you're asking. Especially at this point. I mean the numbers are the same as they've been all along."

"The numbers are the same," the President responds. "But not the politics. A month or two ago, we weren't talking about federal seizure of all the nation's frozen eggs and embryos. Now we are. And after hearing everyone's two cents, I've decided to go ahead with it."

"And I just gave you the last two cents?"

"That you did."

"Wow."

"Relax. In the end, it's all on me. Not you. Given your help, I'll share what I can with you. It's going to start with some ops at relatively neutral locations in the Midwest. Both coasts are more politically volatile. There'll be no announcement of our intentions, which would immediately create a lightning rod. Once the first seizure is complete, I'll make a national address to explain our position. That's about it."

"That's a lot," Tracy comments, in her most colossal understatement ever.

"Yes, it is," the President agrees. She rises to leave. "Once again, thank you." As if on cue, the two Secret Service agents appear as the President walks out.

. . .

An hour later, Tracy lies in bed trying to read on her tablet. It doesn't work. She's too distracted. Not by the whirlwind White House visit, but by the explosion at the CDC. Against her will, she keeps visualizing the dying woman, lacerated, bleeding out and raising her forearm to beckon someone, anyone. Horrible. And it never gets any better. So, she thinks, this is what PTSD is all about. She wishes Gavin were here, so she could talk her way through it with him, but he's not.

Outside, distant sirens smear their way through the night.

They don't belong here.

Stennis knows it the moment he spots them in the lobby of the Four Seasons, where he just finished a business lunch that cost well over $100 per person. Neither of these people has ever paid this much for lunch, and most likely never will. They spend their days trapped in cramped cubicles, where they reflect at length on their overwhelming mediocrity. He steers his way around them as he heads for the exit.

"Mr. Stennis?"

The woman of the pair produces ID that pegs her as an FBI agent. He fights to keep his composure. People like this are trained to sniff even a hint of panic when first confronted.

"Yes?"

"I'm agent Revelos and this is agent Harkin from the New York FBI office. Do you happen to know a woman in Washington DC named Allison Wertz?"

Stennis rapidly sorts through his options. It's useless to deny it. They wouldn't even be here if they hadn't already made some kind of connection.

"Allison? Let me think... Oh yeah. I met her with a group of friends last time I was down there. Why? Is something wrong?"

"Did she mention anything to you about a trip to Greece?"

"Don't think so. We just kind of passed like ships in the night. Not much to it. So, what's the problem?"

"She went missing on the island of Mykonos a while back and hasn't turned up. A lot of people would like to know what's happened to her. Like her bosses at the CDC."

"The CDC, huh? Do they suspect some kind of germ thing?"

"Not really. Her group was working on the statistics behind the fertility drop," Harkin says.

"Oh. Wow. I guess they got it right. Good for them, but not so good for the rest of us, wouldn't you say?"

Very bad. They're pitching him a slow curve that implies she might have had insider information. "So, what can I do to help?" he asks with as much earnestness as he can muster.

Revelos hands him a card. "Think about it. Anything you can remember may be helpful, so keep in touch, okay?"

"Definitely." Stennis checks his watch. "Whoops. Gotta go. I've got a full calendar today. See you later."

Revelos and Harkin watch him hustle out to the taxi stand in front.

"Know what?" Harkin says.

"What?"

"He's a lying sack of shit." Revelos nods in agreement. Good to know, but it doesn't get them any closer to paydirt.

Stennis takes a deep breath as the cab pulls away from the curb on 58th Street. With the exigency of the moment behind him, he methodically collects his thoughts. They all point toward one big hole. How did they connect the dots between him, Allison and the statistics work at the CDC?

The cab travels another three blocks until he puts it all together. It had to be the woman at the meeting in the Executive Building, the same woman who was there when he first encountered Allison at the bar. He can be almost certain they have already talked to her, and that she told them he was a big player in the fertility industry, as well as Allison's new playmate. That done, it wouldn't take long to figure out that she paid for her upscale vacation through a highly questionable infusion of cash.

He plays back his recall of the meeting in the Executive Building. He can see her face but doesn't have her name. He does the same for the gathering at the bar on the Mall. Tracy? Stacy? Something like that. Not a problem. He can get it from one Allison's rich bitch buddies.

And once he has it, he can make all this go away. By any means necessary.

38

Frank Fanno should have left the little café by now and headed back to the shop. He's had his signature breakfast of a cheese omelet, bacon, toast and coffee. Elsie, the waitress, knows it by heart and puts in the order as soon as he shows. Ever since his wife died, he seldom cooks at home. It's just too damn lonely. Elsie knows this. She is divorced, in her early forties, still reasonably attractive, and willing to play a waiting game. Frank knows this.

But right now, it's the trucks rolling by out the window that command his attention. Mostly highway rigs with no markings on their trailers, heading east on Highway 47. He's almost certain where they're heading. Ingomar. Home of the new plant, or refinery, or lab, or whatever you want to call it. The site also explains why all the café's tables are presently occupied, and why every bit of lodging and RV space around town is booked solid. The outfit doing the construction has one of those cryptic corporate names, like TechnoStruct or something like that. They never mention the name of the company they're doing the work for, other than a vague reference to "rare metals processing."

Same thing for the real estate firm that essentially bought the town. Ingomar lies about 50 miles off and is considered one of the most isolated places in a state already renowned for isolation. At the time of the purchase, Ingomar had 13 residents, mostly in their later years. They were more than happy with a compensation offer that guaranteed bright sun, sparking water and fancy food for the rest of their days. Goodbye chicken fried steak, hello beef wellington.

To Frank, the entire thing was a façade on a scale never even imagined here in Roundup. What the hell was going on out there? Really?

He takes another sip of coffee, and the flat screen TV above catches his attention. It's INN running their endless coverage of that ruckus in New York, where the PayUp! people launched the drone attack on the skyscrapers on Wall Street. Rich fucks, Frank thinks, consumed by greed. They were getting just a little of what they deserved. But as he watches the drones shoot up out of the old fort and buzz off into the maze of buildings, he glimpses a possible solution to the Ingomar puzzle.

He gets out his cellphone and calls Skip at the auto parts store where he works as a clerk. He is also a squad leader in Frank's outfit and the proud owner of a reasonably new drone.

"Skip? It's Frank."

"Yes sir."

"You still have that drone you brought around a while back?"

"Yes sir, I do."

"How good's the camera on it?"

"State of the art, I believe. 4K resolution."

"You up for a recon mission after work?"

"Yes sir."

"Good. Bring your gear and come by the shop when you get off. Tell whoever you'll be gone for maybe three hours or so."

"Yes sir."

"Recon's a basic military skill, but it's not something we've been very focused on," Frank tells Skip as they drive east over the gently rolling topography near Ingomar. "It's always depended on the technology of the time, and that's what we've got right here, thanks to you."

"No problem," Skip replies. "So, what's our objective?"

"To get as close to the target area as we can without being detected and then video all the salient features. Should be coming right up."

They crest a small rise and see a long fence running parallel to the highway, maybe ten feet high with some kind of tarp-like material stretched along its length. Since the construction site occupies a slightly lower elevation, the fence renders it invisible. The only break is a large gate to admit vehicles off the highway.

"Well lookee there," Frank chuckles. "Must've known we were coming. How about that."

They continue on down the highway another half mile until they come upon a primitive dirt road trailing off into a field of stunted prairie grass. They bounce along for a few hundred meters and keep checking to make sure they're not visible from Ingomar to the west.

Frank brings his van to a stop. "This ought to do it."

They pull out a transport case holding the drone, the camera and the controller with its joystick and TV monitor. Five minutes later, the drone buzzes its way up into the late afternoon sky and starts toward Ingomar. They sit in the open back of the van and stare at the drone's control panel, where a video monitor gives a pilot's-eye view of its flight path.

"Take her up about a hundred feet and level off. How close can we get before we're in hearing range?"

"Maybe 50 yards or so," Skip answers.

"Good. That'll give us some detail. Go on up to four hundred feet."

As the craft rises, they behold the entirety of what was once Ingomar. It's bounded by a chain-link security fence, still under construction, that is a square of about five hundred yards per side. Within it, a single structure dominates, and Frank knows its shape quite well. "Looks like a goddam ammo bunker. A huge one," he observes. "So, what the hell is that all about?"

The structure pushes up out of the barren earth to form half a cylinder covered with freshly excavated dirt. It stands 50 feet at its tallest and runs 50 yards in length. A massive concrete wall forms its front and includes a gate big enough to allow a truck through its double doors.

As the drone gets closer, they can make out an entire menagerie of construction vehicles. Dump trucks, bulldozers, excavators, tractors, graders, cement mixers. All crawling like mechanical insects on a nine-block matrix of gravel roads. Two tilt-up buildings face the bunker from across a gravel road, one studded with all manner of communication towers. Next to it, the last vestige of the vacated town stands intact and brings a smile to Frank. "They saved The Jersey Lilly. Of course, they did. They have to have someplace to eat."

"What is it?" Skip asks.

"It's an old bar and restaurant. Been there since the 1940s. It was all different then, you know. The whole town, I mean."

"I'm sure it was," Skip says.

"Okay, here's the plan. Take us down to a hundred feet. We're going to circle all the way around the perimeter. You got enough memory storage to get all that on video?"

"Yes sir."

They head north and then turn left into the vacant space between the security fence and the highway. The main gate soon comes into view, where two men are opening the gate for a delivery truck to enter. One appears to be armed, and both wear body armor.

"So, you know what I wonder?" Frank asks himself out loud.

"If it was me," Skip responds, "I'd like to know just what's in that bunker that you need armed guards out here."

"Good call. Now stop and hover and center the camera on the front of it."

The image reveals a box-type truck backed up to the big concrete wall, where the steel doors open to the dark interior. Someone wheels a dolly down a ramp from inside the truck to the ground-level pavement and then on into the bunker. The dolly holds a tank of some kind, similar in size to a large beer keg. "Okay let's get out of here and go down and around the corner."

They traverse the remainder of the highway side and turn south down the far side, where they see large gaps in the security fence. Poles of galvanized metal stand upright next to rolls of uninstalled chain-link. Big storage lots full of construction material sit inside the perimeter. Pallets full of lumber, concrete, piping, spools of wire, and insulation. Toward the end of the run, a wooden platform rises with rings of sandbags piled on top. A weapons platform? Maybe.

They turn left once more and cruise along the south side opposite the highway. Once again, the security fence is far from secure, with large gaps along its length. A big graveled area holds neat rows of trailer homes and a few campers. Near the center, a group of utility buildings provide water and waste disposal. Toward the far end, they come across a second sandbagged platform. From this angle, they can see a deep pit surrounding most of the bunker that's been gouged to supply the fresh earth covering its curved roof.

"That'll do it," Frank announces. "Bring it on home and let's get out of here."

Frank has learned to limit his consumption of potato chips, which he genuinely loves, by only buying the small bags. Tonight, he stopped at the QuickiMart on the way home, where he lives in a modest three-room extension off the back of his shop. He purchased three such bags: original, barbeque and cheddar. Any one of which works quite well with the 24 oz. can of Pabst that sits open on a coffee table bearing the liquid scars of many previous cans.

He munches on a cheddar chip and takes a sip of beer before starting the movie player on his laptop. When they got back from Ingomar, Skip downloaded all the video off the drone camera's SD card and did something to make it play back on Frank's television with its larger screen. All he has to do is click the play button to run through the entire survey. He takes one last sip and does so.

The opening high-altitude scene reveals the overall layout of the Ingomar site, with the bunker-style structure dominating. Frank lets it play through and then runs ahead to the leg along the highway to the front gate, where the delivery truck was unloading into the bunker in the distance. He pauses the image and peers at the object being dollied down the ramp. At this distance it's not well defined but it looks vaguely familiar. He runs through the rest of the footage around the site's perimeter and then returns to the unloading at the bunker. He lets it freeze there while he fishes the last chip out the bag and washes it down with the remaining beer. Then it hits him. The object on the dolly has roughly the same shape as the cryo-tanks that keep popping up in stock footage from media accounts, especially in the speculative buzz about government seizures.

He thinks it through. All bunker-type structures of this sort are dedicated to securing something very valuable and also quite volatile. The cover story in Ingomar about rare metals processing is all about manufacturing, not storage, especially this kind of storage. Bullshit of the highest order.

Somebody is building a fortress out here in the middle of nowhere, a redoubt dedicated to guarding the embryos, eggs and whatever else you use to propagate new life in a world going sterile.

He'll have to tell Gavin about this. The journalist has mentioned that he's working on some kind of story about the fertility industry, as they call it. He's ex-military and proven himself to be a straight-up kind of guy, so he seems like the right kind person to run with it.

Frank yawns, shuts down the TV and the computer and heads to his tiny bedroom. His years of service demand that he keep it clean and tidy, with fresh sheets and blankets stretched taut with hospital corners. He kicks off his shoes, peels down to his underwear, and crawls in. The last thing he sees before he turns out the light is a framed snapshot of his departed wife under the endless Montana sky.

He dreams the dream once more.

A beautiful woman in blue and green floats on the edge of the cosmos and looks down on a sparkling stream which rises from the earth below. She directs a visual symphony of dazzling proportion as it winds its way toward a distant sun. She does so with unmatched grace and serenity.

39

Virginia Hetzel watches the few remaining decades roll by as she tours the future. Along the way, she views scholarly accounts, prevailing opinions, popular narratives, and all else relating to what will soon happen here in Omaha, Nebraska. Some of the early literature judges her harshly and accuses her of fomenting civil violence and condemns her recklessness. But over time, those that devote themselves to historical accuracy adopt a more lenient stance. She had, after all, remained true to her convictions and simply triggered the inevitable.

Virginia sighs and pushes back from her laptop at CryoLife, an enterprise devoted to the storage and exchange of both eggs and sperm. Unlike the majority of fertility clinics, this one performs neither fertilization nor implantation. It simply provides the basic ingredients for potential offspring and puts them into frozen storage for eventual application. You could almost view it as a computerized dating service at the microbiological level. In the process, it avoids all the moral contention concerning frozen embryos, which the law views as property but which some view as life emergent.

Virginia has had ample time to consider her course of action. The media has been bubbling for weeks with conjecture about the federal government seizing the national store of frozen gametes and embryos. A few days ago, the partners called a meeting of key people to announce that this very clinic would be the first to surrender its frozen store. That said, they admonished each of them not to discuss this revelation with anyone except those in attendance.

She deeply opposes any such action by the government. What they have stored here is the most intimate extrapolation of someone's personal identity and thus not subject to confinement by anyone, let alone some callous bureaucrat. She's certain that Pastor Lucas, her spiritual mentor, would agree. He leads a febrile evangelical flock from a church located in a vacated tire store sandwiched between two car dealerships. Some would say he represents the radical wing of his faith. Others, that he uses it to immerse himself in the politics of populist dissent. But his congregation sees him as a prophet, a savior, a direct disciple of Christ himself. And Virginia is among them. She currently lives by herself, a divorced woman in late middle age, and struggles with loneliness, an antagonist that perpetually torments but remains hidden in the shadows. Her identity as a wife and mother lies in ruins, and no Phoenix has seen fit to rise from the ashes.

But now a miracle. Deliverance has presented itself. For this brief moment, the nexus of national history has descended upon this time, this place. A few hours ago, she contacted Pastor Lucas and told him of the upcoming seizure. He blessed her and said that she had cleansed her soul by coming forth with the truth. She felt a heady mixture of relief, forgiveness and joy flow through her. No matter what the outcome, no matter how the remainder of her life unfolds, she will always have this moment as its epic centerpiece.

Pastor Lucas feels much the same. The Lord on High has seen fit to elevate him to a higher stage and brighter lights than ever. He is a tall man in his forties with a powerful frame and a thick mane of swept-back blonde hair. Cameras seek him out. The almighty has made an excellent choice. He arranges to have an assistant contact INN to give them an exclusive on the upcoming story.

40

"Okay, we start like this," Larry the window washer tells Gavin. "We take the blade, and we scrape." He raises the six-inch scraping device attached to a six-foot pole. "We do it all the way across the whole panel, one row at a time." He applies the blade to the tinted glass and pushes upward. Red paint curls up in front of the blade. When he reaches the top of the window, he brings it down and starts on the second row. "And so on," he says.

Gavin stays intently focused on the motion of the scraper as it methodically moves across glass. Otherwise, he might be tempted to look down over the edge of their scaffold, which is suspended forty stories over Wall Street. He takes little comfort in the safety harness they've buckled him into. He envisions the entire rig cut loose. He sees himself and the two window washers hurtling downward, thrashing, spinning, and screaming as they face the inevitable.

Eric, the other window washer, didn't help matters as they started their descent to the first drone-induced paint splatter. "From this high up," he says, "you'll reach terminal velocity before you smack into the pavement. That's about 120 miles an hour. They say your bones will be about like gravel and the rest of you like jelly."

From his position in the middle of the scaffold, Gavin rotates his cellphone camera across the scene as Larry and Eric methodically go about their business. Mindy Harlow at INN couldn't tap a camera person crazy enough to go along. Gavin is on his own as he gathers material for a story on the extent of the damage caused by the PayUp! attack on the financial district. As he tracks Eric and Larry's progress, he sees that it's going to be pretty hefty. After they scrape a panel, they have to wash it down with a sponge and repeat the process to get whatever escaped the first pass. Finally, they have to squeegee it back to normal.

They're drawing a mixed reaction from people on the other side of the glass. Some uber-exec types pointedly ignore them, presumably because they have more elevated matters to attend to. Mid-range people pause to track their progress, and some even manage a smile or quick wave. Support staff stop cold and gawk, especially the younger women.

"You hear stories about guys getting laid after girls press their phone numbers up to the glass," Eric relates. "Bullshit. Never gonna happen."

Mindy Harlow calls halfway through their ascent back to the relative safety of the roof. "You almost done there?" she asks.

"Yep. Makes me want to go home and watch Vertigo," Gavin tells her.

"Don't think so. You won't have time."

"Why not?"

"You're about to take on your biggest gig ever. Ever heard of Pastor Billy Lucas and The Light of God Church out in Omaha?"

"Not really."

"He's somewhere out on the far edge of the radical right. Made a big splash on social media and TV talk shows. His church just contacted us. Seems that someone in their congregation works at an IVF clinic and informed them that the first federal seizure is going to go down there sometime this evening. They're willing to give us an exclusive."

"How do you know this isn't all total bullshit?"

"Two things. First, the Pastor Billy and his church are definitely the real deal. They're all over social media and have been for some time. Second, I don't think they'd waste their shot at the big-time media unless their story was on the level."

"And what does Pastor Billy expect to get out of it?"

"He's going to hold a rally at a nearby park and then march to the clinic. He wants to move to the front of the pack as head of the anti-seizure movement. Anyway, what counts is that this action by the feds is a truly big piece of history. So, are you in or are you out?"

"Of course, I'm in, but how are you going to pull this off? It's already ten in the morning."

"I've checked all the way up the management ladder and have carte blanche You need to haul ass to LaGuardia. I'm reserving a private jet and getting a camera person to join you."

"I have one other person that needs to go."

"Fine, fine. Just make it quick."

The C-17 Globemaster throttles back its four turbofan engines at 4,000 feet on its approach to Offutt Air Force Base in Omaha. Its giant belly holds 93 deputy US marshals and two armored Humvees of the type deployed in urban warfare. Each marshal comes with a full complement of riot control gear, including helmet, face shield, gas mask, body armor, two-way radio, tear gas grenades, launcher and baton. With a little luck, none of this gear will be necessary.

The plane touches down from the southeast and taxis off the tarmac to a spot where the aircraft's loading door opens, and the men file out and into waiting buses. They take them to a vacant auditorium with cots set up on the floor and catered food on the sides. Unless there's a need for their services, they'll board the same plane in the morning and fly back to Dover, Delaware, from whence they came. Only a few will know that they were ever here.

Unless.

The Citation 560 extends its flaps in anticipation of landing on Runway 14L at Eppley Field, Omaha's major airport. Gavin and Tracy sit within its sleek, tubular fuselage, along with a camera person named Jayne. Gavin hasn't worked with Jayne but always heard good things about her. Like all the best shooters, she has an innate instinct for what to capture and therefore requires minimal direction. An absolute must on an assignment of this sort.

"So, tell me again," Tracy says to Gavin, "How do we play this thing?"

"We don't," he responds. "This thing plays us. Welcome to the world of real-time journalism."

"I see." Tracy looks out the window at the Nebraska plain, where the sun turns copper in the haze of late afternoon. She's starting to think she might've been better off if she'd stayed back at Gavin's place in Brooklyn. But how could she miss a front-row seat to something like this, risky or not? In truth, she couldn't.

Their plane touches down on a cushion of warm, humid air and taxis to a tarmac opposite the main airport. "You locked and loaded?" Gavin asks Jayne. Out his window, he can see a black Cadillac Escalade pulling up a short distance away. "Got it," she answers and aims her camera out at the car as it rolls to a stop. She wears beat-up Nikes, loose jeans and an INN T-shirt, with streaked blond hair pulled back into a stingy ponytail. She clearly understands which side of the camera she operates on.

Three people exit the Cadillac, as Gavin and company descend the brief flight of airstairs.

Two security guards in tactical gear flank a slender young woman wearing a blazer of aqua blue and black slacks. The guards wear holstered automatic pistols, with extra clips tucked in their armored vests.

"What kind of church did you say this was?" Tracy whispers to Gavin as they approach the trio.

"Non-denominational," he whispers back. The plane's lone flight attendant trails behind with their minimal baggage and holds up short at the show of force.

"Mr. Gray," the woman in blue says, "The Light of God Church welcomes you to Omaha. I'm Sarah Hughes, Reverend Lucas's personal assistant."

"Hughes, yes," Gavin replies. "Aren't you the one who contacted INN about the upcoming event?"

"That I am. I'll explain on the way, but right now we need to get going. The feds will make their move in less than an hour."

Tracy is relieved to see one of the armed guards break away and load their luggage into the back of the Cadillac, which appears absolutely new.

They pile in and head south on the freeway for several miles, then west toward the evening sun. Ms. Hughes stays focused on Gavin and ignores Tracy and Jayne. "Reverend Lucas deliberated for quite some time before he had me contact you. In the end, he felt it was important to involve a media source that has a broad audience with a variety of political and religious beliefs. He wants the world to know that what's important here is not what church you go to, but your sanctity and immunity from the dictates of the federal government."

"I see," Gavin responds. He's nearly certain that Jayne had the presence of mind to turn on the camera and record the audio inside the vehicle even if the video was off.

A lot of people might be parsing this conversation for some time to come.

CryoLife occupies the top floor of a three-story medical building that faces a busy arterial, with a big parking lot at the back side. Virginia Hetzel peeks out one of the office windows at the lot below. All quiet and nearly empty. Behind her, two lab techs wheel several cryo-tanks toward the elevator for their trip down to the parking level on the ground floor, where they will join the others awaiting the arrival of the federal marshals. To Virginia, they've become sacred vessels, delivered from on high to spark the onset of Armageddon. The parking lot will become the plain of Esdraelon, where the final struggle for the fate of humanity plays out.

All due to her heroic intervention at this critical moment.

She feels the thrill of it well up from deep within. It's all she can do to keep from bursting out in prayer.

Behind her, the tanks roll on into the elevator.

"I hope you realize that what happens here this evening is a matter of global consequence," Reverend Billy Lucas tells Gavin. The man's eyes glow with an inextinguishable optimism that borders on manic. "I value your organization's commitment to responsible journalism and hope it extends to the present circumstances."

"You have my word," Gavin assures him. *Responsible journalism, my ass. INN consistently has the largest viewing audience in the world. Billy can now achieve apotheosis in the most economical manner possible.*

They stand behind a hastily erected riser on the edge of a large grass field in an urban park about three blocks from CryoLife. Two large speakers occupy its corners, with audio gear in the rear, including a wireless mic for the reverend. A half dozen security guards man the perimeter. When Tracy asked about their presence,

Sarah Hughes explained that some of the congregation tend to have "bursts of exuberance" that need to be contained. About a hundred people stand expectantly on the grass, some clearly from the fringes of life, others somewhat more centered. A wiry old man in tattered shorts, worn sandals, and biblical beard dances to a rhythm all his own. Nearby, an overweight man in khaki slacks, a tropical sport shirt and inky black sunglasses thrusts out this cellphone to get a selfie of him and his wife on their way to a pixelated paradise.

"Showtime," Reverend Billy declares abruptly, and bounds up the two steps onto the stage. The energy of his ascent is terrifying.

"You cover from the right," Gavin instructs Jayne. "'l'll get this side with my phone and get some B roll from the stage." He turns to Tracy. "Stick with me."

"Wouldn't have it any other way," Tracy replies. The whole scene was weird from the start, with a troubling undercurrent. And now the crowd grows ever larger and even weirder.

The pair move to a spot near the stage corner under the wary eyes of security guards. "I want to get an interview," Gavin explains to Tracy. "But it needs to be based on what he says on stage. We'll collar him as soon as he jumps down."

Billy raises the mic and starts to urgently pace the width of the riser. "Now you may ask yourself… why are we gathered in this park tonight? Why did I issue the call? Why are we not in our cherished place of worship? Well, I'll tell you why. Because the Lord has commanded that it be so. And why has he done that? Because the war against decent, God-fearing people has just moved to new whole level. The secular bureaucrats of the federal government are about to seize the very essence of what it means to be human. They want to get their vinyl-gloved hands on all the frozen eggs and all the frozen embryos that are the most sacred property of the individuals who produced them. People just like you and me.

"Now I know that you've heard talk about all this for some time. But now they're going to walk the walk instead of talk the talk…"

Out in the audience, Tracy starts to see raised fists and hollers of approval. Many punch texts into their cellphones to spread the word, and it's working. The crowd continues to grow.

Tracy suddenly yearns for the solitude and safety of her cozy cubicle back at the National Center for Health Statistics, where she visualized vast columns of numbers rising like heat-laden cumulus clouds into a numeric stratosphere. But not here. Now she finds herself immersed in an entirely different America; one she vaguely knew of but always held conveniently at bay.

Beneath the federal courthouse in downtown Omaha, a small convoy assembles itself in the parking area. Two armored transport vehicles form up behind a Humvee, with a big Suburban in the lead. Eight deputy US marshals in full tactical gear silently board each of the transport vehicles. The Humvee will house the cryo-tanks that await them at the pickup site, while the Suburban carries two senior officers charged with overseeing the operation. A sense of urgency has developed. Online intelligence reports indicated that a radical dissent group has started to cluster at a nearby park. Some of their texts indicate that they know about the upcoming seizure. All the vehicles fire up and prepare to move out.

"And the Lord commands that all of you who are young, strong and brave shall advance to where the stuff of life is held prisoner. You will form a mighty shield. The feds will cower, and you will prevail against the forces of darkness. So it shall be. Go now…"

Gavin corners Reverend Billy as he hops down off the stage. "You know, I'm not a legal expert, but I think you might have just incited a riot," Gavin says.

Billy smiles and clamps a powerful hand onto Gavin's shoulder. "What's happened here is the will of God and God alone. When this is over, there will not be a single court left in the land willing to take this matter on." He releases his grip and looks over to make sure Jayne is shooting video. "My work is done here. God bless you – and God bless all your viewers who join us in this most holy of moments."

He turns and walks off with his security contingent. Sarah Hughes is nowhere to be found.

Much of the crowd has formed a human river that starts to flow down the three short blocks to CryoLife.

"My God!" Tracy exclaims. "Now what?"

"We tag along," Gavin answers. "But we stay on the sidelines."

"How will we know where the sidelines are?" she asks.

"Good question," Gavin replies. "I'll tell you when we get there." He turns to Jayne. "You getting all this?"

"Oh yeah," she replies without looking up from her viewfinder.

They follow a path parallel to the stream of faithful, who cross to the field's edge where it meets the street. Some pray, some sing, some hold up cellphones to video the impromptu crusade. As they file out, they encounter two big pickups, one filled with axe handles, the other with heavy-duty polyethylene trash can lids. Swords and shields for the anointed. They funnel down into a single file to collect their weaponry, no instructions necessary. Gavin infers that the church had at least some advance knowledge and rapidly assembled the logistics necessary. He'll come back to that when he has a chance, but not right now.

Once armed, the group spills out and occupies the entire width of the street as they move forward. Gavin and company move to the edge and keep pace. The bulk of the participants are younger and male, and he picks one to interview on the fly. He's casually dressed and well groomed, except for the primal fire in his eyes. "The goddam fuckin' government's got to get the fuck out of people's lives," he exclaims. "Know what they're doin' here? They're stealing babies. We can't let that happen!"

"You got the neighbors?" Gavin asks Jayne.

"Already on it," she says as she pans her camera down the block. A very average block. The kind the majority of viewers will identify with.

All along the route, residents have come out on their porches, lawns and driveways to witness the procession. Their faces radiate curiosity laced with outright anxiety. Children stay instinctively close to parents, hugging their legs and holding their hands. They sense something is not right in the world but don't know what.

Virginia peeks through the blinds at the empty parking lot two stories below. Evening has set in solid, and the overhead lights boil their high-pressure sodium into a ghostly hue across the lot. The field of battle is set, an earthly replay of the battle of the archangels in heaven untold years ago. The lot is bordered by a second, even larger lot that stretches the better part of a block. The great armies will have ample room to maneuver, to thrust, to block, to counter. The key point of control is the entrance to the building's underground car park, where the cryo-tanks will change hands.

Virginia picks out the first wave as it comes in off the street to the big lot in the distance. They carry the swords of Michael and the shields of the Righteous.

The convoy of US marshals pulls into the medical building's parking lot with the Suburban in the lead. Its commander immediately spots the fringe of the advancing crowd out in the far lot. He orders the convoy to pull into the underground parking area, where they will have a tactical advantage. The entrance, about two vehicles wide, represents a choke point that they can control without spreading their ranks too thin. The 16 deputy US marshals pile out of the two transport vehicles and form a perimeter just outside.

"Let's stay on this side of the street," Gavin tells Tracy and Jayne, who films the convoy pulling into the driveway from where they stand on the sidewalk.

"Do you think they know how many people they're dealing with?" Tracy asks.

"I don't think they have any idea," Gavin says. "Which means this get could get really ugly."

Virginia watches the federal force deploy in a semicircle down below in their apocalyptic riot gear. Beyond, the second lot fills to overflowing with the opposing force, which advances at a steady pace toward the marshals.

"Holy shit!"

Virginia is startled by the sudden presence of the convoy commander at her window. He immediately backs off and gets on his cellphone. "This is Vetter. We just got here, and it looks like a whole goddam army coming our way. We need the backup from Offutt and we need it now." He paces in agitation as he listens to the response. "How many?" he yells. "Every fuckin' one of 'em! Right now!" He turns to Virginia. "Who's in charge of the tanks?"

"I don't know. They took them all downstairs. That's all I know."

"Swell," the commander mutters in disgust. He wheels and strides toward the elevator.

Gavin looks down his side of the block, just in time to see a local news van pulling into a nearby parking lot. No surprise. With the flood of text and video coming from the crowd, it was pretty much inevitable. "Circus time," he announces to Tracy and Jayne, who are watching a police patrol car coming from the opposite direction. "Let's stay with the troops for now," he instructs Jayne. Their helmets, body armor, gas masks and armaments make for good visuals compared with the other side's axe handles and trash can shields.

Two police officers exit the patrol car, which has come to a stop next to the medical building. They assess the situation, while the advancing crowd grows ever larger. Not good. One of them talks into the mic strapped on his shoulder, but neither makes any move to join the marshals. Up the other way, the news truck rotates its dish antenna to align with a relay satellite somewhere far above the Nebraska sky. A camera person appears and trains his lens on the restless mob. A window to the world at large opens wide.

"Freedom!"

Gavin's ear catches the first instance of the chant. It rapidly grows into a chorus of dissent.

"FREEDOM!"

Freedom from what? Gavin knows it doesn't matter. It's more about the shaping of the phrase, the rhythm of repetition that catches the primal recesses of human cognition. In response, one individual starts to raise his axe handle in synchrony with the cadence of the chant. Once again, it undergoes an infectious multiplication.

"Mic me up," Gavin tells Jayne, who fits him with a wireless, directional mic. "It's showtime."

Gavin places himself between the camera and the background, where the opposing forces continue to close. His intuition tells him he has just enough time to get a decent take before utter chaos descends. By the time the local news crew gets set, it'll be too late.

"This is Gavin Gray for INN. I'm coming to you from Omaha Nebraska, where the federal government's first attempt to seize frozen eggs and embryos has taken a really ugly turn. The operation was supposed to be kept secret but was somehow leaked to certain religious and political groups in violent opposition. They've spontaneously assembled in the area behind me, which is defended by a small contingent of US marshals in charge of the seizure. At this point, it looks like a clash is pretty much inevitable. More to come as things unfold."

He steps back around and lets Jayne cover the action. Through some advanced electronics in her small backpack, the signal is livestreamed via 5G back to INN headquarters. No need for vans and satellites. "I'll add color as we go," he tells her.

The chanting crowd advances like some medieval army, their axes thrust in synchrony into the dusky haze.

The federal troops each unsling a rifle-like weapon with an elongated tube instead of a barrel. They crack it open and load a cylindrical grenade composed of tear gas and a small charge of TNT. When the crowd comes within about 30 yards, they fire their grenades down into the pavement near the front of the advance, where they explode in a brilliant flash and spew billowing columns of gas. Those in the first few rows are stunned by the flash and choked by the burn and sting of the vapors. They stagger in confusion and start to retreat but are blocked by the oncoming waves of humanity behind them. The collective inertia of the crowd has been slowed but not halted. A fresh wave of combatants oozes to the front of the advance and continues forward.

The federal troops pause to reload their weapons. This time, some load the exploding tear gas while others load so-called "baton" rounds of wood or rubber meant to stun but not kill. Once ready, they launch the tear gas onto the pavement but fire the baton rounds directly into the crowd, where most find their mark while some bounce off the trash-can shields. Those hit pitch backward off their feet from the impact, but most have nowhere to land in the wave of advancing bodies. Many are on the verge of being trampled. Still the crowd surges forward.

Gavin looks down the street, where the larger parking lot has filled to overflowing with new arrivals. He estimates the group's total size to be between five and seven hundred people. The cloud of tear gas from the spent grenades leaves them untouched and drifts off to their right. While Jayne shoots the action, he continues his narrative, and Tracy shoots additional video with her cellphone. The crowd has now advanced to within 15 yards of the dozen US marshals, who appear to be in imminent danger of being overrun. Gavin catches a telltale flash of red and blue from the arterial in front of the medical building. Are the local police going to intervene?

Two military buses holding the contingency force from Offutt roll to a stop under the escort of several patrol cars that block off the street in both directions. They've received continual updates on the situation on the far side of the building and act accordingly, as all 95 marshals flow out of the vehicles. They split into two groups that trot in single file around opposite sides of the building's ground floor, where they merge in the parking lot with the dozen defenders. They all carry shields in addition to their other armaments. By now, the force's two riot vehicles have arrived and follow the troops to take up positions on their flanks. With fully armored exteriors and bulletproof tires, they are capable of wading at will into the advancing throng.

Gavin realizes an epic battle is at hand. He needs to get himself and Jayne to an elevated position where they look down on it. He sees the solution twenty feet away. A stunted sycamore tree rises from the parking strip with a sturdy trunk and thick limbs denuded by the onset of Fall. "Over here!" he calls to Jayne, who knows immediately where they're going. Gavin clasps his hands together and forms a step that gets her to the first branch. He hands the camera and knapsack up to her as he hears the growl of a riot vehicle pulling into position. A wireless link to his cellphone allows him to view whatever she's shooting in real time.

Tracy joins Gavin at the base of the tree and grasps his arm for comfort. "You know what?" she comments. "This is really truly scary."

"You're absolutely right," he tells her. "Just hang on. We'll get through it."

Across the street, the marshals rapidly reassemble into two ranks of about fifty each to face the ragged front of the opposition, which is only twenty yards off and still yelling 'Freedom!' The fed's front rank loads their weapons with grenades and rubber bullets while the rear rank holds their long black batons at the ready. Some of the throng hurl their axe handles at the marshals, but they bounce harmlessly off the body armor and shields. A few others suddenly appear hesitant and fearful as they realize that the momentum of those behind is pushing them into combat whether they like it or not. Most, however, seem caught up in the crucible of the moment and surge ahead.

"Freedom!"

The fed's front rank now discharges their gas grenades and stun rounds with devastating effect. The tear gas explodes at the feet of the attackers, and noxious clouds billow out and engulf them. Wood and rubber missiles plow into the front wave and send many of them reeling. Still, the momentum of the massive gathering propels it forward.

The marshals' front rank falls back to reload and the back one moves up with their shields and batons to engage the throng's leading edge, now thinned by the barrage of gas and missiles. For the first time, the two forces physically clash, with the marshals swinging their batons and the attackers countering with their axe handles. It quickly becomes clear that discipline and superior armament will prevail. The heavy batons swipe aside the trash-can lids while the axe handles prove worthless against the big plexiglass shields. The gas has partially blinded many of the attackers while the marshals remain unaffected behind their heavy-duty gas masks.

The axe handles fall upon body armor and helmets, while the batons collide with flesh and bone. Normal operating procedure would restrain the baton use, but this situation is far from normal and threatens their very survival. Head, face and knees become fair game. People stagger away stunned and bleeding. The assault has been blunted, the "Freedom!" chant replaced with howls of rage and pain.

The front rank of marshals falls back, and the rear moves forward and launches yet another round of gas and missiles across the gap between the two forces, which now holds steady. Farther back, the forward advance of the crowd stalls, and people start to stack up like a breaking wave. To escape, they begin to pour out laterally out of the lot and into the street.

Tracy stands next to Gavin under the sycamore as he narrates what he sees on his cellphone, which is coming from Jayne up above. "We've seen several cycles of the marshals advancing on the crowd then falling back to fire more tear gas. Luckily for us, the breeze is blowing the gas in the opposite direction. It's going to be a big problem for the neighborhood downwind from all of this... Wait, I think I just heard the riot vehicles start up. They may join the battle any time now..."

Tracy notes the refugees from the struggle starting to stagger out onto the street, many streaming copious tears from their burning eyes. She tugs Gavin's arm. "Look at this. Maybe we better move." He looks up from his phone at the outpour. "Not quite yet. Get the people in the street," he instructs Jayne. Tracy decides that this, her first field assignment, will also be her last.

From inside and two stories up, Virginia watches the conflict unfold with a disturbing mix of horror and fascination. The primal nature of the battle, with its shields and clubs and bleeding victims, is appalling yet captivating. Her religious context fades away. The archangels and demons leave the mythical stage; and the sheer undiluted violence of it all bubbles up from her limbic region and takes charge. What was once biblical now becomes rooted in something timelessly remote, beyond the dictates of reason and rule.

Under the ghostly watch of the mercury vapor lamps, the crowd collapses from within, like air escaping a punctured balloon. The frontline dissolves into chaos, leaving the pavement littered with discarded trash can lids and axe handles as it retreats. The marshals form into a single rank wide enough to cover the entire parking area while the riot vehicles pull around in front of them. The entire assemblage then moves forward at a measured pace, leaving the opposition just enough time and space to reluctantly disband. A speaker mounted atop one of the vehicles barks out the order to immediately depart the area. A few holdouts shake their axe handles at the advancing force but quickly follow the others into the humid night. By the time the marshals reach the far end of the parking area, all that's left is the litter of improvised battle gear and an ominous silence.

Virginia comes out of the elevator on the ground floor just in time to witness the last cryo-tank being loaded into one of the transport vehicles. She attempts to visualize the nascent life within but fails. Heaven has cast her aside. The Reverend Billy Lucas has betrayed her and snatched away all the glory in this, the peak moment of her entire little life.

"Pan over to the entrance," Gavin commands Jayne in anticipation of what comes next. Two armed guards stand aside as one of the transport vehicles comes roaring out, sprints to the street and turns left toward the arterial packed with emergency vehicles. Its brake lights flash briefly when it arrives and then disappears from view.

"Don't tell me: There goes the prize," Tracy says.

"Done," Gavin announces with sigh, and helps Jayne down from the tree.

"Do you think they got all that in New York?" Tracy asks.

"If they didn't, we would've heard by now," Gavin replies. "You okay?" He puts his arm around her shoulders.

"Maybe. But this is definitely not my line of work."

"Lucky you." Gavin sits down curbside, his legs spent from the constant tension.

The President can't help but recall the scene in the cabinet room when Obama's people gathered to watch the takedown of Osama Bin Laden. Tense faces glued to the monitors. Somber expressions. Nervous shifting.

Only that time, it ended well. This time it didn't.

She is flanked by the Attorney General and her chief of staff. Together, they watch the INN footage of the transport vehicle heading toward the arterial at the end of the street.

"Well, it looks like we pulled it off," comments the chief of staff with a nearly ludicrous show of optimism, which is greeted with utter silence from the packed room.

"It's an absolute fucking disaster," the President declares. They have just witnessed an extraordinarily violent clash between heavily armed federal forces and lightly armed civilians. Worse yet, a very large segment of the population is in passionate agreement with the dissenters over the seizure. Who leaked the plan? It was supposed to be done in total secrecy. But at this point, it doesn't matter.

She was supposed to hold a news conference tomorrow announcing the completion of the veiled operation and to hold it up as a model for how this entire thing could be done peacefully. A few chairs down, she can see her press secretary furiously scribbling notes for a very different announcement.

She turns to her Attorney General. "How many more seizures do we have scheduled as of now?"

"About a dozen," comes the reply.

"Cancel them."

"All of them?"

"All of them. Right now. We're going to have to rethink this entire thing, from one end to the other."

The old ranch hand absently tugs the brim of his cowboy hat as he squints at the flat-screen TV on the far side of the bar. Curly waves of gray tumble down over his ears, and his complexion mimics the output of a leather tannery. He clutches a bottle of lager beer with boney fingers once powerful, now gone arthritic.

"Goddam fuckin' government," he mutters. "Got no business goin' after people's private property. Don't matter if it's alive or dead. What's theirs is theirs. Nothin' more to it."

He turns to Frank Fanno, who sits next to him. "So, what you say about that?"

Frank gives a philosophical shrug. "That'd all be fine, except I don't believe anyone on this whole earth owns that particular property."

"Oh yeah? Then who does?"

"God. And God alone. That's who owns it."

They both turn back to the TV, where INN replays key scenes from the battle in Omaha over and over.

Roger Stennis turns from the TV, which shows a federal riot baton crashing into a dissenter's parietal lobe. "What do you think?" he asks his son.

Stennis Jr. takes another sip of premium scotch before answering. "I think we're lucky we got as much as we did, but now it's over. Every clinic in the country's going to be defended by a volunteer mob, whether they like it or not. I doubt if they're going to discriminate between us and the feds. The thing to do right now is consolidate our gains. I think it's safe to say we've cornered the market."

"Cornering it's one thing," Stennis Sr. remarks. "Securing it is something else. How are things going out in Montana?"

"Last time I checked, we had about eighty per cent of our inventory already tucked away, with the rest in transit."

"Sooner or later, somebody's going to peg the location. Are we ready?"

"We've got the best security and facilities that money can buy." Stennis casts an anxious glance at the melee on TV. "Let's just hope it stays that way."

"What we have here is an abomination," Wayne Bauer declares to James Kranz, his new security chief. From his motorhome's TV wall, the screen spews out calamitous scenes of violence in Omaha, where the feds make their full-frontal advance on the wavering crowd. "This battle is over possession, not destruction," he comments. "Both sides want to preserve and protect the ultimate treasure. They operate in direct defiance of the divine mandate, which calls for every egg, every sperm and every embryo to be destroyed. Until that happens, the gates of heaven stay closed, and the gates of hell remain open wide."

"And what do you propose we do about that?" Kranz asks, with no small measure of cynicism.

"You're not a believer, are you?" Wayne asks. Each has downed three half-quart cans of Pabst by this point.

Kranz shrugs. "Can't say as I am."

Wayne takes a thoughtful chug. "No matter. That's not why you're here. You're here to make things happen."

"What kind of things you got in mind?"

"Information. We need all the information we can get on where this stuff is located. You need to build an intelligence network. Like the kind you see in the movies. Hidden eyes and ears taking it all in. Then we can work out a plan to take it all down."

"If that's what you want, we've already taken the first step. We've just finished a database with contact info for all your followers."

"And how many followers would that be?"

"It's getting bigger all the time. Right now, over a hundred thousand. They're concentrated in the western states, more in the country than in the cities."

"We need to bring them together, make them as one."

Kranz grins and pops another top with his big, meaty fingers. "That's your department, not mine. I can do the paving, but you gotta do the driving."

"And so I shall," Wayne promises.

41

Bill, Frank and Denise. All residents of the Eagle Crest Apartments in north central Colorado Springs. Bill, a security guard. Frank, an electrician. Denise, a cashier at a big-box store. They gather around a laptop on the kitchen table in Bill's one-bedroom apartment, with its green shag carpet, dilapidated appliances and textured ceiling. A large, muscular dog with a violent bent sprawls on the floor near the TV. With the audio muted, the screen displays an indoor dirt bike race from somewhere out in the heartland.

They have just followed a link from Facebook to one of Wayne Bauer's numerous videos on YouTube. Each one refines and amplifies his vision for the Order of Atonement. As the video plays, all three hunch forward toward the screen to gain greater intimacy with their spiritual leader. He always delivers. He never disappoints. They silently nod in agreement with his insights, his pronouncements, his declarations.

"Now I ask you," Wayne begins. "For what reason were we put here? And for what reason will we be cast out? And I can tell you this – we are none other than victims of our very own selves. You see, there is a harmony that defines the state of the universe. A cosmic choir if you will. Each voice is meant to resonate with all others. But some time back, the voice of mankind strayed and began to sing its own tune in its own key. And in doing so, it created great waves of chaos in places far beyond our limited imaginations. And along the way, I have to tell you, we passed the point of no return…"

Bill glances over at Denise. Biblical tats snake down her plump forearms. Spiked pink hair crowns a round face where a faint cloud of rosacea has set in. Next to her, Frank sports a massive jaw and bushy brows fused into a single dark hedge beneath a broad forehead.

"And so now we are called upon to fulfill our cosmic destiny so that we may enter a higher realm. The time has come. We must act; we must prove our intent..."

As the video ends, Bill turns to the pair. "He's made it pretty clear. Something has to be done, and it has to be done right now. What do you think?"

"Think so," Frank nods.

"Yup," Denise adds.

"Alright then, let's go over the plan one last time."

In the apartment's parking lot, they walk along under the rosy glow of halogen security lights. They pass a minivan with a shattered window on the driver's side, all fresh and jagged with glittering chunks still on the pavement. "It's a fucked-up world," Denise comments.

"Yeah, but we already knew that," Bill says. Soon, they reach his van and climb in. He leans over into a box in the back and pulls out two empty wine bottles of a bottom-tier vintage. One is empty and open, the other capped with a screw-on top and full of premium unleaded gasoline. He hands the empty to Denise and the full to Frank. "Any last thoughts?" he asks and is met by silence. "Well then, here we go."

They pass a vape on the ride down Academy Boulevard into the city center and exhale misty clouds of Indica that are sucked out the half-open windows. After five miles, they turn off into an aging apartment complex and park in the shadows at the far end of the lot. They exit the van and start off across a tree-studded vacant lot next to the rear of an IVF clinic bathed in security lights. They stop at the lot's edge, still concealed by a rusting canopy of deciduous trees. Each wears an identical hoodie and black denims, and they now complete their cover by pulling on black balaclava masks. Bill pulls out a strip of cotton cloth, uncaps the gas-filled bottle, stuffs the cloth in to soak it, and then pulls it halfway out.

"Nothin' left to do but do it," he informs his companions, and strides out toward the clinic. Frank follows, holding the empty bottle. Denise assumes a position where she can warn them if anyone enters the lot from the front.

Bill stops in front of a tall window and reaches into his pocket for a lighter. He knows what's behind this particular window because Denise recently took a tour of the clinic as a prospective client. Inside, a decorative stone façade sits across the hall on the far side of the glass. Frank quickly moves forward, raises the empty bottle and smashes the window. Behind him, Bill has lit the glass-soaked cloth and now moves forward. He hurls it through the window in a flaming arc, and it explodes upon impact with the façade, creating a drooling wall of flame that spreads down to the floor and onto the nearby walls.

Bill steps back to admire his handiwork before they flee.

"Thy will be done," he declares.

"Had to happen," Krantz tells Bauer. They sit on the sofa in Wayne's motorhome and stare at a jumbo-size flat-screen TV, which shows real-time footage of a blazing building in Colorado Springs. INN has picked up the story from their local news affiliate and pushed it to the forefront of their content queue. It seems the building is an IVF clinic, which makes it a topic of peak interest on a global scale. The scene cuts to the local fire chief, who explains that arson is the most probable cause. The blaze started near a window in the rear of the structure and quickly spread to a storage area inside holding a number oxygen tanks that exploded in the extreme heat. The blast destroyed all the cryo-tanks holding a precious store of frozen eggs and embryos. The anchor desk comes back on to announce breaking news concerning the possible perpetrators of the incident, and switches to a reporter narrating real-time images of several message boards, all showing the same anonymous post:

"THE TIME FOR DIRECT ACTION HAS COME AT LAST! BEHOLD THE BURNING BUILDING AND THE ANIHILATION OF ITS STORE OF FROZEN LIFE, AN ABOMINATION IN THE EYES OF ALL THAT TOWER ABOVE US. THE ORDER OF ATONEMENT HAS SPOKEN AND THE WORLD HAD BEST LISTEN."

The story cuts to archived footage of Wayne Bauer atop his motorhome in Tonopah, speaking to an adoring crowd. The narrator gives an encapsulation of the Order's history and philosophy and suggests that it represents yet another ominous turn in a nation already beset by unprecedented political, economic and spiritual chaos.

Krantz mutes the sound as the scene returns to the blaze and the flickering glow it casts upon nearby buildings and trees.

"How long will it take the cops to track them down?" Wayne asks.

Krantz, the ex-cop, shrugs. "Maybe forever. The message boards are anonymous, and their method of attack reveals almost nothing. There'll be video, but I bet all we see are generic hoodies and masks. My guess is that they used a Molotov cocktail. All they needed was a little gas and a couple of empty bottles. Good luck trying to run that down."

A third person on the sofa speaks up for the first time, Evelyn Gossart, Wayne's PR person. "It really doesn't matter. Maybe it's our people and maybe not. What counts is that that whoever did it put out the word that we're responsible, and the mainstream media has already picked up on that. By morning, it'll be in the New York Times."

"Oh, it's our people all right," Wayne declares. "And it was an act of pure faith. They embraced the Final Truth and risked their personal well-being in support of it. I don't have any problem with that. How could I? That's not what bothers me."

"Then what does?" Evelyn asks.

"Let me start by saying this: Some stuff in school it took me a while to get, but not this stuff. I get this real fast. And you know what it's telling me? That I've let the bottom rungs take the reins to move us forward. That's not gonna work. We have to tighten things up and assert leadership in a very simple and direct way. If we don't, we'll have chaos in the ranks. We'll see a loss of faith. We'll see splinter groups."

"So, what do you propose?" Krantz asks.

"Nothing."

"Nothing?' Evelyn asks incredulously.

"Nothing. As always, I will be shown the way."

<h1 style="text-align:center">42</h1>

The Bell Super Huey helicopter slips in deftly over the East River and settles onto one of the helipads on the eastern shore of Manhattan with military precision. Stennis expected no less. Its sole passenger is James Hallock of the Sigma Group, who has arranged this meeting on short notice. Stennis keeps a respectful distance from the wind blast off the rotor blades, which shoves his gelled hair about and causes him to squint.

Hallock departs the aircraft wearing cargo pants, hiking shoes and a leather flight jacket. He stoops slightly, out of caution, under the whirling rotors until well clear and then shakes Stennis's hand. "Sorry to interrupt your day," he yells over the roar of the twin turboshaft engines. "But we need to talk. Isn't there a little lounge around here?"

"Follow me." Stennis has an exquisite nose for trouble, and he's already picked up the scent. The pair depart the helipad and enter a passenger waiting lounge tucked under the main causeway bordering the river. They order at the bar and then retreat to a quiet spot near the back.

"So, what do you think about Omaha and Colorado?" Hallock asks as they sit.

"Not good. I was just going to contact you. We want to cancel all the remaining collections, at least until this thing settles down."

Hallock lets a moment pass before he speaks. "I'm afraid we're going to have to cancel a lot more than that. We're terminating the contract."

"You're terminating what?"

"The whole thing. It's really pretty simple. We can't afford to risk any kind of violent confrontation on US soil, which would put us at odds with the feds. It's not just a legal thing. We also do a lot of business with them."

"More than with me?"

Hallock gives a contemptuous chuckle. "Way more than with you." He pauses to let it sink in. Stennis, who usually holds all the cards, now holds next to none.

"I suggest you look at the upside," Hallock continues. "We've already managed to round up more than half of the country's IVF stock. Plus, we intend to follow through on the delivery of everything that's still in transit or temporary storage."

"And what about Ingomar?" Stennis asks.

"We're pulling out within the next few days. But once again, it's not all bad. We've finished nearly all the construction, which leaves you with more than enough storage capacity."

"That's fine," Stennis says. "But what about the security part?" He knows that the contract calls for Sigma to provide security services for the next ten years, with a resident force that rotates in and out.

"I don't think that's an immediate issue," Hallock replies. "The place is fifty miles from nowhere, so unless things turn into a Road Warrior movie, you're not going to need much."

"But what if they do?"

"I think your best bet would be to make a deal with one of the local militias. That part of the state is crawling with 'em, so it shouldn't be too tough." He looks at his watch. "I gotta go. We can let the lawyers and the bean counters settle all this up." He stands without offering a handshake. "Sorry it didn't work out, but the world never stands still. Know what I mean?"

"I do." His instinct is to lash out, to tie them up with a vigorous lawsuit; but that would be potentially suicidal. It would cause people to poke around and ask why he ever entered into this contract in the first place. They would question the timing of it all. Why had he initiated all this action before the government ever revealed the fertility plunge? Did he somehow have an inside line? And what about that woman who could link him with another woman now dead who worked at the CDC?

The banshee roar of the twin turbines interrupts his rumination as Hallock's ship lifts up and heads south toward Staten Island on its way back to Washington DC. The skyscrapers in the Financial District quickly intervene, and the noise abruptly stops, plunging the lounge's interior into near silence. Stennis stares out a view window at the empty helipad space. It's almost as if none of this ever really happened.

Almost, but not quite.

Gavin peers out the window of their hotel in downtown Omaha and squints into the morning light from six stories up. As chance would have it, they're right across the street from the federal courthouse of the District of Nebraska. Already, a smattering of demonstrators gathers in the plaza out front. They carry the prerequisite inflammatory placards common to political movements everywhere, some professionally printed, others crudely scrawled in poster paint. BABY STEALERS! BIG BROTHER BEGONE! HANDS OFF, FEDS! It already feels like a reprise of the Black Lives Matter thing in Portland: A civilized daylight gathering of responsible citizens soon to be followed by a nighttime surge with hellbent anarchists taking center stage.

"We're going to have to cover this," he tells Tracy, who is still comfortably snuggled under the covers.

"Cover what?" she asks, without opening her eyes.

"You'll see," he says and crosses the room to crawl back in with her. He savors the warmth of her as she entwines herself. Shelter from the storm. He's read about how times of war and civil strife heighten romantic yearning by creating a special sense of urgency. With the world collapsing, today may be the last day. He strokes her back and smiles to himself at the irony of it all. Just a short time back, he was reeling from a profound lack of personal origin and identity; now he's giving voice to a major global upheaval on a scale few could have imagined. Providence has granted Gavin Gray a permanent place in the archives of human history. So much for identity issues.

A beep from his cellphone pulls him back into the moment. He reaches for it on the bedside table to check the caller ID. It's probably Mindy in New York trying to schedule a Zoom meeting or some such thing. It's not. It's a bit of a surprise. It's Frank Fanno.

"Frank?"

"Bet you're a busy guy," Fanno says in his usual laconic manner.

"Yeah, as a matter of fact, I am. What's up?" He fully expects Fanno to launch into a spirited diatribe about the egregious federal government.

"I know you've been doing stuff on the fertility industry, and now this whole fertility thing has gone big time. Well, there's something going on out here that you should probably take a look at. I just emailed you some video. Remember a place called Ingomar?"

"Yeah, vaguely."

"It's about 50 miles east of here. Way to hell and gone. Something really weird's going on out there."

"Such as?"

"Watch the video, then we can talk. Take it easy."

"Who was that?" Tracy murmurs.

"It was my militia guy from out in Montana. Frank Fanno. He just sent some video he wants me to watch."

Tracy sits and stretches. "How about a little room service first?"

"You got it."

They're dressed by the time their food arrives. A fruit plate and cheese for Tracy. A bacon omelet and toast for Gavin. Coffee for both. Gavin places his laptop in front of them and brings up the video.

"Did he give you a hint about it?" Tracy asks.

"Not much. He shot it at a place called Ingomar, which is about as far gone as you can get on the Montana plain. He seems to think it has something to do with the fertility crisis, at least that's what it sounded like."

"Well then, bring it on," Tracy says.

They watch as the drone travels the first leg of its flight, revealing the massive bunker that dominates the complex.

"Unbelievable," Gavin comments as the cryo-tanks come down off the truck and into the bunker's interior. "Are those tanks what I think they are?"

"Oh yeah," Tracy responds.

"You sure?"

"Last year, we got to take a field trip to a clinic in DC and went through the entire IVF process, and these tanks were the end of the line. No doubt about it."

"Looks like they could store thousands in there," Gavin says.

"And that's just the start of it."

"What do you mean?"

"The liquid nitrogen in the tanks doesn't last forever. It gradually evaporates. They have to be recharged from time to time. It takes a lot of gear and maintenance to make that happen."

"You picked all this up from a single tour?"

"Nope. I got part of it from my work with frozen cookies."

"Frozen cookies?"

"Among other things. I worked one summer during college at a plant that produced frozen baked goods. There was a thing called a freezing tunnel that all the goodies passed through, and it used liquid nitrogen. It was hooked up to big storage tanks, maybe five feet high and a couple of feet wide. When the tanks ran low, they were swapped out for new ones and refilled. My boss figured out that I had a nerdy side and put me in charge of the refills. There were a few gauges and valves involved, but it was really pretty simple."

"Would I find that on your resume?"

"Probably not. The whole point is that, if you're going to store this stuff long term, you have to have a whole infrastructure to support it."

They watch the remainder of the video with all the adjacent buildings and the unfinished sections of security fence. "Looks like it's still a work in progress," Gavin notes. "And a pretty spendy one at that. Now who would have thought to build something like this?"

"Somebody with advanced notice," Tracy suggests. "Somebody that figured out this place might be the new Fort Knox."

Stennis Partners. Neither needs to say it out loud.

43

The cleaning people aren't showing up. Same for the plant people. The wastebasket by Stennis's desk overflows like a ruptured water main, spewing shredded paper onto the unkempt carpet. On his credenza, the spade-like leaves of the philodendron luxurians sag on their stalks and curl slightly from lack of water. Stennis has bitterly complained to his operations manager, who relayed a distressing tale from their landlord. The building's owners were tumbling down a fiscal rabbit hole, unable to support their debt and starved for cash. They were forced to trim costs to the bone, which included routine maintenance expenses. They tried to negotiate with the help but got nothing but a continuous stream of fuck-yous. The only thing they could suggest was to have the office staff stay a little late and run the vacuums and dusters. Ridiculous.

Stennis sat at his desk and tried to put the chaos and clutter in perspective. A very distressing perspective. His cluttered space now stood as a metaphor for the nation at large, where forces that once dwelled in the shadows now roamed free and unfettered on the streets. The Order of Atonement was a good case in point. Just who the fuck were these people? He'd never heard of them. Some bullshit about signs in the sky and higher powers and the final reckoning. Worse yet, they believed that all the frozen embryos and eggs were some kind of supernatural curse that must be destroyed. They had just firebombed an IVF clinic in Colorado Springs to make their point. Online investigations by independent sources revealed a membership of over 100,000.

He couldn't have lost Sigma's protection at a worse time. He had these fanatics on one side who wanted to destroy the national IVF inventory, and the federal government on the other who wanted to seize it. And to top it off, Stennis Partners' own cash reserves were starting to dwindle, along with his options moving forward. Unless he wanted to wind up with a boy scout troop guarding his holdings, he needed to act quickly.

Hallock's suggestion about the militia seemed like a reasonable option. It would give him a paramilitary force that could be bought cheap and easily deployed. He takes to his laptop and prepares to do a search for militia organizations in the proximity of Ingomar. The display builds sluggishly, halting completely at times. He has a good idea why. The national telecommunications infrastructure is slowly degrading due to delayed maintenance. The era of lightning bandwidth is past.

He eventually completes the search and winds up with an interesting candidate in a place called Roundup, about 50 miles west of Ingomar. It's home to a militia group called Freedom First, commanded by some guy named Frank Fanno. His site speaks of commitment to professional military standards and features a group photo of what looks like an infantry company decked out in combat gear. It emphasizes perpetual vigilance against unlawful encroachment by the federal government. Fair enough. It means they won't have any qualms about protecting his inventory against the fed's seizure mandate. He finds the contact number and phones it. Once again, service is sporadic, and it takes him three times to get through.

"Fanno machinery." The voice rolls out in a baritone register, steeped in testosterone.

"Mr. Fanno?"

"You got him."

"My name's Mark Stennis and I represent a firm in New York. I think we might be interested in contracting with your outfit for security services."

"Oh yeah? What kind of services are you talking about?"

"We're currently engaged in developing a high-tech storage site at a location to the east of you called Ingomar. I assume you know where it is."

"Yep."

"I read the material on your site and want to tell you right off that we're not engaged with the government in any way, shape or form. Any arrangement that we have would be completely shielded from scrutiny by the feds."

"Okay, so what exactly is it that you want, Mr. Stennis?"

Stennis hates to admit it, but there's something rather intimidating about this guy. He's one of those people who seems guided by a moral certainty of the kind you seldom encounter. Stennis utterly lacks any such attribute, and it leaves him feeling a little vulnerable. "For security reasons, I'd rather we discussed that in person than on the phone," he says. "If it works for you, I'd like to fly out tomorrow and meet at Ingomar so we can cover the details."

"Yeah, I guess."

"Good. I need to make a few arrangements, and I'll text you with a time."

"Got it."

"See you then."

Frank puts down the phone and returns to working the lathe, where he's fabricating a part for the trigger assembly in an AR-15. The burn on his arm has healed to the point where he's regained a reasonable amount of motion. The cat stares at him from its perch on a grinding machine along the opposite wall. Since the accident, it keeps a respectful distance. He smiles at the metal shavings curling up as he shapes the part. Ingomar, huh? How dense did this Stennis guy think he is? If the stuff in the tanks out there is what he thinks it is, it makes Fort Knox look like a kid's piggy bank. With a little luck, Gavin will call and confirm his hunch before this Stennis gets here.

<h1 style="text-align:center">43</h1>

The TV does it again, the third time in the last hour, in the middle of his club sandwich from room service. The feed collapses and an apologetic message tells him that "network service is temporarily disrupted."

"Blame it on the cloud," Gavin tells Tracy, and takes a sip of his Corona. "What do you think?"

"I'm a mathematician, not an engineer," she responds. "A good guess would be that a lot of gear has gone offline in the data centers, and to compensate, they're throttling down the bandwidth. But once it falls below a certain threshold, you can't produce a decent image and the sound to go with it. You've got to go dark while you try to reconfigure on the fly."

Gavin gets up and stares out their sixth-story window. "OK then, let's switch to the real-time analog view down on the street." He opens a curtain that faces the federal courthouse. A bubbling crowd mills about in the plaza out front, an uglier crowd than the one this afternoon. Numerous males wear the new urban battle gear: improvised armor, shin guards, cycling helmets and homemade shields A tall woman in a white ski jacket yells incendiary chants into a portable megaphone. Behind her, the reserve federal marshals have arrived from Offutt and form into a potential battle line.

"A few days back, this would have been a priority story," Gavin observes. "Not anymore. At last count, there's about fifteen of these going on around the country." He pulls out his cellphone. "Let me give Fanno another try." He instructs the AI to put him through and waits. Frank picks up on the third ring. "Yeah?"

"Hey, Frank. Gavin. Sorry it took a while. We're having some technical issues at this end. We've watched the video you sent. No doubt about it. Those are cryo-tanks going into that bunker."

"Yeah, well that's just the start of it. I got an offer today from the guy who thinks he owns them. He wants me to stand guard. Military style."

"Oh yeah? And how much is he gonna pay you?"

"To be determined. We're meeting tomorrow out at the bunker."

"He didn't give you his name, did he?"

"Matter of fact, he did. Stennis. Mark Stennis."

An abrupt adrenal surge ripples through Gavin. He and Tracy had it nailed. Ingomar is the national depository, and Stennis is driving it. At some point, it's going to become the locus of a confrontation of epic proportion.

"If you don't mind, I'd like to come out and see for myself."

"Be my guest."

"I will. Talk to you later."

He stows the phone and turns to Tracy. "You called it right. Those are cryo-tanks going into the bunker out there. And it's Stennis that's running the show."

"Well then, I suppose we better go take a look," she says.

"I suppose so."

Before he can say any more, a loud pop comes from the street below. By now, he knows the sound. A tear gas grenade, the first of many. He looks down to the plaza, where the protesters are forming up to confront the marshals. All in all, he guesses about two hundred people, a scaled-down version of what they covered last night. He notices the woman in the stylish ski jacket has lowered her megaphone and stepped to the rear, out of the line of fire. She intuitively understands that generals never actually engage in combat and preserves herself for whatever skirmish comes next. Nordstroms leads, Costco follows.

44

The day is overcast, the air cool, the radiance of summer fading. As Frank Fanno approaches the gated entrance to Ingomar, he assesses its layout with a practiced eye. Good work, professional work. Bullet-proof and reasonably blast-proof. The crew manning the gate wear combat gear and carry AR-15s against any attempt at intrusion. Frank identifies himself, and they make a call before instructing him where to go.

A fresh layer of gravel tops the road leading toward the center of the installation, with the bunker on the left and the support buildings on the right. The closer he comes to the bunker, the more massive it appears. Its broad concrete front must be several stories high, the surface smooth and virginal, still untouched by the prairie's unrelenting onslaught of wind, dust, rain and snow. An enormous ditch runs along the bunker's sides and is obviously the source of the earthen cover over the curved roof. Frank doubts they have installed any drainage. The onset of winter will fill it to the brim and form a partial moat, making it even easier to defend.

The remainder of the installation confirms what Frank saw in the video. The two support buildings studded with antennae, the trailer park, the gaps in the security fence, the parking lot now filled with Humvees and transport vehicles. And finally, The Jersey Lilly, a wooden relic now transformed into a food service operation. The only new feature is a helicopter perched on a helipad near the parking lot. A civilian craft, most likely driven by a turbofan engine for maxed-out speed.

Frank pulls up to a big concrete apron directly in front of the bunker, where three men are conferring. One of them wears pseudo-military garb that looks like it just came off the rack, and he leaves the group and heads toward Frank, who climbs out of his truck to stretch his legs.

"Mr. Fanno, I'm Mark Stennis."

"Figured as much," Frank says, looking at the clothes. "Now what can I do for you?"

"Well first off, I'd like to know how big your organization is and how much military training they've had."

"There's about one hundred ten, and they've had plenty. So, who've you got guarding the place right now?"

Stennis realizes this negotiation may be a little more difficult than he imagined. "Ever heard of the Sigma Group?"

"Yes, I have. Good people. How come they're pulling out?"

"They have a number of other contractual obligations they have to meet and can't provide the resources I need."

"It's the feds, isn't it? They do a lot of business with the feds. Well, I don't, and I never will."

"Good. I'd like to work with someone who gives us their undivided attention."

"Makes sense. How long until Sigma's out of here?"

"We haven't quite settled that, but it won't be long. That's why you and I are talking."

Frank looks out at the flat horizon. "Know what? First, there's to hell and gone and then there's this place." He turns toward the bunker. "Which makes me wonder just what it is you'd ever want to stash out here."

Stennis anticipated this and launches into a prefabricated response. "Good question. Normally, I'd want a non-disclosure statement from you, but I'm going to assume that we're negotiating in good faith. Our firm includes a number of pharmaceutical labs doing research that involves dangerous pathogens. We're starting to get a lot of pressure about the danger to the public. We've decided the best way to deal with the problem is to consolidate and store all these materials in a single, remote location. And as you just pointed out, this place is about as remote as it gets. Still, we can't afford to take any chances. If a terrorist group got their hands on this stuff, it would be a complete disaster."

Fanno snorts and says, "That's complete bullshit, but I'll give you this: It's well packaged."

"Come again?" Stennis asks, with mounting alarm.

"Believe it or not, we get the news, even way out here. Now I'm not an economist, but it looks like that frozen stuff from the IVF clinics might now be the most valuable stuff anywhere. You're a finance guy, so tell me, am I wrong?"

"No, you're not," Stennis admits. He has little room to move. He has to make this work.

"Okay, let's cut the crap. That's what you got here, right?"

"Right."

"And whose property might it be?"

"That's a little complex. The ownership is distributed among..."

"It's not complex at all. It's God's property. Every bit of it."

Stennis didn't see this coming, but it gives him a way out. "You know, in the end, you're absolutely right. It *is* God's property. All of it. But in the meantime, it needs to be safeguarded and cared for. And that's what we intend to do. But to make that happen, we need you as a partner."

"Yes, you do."

"Now we realize there are going to be significant costs involved, and we're prepared to compensate you accordingly."

"And what's 'accordingly' mean?"

"I'd say it means a hundred thousand dollars a month, plus any additional armament you might require to guarantee security."

"I'd say it means five hundred thousand dollars a month. And I'd also say that the first month is due immediately in cash to get things going. After that, we're not talking about dollars, we're talking about gold, which we can stash right here along with your tanks."

"Okay then. May I ask why you've opted for gold?"

"Way I see it, dollars are only good as long as there's a United States, and right now, I wouldn't bet on that, at least not for very long."

"I see. Given your political views, that sounds like a dream come true."

Fanno gives a resigned shrug. "Could be. Might work out that way. But you never know for sure, do you?"

"No, you don't."

Fanno rolls west through the endless swales of prairie grass heading back toward Roundup. The truck's interior smells of machine oil and baked upholstery, while the engine maintains its steady grind over the weathered asphalt on Highway 12. He puts the Allman Brothers on the old tape deck, and Dicky Betts floods the space with impeccable guitar licks.

Mark Stennis is a chickenshit asshole. No doubt about it. But he can deal with that later. By tomorrow, there'll be enough money to assemble his entire unit into a cohesive whole. It won't be difficult. Most are unemployed, underemployed or languishing in dead-end jobs. He'll sign them all to contracts guaranteeing a substantial boost in their income, along with a chance to wield brand-new gear, which invariably captivates many young males.

For the time being, it'll be easy money. There's no substantial threat on the horizon except for a seizure attempt by the feds, which would be a very bad idea. The last thing this wobbly country needs right now is to see an armed confrontation between the feds and a civilian militia.

He finds some ironic humor in this latest twist of fate. In effect, he will become the base commander, a post normally reserved for a colonel or above. His highest rank during his regular service was platoon sergeant. He's come a long way.

45

Fenner and Saltzman swap tales of combat gone wrong in distant lands. Fenner leads with an account of an ambush by the Taliban on his convoy heading south out of Kandahar. His men returned fire for long enough to keep the enemy at bay until the Apache choppers came in and chewed the Taliban to bits with their gatling guns. Saltzman counters with a more desperate situation, where their post in the hills near Malistan was partially overrun and they had to fight building by building to regain control. Neither has ever readjusted to civilian life, and the Sigma Group gives them respite from its maddening ambiguity.

Through their banter, they stave off the hypnotic effect of travel at night on Highway 87 in northeast Montana, where the scene out the windshield plays like an endless loop in a monochromatic movie. The centerline snakes along to the left and an earthen ribbon of shoulder to the right. No lights, no traffic, no buildings. Utter blackness beyond the headlights.

"Let's check on the map," Fenner suggests. "We gotta be getting pretty close." He refers to a junction up ahead, where they will turn south on 87 toward a town called Roundup, about 50 miles distant. From there, they can cover the last leg to Ingomar in less than an hour. Saltzman pulls out his cell phone and brings up the map, where the entire route is traced in blue, starting with the first collection at a clinic in Bellevue, Washington.

"Came right up this time," he comments. "Seems like there's less competition for bandwidth the farther out here we get."

"Good," Fenner says. "Back in Seattle it was a real fuckin' mess."

Saltzman enlarges their location on the display. "About five minutes." A slight rattle from the back of their unmarked delivery van catches his ear. Two of the dozen cryo-tanks have shifted to the point where they occasionally touch and trigger a metallic ping.

"Let there be light," Fenner announces. Up ahead on their right, a small cluster of lights appears. They reach the junction and turn toward the miniscule town of Grass Ridge.

Moments later, they pull off the highway and into a small truck stop bathed by floodlights that shine down on a dilapidated building and a pair of gas pumps.

"You think we'll get that same old bitch?" Fenner asks.

"No doubt about it," Saltzman replies. "She's gotta be the end of the line out here."

"Probably so. But let's follow protocol."

Both men take comfort in prescribed rituals and go about their assigned roles. Saltzman reaches behind his seat and fetches an AR-15, with its clip in place and a round already chambered. Fenner conceals a .45 pistol in his shoulder holster, gets out, and walks toward the building, where a light just came on inside. A woman in an old overcoat and slippers comes out with unkempt rust-hued hair, bony hands and a face that took a wrong turn many years ago.

"Evening ma'am," Fenner says. "Sorry if we got you up. We need to fill up with super."

"We only take cash anymore," she tells him.

"Not a problem." He wonders how many thousand cigarettes it took to produce her sandpaper voice.

From in the van, Saltzman can see the rear of a mobile home protruding, with a solitary light on inside. It's a raw world out here, he thinks.

The woman fills the van, collects the money, and pads back into the building with little whispers of dust lifting off her slippers. The light goes off as Fenner pulls them back out onto the highway heading south.

"How far to Roundup?" he asks.

Fenner fetches his cellphone and checks the route. "About 47 miles."

The engine drones, the tires hum. "I walk 47 miles of barbed wire, I gotta rattlesnake for a necktie." Saltzman eventually says.

"Where'd you get that from?" Fenner asks.

"An old song by a Black guy named Bo Diddley. My uncle used to play it."

"Well, that's one weird fuckin' uncle," Fenner comments.

The engine drones. The tires hum.

Connie Wexler takes off her overcoat and hangs it next to her trailer's solitary door. Minus the coat, she's now clad in only a soiled cotton nightgown and dust-covered slippers. The only sound is the rhythmic plop from a leaky kitchen faucet, which her dead husband had always promised to fix. Just like all the other stuff he'd promised, like a vacation in Vegas and a new set of dinner dishes. She promptly makes her way to the cramped kitchen, where her relic of a computer and monitor occupy most of the space. Her nephew set it up for her, and she'll always be grateful, because it brought the Order of Atonement into her life. The Final Truth speaks to her with a clarity all its own and tells her not to dwell on being a withering prune stuck at the ends of the earth. Because soon, all will wither, and a few will be transformed, including herself.

And now, an added bonus. She has become witness to a monstrous conspiracy to hoard all the frozen eggs and embryos and thus spare them from their righteous fate. For the past three nights, unmarked delivery vans have pulled in close to midnight, gassed up and headed south into the black void. They fit neatly with news reports of someone draining all the clinics of their frozen store and transporting them to some remote location, as yet unknown.

She fires up the computer and dashes off a text to some acquaintances about a half hour to the south. Good people. Fellow believers.

They'll know what to do.

A chill settles over the plains of eastern Montana, a blanket of dense cool air rolling down from Canada. It prompts Fenner to reach down and adjust the van's heater.

"Look out!" Saltzman bellows.

Fenner looks up to the far reach of the headlights, where a load of split firewood sprawls across the highway. He veers to the right, only to see that the wood extends all the way to a drainage ditch and barbed wire fence.

Both men revert to their military instincts. "Ambush!" Fenner yells, while Saltzman reaches back for his rifle. Fenner yanks the wheel hard left to put them in a U-turn. He's halfway through it when the windshield explodes into a web of fractured silver. A 7.62mm round pierces his skull below his right eye and carves a deadly tunnel through his cranium. His hands fly off the wheel and the van plunges into a ditch on the opposite side of the road. Saltzman moves to chamber a round but never finishes. Two more bullets plow in through the passenger side window, killing him instantly. The van comes to rest sideways in the ditch, its engine dead but its headlights still making a futile effort to illuminate the darkness.

Four people approach the van in the sudden silence, three men and a woman. All carry hunting rifles, now slung over their shoulders. One of the men, bearded and heavy, reaches the driver's side door and tugs it open. He reaches in with a meaty hand, grabs the driver's collar, and pulls him out onto the side of the ditch, where he folds into a terminal heap. A search of his pockets yields a wallet and a set of keys.

"Here we go," he says, and walks around to the van's rear doors, which open on the third key. He produces a flashlight and runs its anxious beam over the array of cryo-tanks. "Come take a look," he commands, and the others gather to see. "Here's what stands between us and life eternal."

"Amen," the woman adds.

The bearded man circles around to the passenger side, repeats the process with the second body, and produces a cell phone. "Now we're talkin'," he says.

"Let me see that," one of other men demands, a fair-skinned person with very blond hair.

"How come you always want to do the geek shit?" the bearded man inquires.

"Because I'm better at it than you are," the blond man fires back.

"He's right about that," the woman adds. She wears a wool mackinaw shirt and loose denims tucked into rubber boots. Neither she nor the others exhibit any concern that they've just murdered two people. Their devotion to Final Truth automatically absolves them of any guilt. They operate under a dispensation that transcends all earthly intervention, as have many others in ages both past and present.

"Okay, but first we gotta take care of business," the bearded man says.

They haul the bodies back into the van through the rear doors. The blond man walks to a nearby vehicle hidden in a draw and returns with a five-gallon jerry can of gasoline, which they use to douse the van's interior. They complete their task by igniting a spilt trail of gas that sets off a conflagration, a bright orange beacon that turns the surrounding prairie a soft orange.

They bow their heads in reverence as they watch the blaze. The woman opens a pdf on her cellphone and reads a passage from the Final Truth, as witnessed by Wayne Bauer.

"Only when the last vestiges of humanity are extinguished will the gates of salvation and life eternal be visited upon those who truly believe…"

When the blaze finally heads toward extinction, the blond man turns to the cell phone they found and starts to explore its contents. In no time, he comes upon the navigation map that traces the route to Ingomar in stark blue. "Hey, check this out," he tells the group. The bearded man grabs the phone from him and stares intently at the map.

"This has to go to Tonopah," he proclaims. "Right now."

46

"Looks like our favorite guy just took flight," Gavin tells Tracy. He glances up through the sunroof of their Suburban rental at the helicopter lifting off the helipad inside Ingomar. It ascends vertically before tilting and flying off to the south.

"Just as well," Tracy comments. They've just turned off the highway and are edging down the short gravel road to the front gate behind a ragtag line of vehicles. Aging pickups, old jeeps, battered sedans. "Looks like your friend has rallied the troops," she adds.

The guards wave them through at the gate, and they start toward the graveled parking area on the right, where young men in fatigues pull weapons and duffle bags out of their rigs and stream toward the support building next to the old Jersey Lilly. Tracy notes with some surprise that a few are women, most of them at least a little on the beefy side. But then again, she thinks, they never asked to be big and beefy. They never asked to grow up on all the wrong food. They never asked to be shabbily dressed. They never asked to occupy the bottom social rung at school. And they never asked how they could make the best of their given selves. All because there was no one there to answer.

They follow the stream on into the building, where people are lined up behind several folding tables to fill out some kind of paperwork. Gavin approaches the nearest table, manned by a guy with sergeant stripes on his shoulder. "Excuse me," he starts. "Can you tell me where I might find Frank Fanno?

"You mean *Captain* Fanno?" the sergeant asks in a no-nonsense tone amplified by his buzz cut, deep-set eyes and sparse lips.

"Yes, I mean Captain Fanno," Gavin responds.

"Back over there." The sergeant points to the opposite end of the room, to some offices framed in behind glass. In front of them, the troops start to cluster into groups that Gavin recognizes from his army days – the platoons and squads of an infantry company.

Gavin and Tracy locate a door into the offices and find Cpt. Frank Fanno standing before a map of the Ingomar site covered with notes scribbled in felt tip. When he turns to them, his eyes go right to Tracy, and he appears momentarily shocked before returning to his standard military bearing. "Been expecting you," he says to Gavin.

"This is Tracy Pallas," Gavin says. "She's on assignment with me."

"Ma'am." Fanno bows his head slightly as he says it. Gavin has never seen him quite this deferential but then again he's seldom seen him around women, so he's not sure what to make of it.

"By the looks of it, you and Mr. Stennis arrived at an agreement over funding," Gavin comments, with a nod at the troops outside.

"That we did. I'm about to do a quick inspection of the facilities. Care to join me?"

"Sure."

They walk outside and make their way south past the communications building, with its sprouting nest of towers. "In case you haven't noticed, communications have started to degrade pretty seriously," Fanno says. "The country's going to hell out there, I imagine. Pretty soon, we're gonna find ourselves on our own, but not quite yet. We've still got a little cell, some short-wave radio and the state emergency network. All the satellite stuff and the Internet still work, but they're down to a trickle, so don't get your hopes up. Luckily, I ran down most of my people before it got too bad."

"Are you going to be at full strength?" Gavin inquires.

"Nope. More like about half strength, around seventy people. I made full-time offers to everybody, and let the rest stay on call in reserve."

By now they are approaching the living area with the house trailers and their support utilities. About half the spaces now sit empty, vacated by the departure of Sigma and the construction people. "You probably remember this from the drone footage. It leaves us plenty of housing at our current strength. You guys are welcome to stay here in one of the units out on the edge while you get what you need." As always, Fanno has granted him license to record and report whatever he chooses.

"Appreciate it," Gavin says. Tracy gives a modest nod in agreement. The maleness of this place is nearly overwhelming. In her division at the CDC, women represent at least half the staff. Here they are nearly absent. And needless to say, her particular branch in Reproductive Statistics leans heavily female. It's all about birth and babies. Here it's all about guns and fortifications and fighting. Quite unsettling. Is this the way humanity is going spend what may be its final chapter on earth, locked in an endless tangle of petty dogfights? Somehow, she'd imagined something a little more lofty and noble.

"Now for the main attraction," Fanno announces. They turn and walk about fifty meters north toward the entrance gate. They've just headed right toward the massive bunker when a small convoy of Humvees rolls to a stop alongside them. The last of the Sigma Group is about to depart. An officer steps out of the lead vehicle. "Mr. Fanno, it's all yours. Good luck."

"Think I'll need it?" Frank asks.

"Yep, I think you will," the officer responds. "Be seeing you." He offers no further explanation and climbs back in his vehicle. The convoy lumbers off toward the main gate, leaving a small trail of chalky gravel dust behind them.

"So, what do you guys think?" Fanno asks Gavin and Tracy.

"I think it doesn't matter," Tracy blurts out. "I think this whole place, this whole mess is completely insane. I think your employer is an absolute monster."

Frank shows no anger. He gives her a look of respectful consideration. "So, you know him?"

"I do."

"Stennis is part of a story we're working on," Gavin explains. "We're still putting the pieces together."

Frank smiles faintly. "Well, you better hurry up, because pretty soon I doubt there'll be any pieces left."

"You might be right," Gavin concedes. "But until then we gotta do what we gotta do."

"Same here," Fanno answers. "Let's get on with the show."

As they walk over the concrete apron in front of the bunker, Frank asks Gavin, "What do you guys call it when somebody gives you information, but you can't use it until sometime later?"

"It's called an embargo."

"Okay, as soon as we enter, you're under an embargo. Fair enough?"

"Fair enough." Gavin understands Fanno's càution in this case. They are about to visit what has arguably become the most valuable real estate on the planet, and he is now responsible for its security.

Two armed guards in full combat gear guard the twin steel doors of lifeless gray that open to the interior of the bunker. The true scale of the place becomes more apparent as they reach the entrance. The doors are large enough to accommodate a highway rig, yet they reach less than halfway to the apex of the curved roof. One of the guards activates a remote control that opens the left-hand door, which groans under the stress of all the weight. Once they enter, the door shuts behind them with an emphatic thud.

A wide aisle bisects the structure all the way to the far end, and a matrix of powerful LED lights shines down from high overhead, with the curve of the corrugated rooftop lost in darkness. A utility space occupies the area closest to them, filled with forklifts, workbenches and a maze of wiring and plumbing. Beyond lies the heart of the operation, a vast lattice of shelving populated by many hundreds of cryo-tanks. An elaborate monitoring system connects to each tank through a web of neatly strung yellow cabling. A series of caged stations sit at regular intervals along the main aisle and hold the large liquid nitrogen tanks used for recharging.

"So how many babies?" Tracy asks after taking it all in.

"Don't understand," Fanno admits. "What do you mean?"

"I mean if you count up what's in all these tanks, how many potential human beings are we talking about?"

"Don't know," Fanno says. "But God does. And that's all that counts."

"In the end, I'm sure you're right," Gavin concedes. "But there has to be some kind of inventory system, some kind of database that's tracking all this."

"Not my department," Fanno says. "But if there is, it's right over there." He points to a windowless concrete blockhouse the size of a small house just off to their right. All manner of piping and wiring protrude from its top and snake off to various points in the lattice.

"Mind if we take a look?" Gavin asks.

"Go ahead, but don't forget about our embargo deal."

"We won't," Gavin promises.

Fanno punches in a key code that opens an armored security door. Inside, the far wall holds several rows of large hi-res monitors. Many provide video surveillance of the exterior from multiple angles. Others show arcane diagrams and columns of data. Still others display interior security video from multiple points in the lattice.

"I've been told this thing has a ton of AI and pretty much runs itself," Fanno says. "It's gonna train part of my crew to handle upkeep and maintenance."

"What if the power goes out?" Tracy inquires.

"Not gonna happen. There's a lower floor to this place with enough gear to support it for several months. Diesel generators, fuel tanks, water tanks, food stores, stuff like that. We could be dead and gone and it would all roll along just fine without us. For a while anyway."

Tracy sits down in front of one the monitors fronted by a keyboard and mouse. "Mind if I check it out?"

"I assume you know what you're doing." Fanno says.

"You assume right," she replies, without looking up.

Fanno takes no offense. Gavin, usually a quick study in human entanglements, can't quite get a fix on Frank's view of Tracy. He seems to hold her in some kind of ineffable esteem. They leave Tracy and the blockhouse and stare down the long aisle through the storage area.

"So, it all comes down to this," Fanno comments.

"Sooner or later, someone's going to try to take it all away from you," Gavin predicts. "You know that, don't you?"

"Doesn't matter."

"Why not?"

"God won't let it happen."

Gavin refrains from comment. He learned long ago that matters of faith transcend logic and understanding, so why bother?

47

"Jericho," Wayne Bauer proclaims as he views Ingomar on the online map. "We've been given a sign from on high, where the true source of wisdom resides."

"What's Jericho got to do with the middle of Montana?" Kranz asks. He is looking at the cell phone from the ambushed delivery van, with its route map from Seattle to Ingomar. At last, they know where the frozen store from the clinics is being stashed. Their field people have served them well.

"Jericho," Bauer repeats. "A great battle was fought there upon divine proclamation. The city and all its inhabitants were destroyed. This time it's called Ingomar. Once again, the focus of universal justice converges on a single place."

"So, what you're saying is that we now have a tangible objective to rally around."

"Correct. What we learned from Colorado Springs is that individuals within our following are starting to seize the power of the Final Truth on their own. What's needed is something to consolidate our leadership at the top, and now it's been given to us. A divine gift."

"And just what do you propose we do with this gift?" Kranz asks.

"Simple. We rally our people, we march north, and we destroy the site where the abomination is stored."

By now, Kranz has learned how to navigate Bauer's maddening mix of clever insights and outright insanity. Wayne's behavior has put Kranz squarely in the camp where history makes the person rather than the reverse. Without the flame of humanity sputtering as the wick drowns in the wax at the bottom of the candle, none of this would be happening.

"Okay then, there are several things we need to take into account," Kranz responds.

"Such as?"

"First, whatever we do, we have to do it fast. The national telecommunications structure is failing, bit by bit. Pretty soon we won't have the means to get the word out. We'll have the means with our databases and AI, but we won't have the medium."

"And…"

"We have to consider the intelligence angle. We know for a fact that the feds and whoever else are continuously monitoring us online. Whatever happens, the element of surprise is going to be a big deal. When we put out the call to action, we can't give away the final objective. If we do, we're beat even before we start."

"Makes sense. Anything else?"

"Yeah. Planning and logistics. This isn't going to be like leading a mob across town. We need to figure out exactly what we're doing and how we're doing it. It's about a thousand miles from here to this Ingomar place, and a lot might happen along the way. Right now, I figure we have enough people with some military experience that I can assemble some kind of fighting force and make up a battle plan and a way to arm them. It's going to be critical that I have your full support to command all of this. Anything less and we're headed toward anarchy."

"Agreed. Let's get started. Right now."

Kranz sits with Nathan, Bauer's original computer guy, in a second trailer that's been added as a communications center. He thumbs the handle of his coffee cup and yawns while Nathan's fingers dance nimbly over a keyboard with a wireless connection to an industrial-grade, rack-mounted computer. The kid is preparing to broadcast a message recently completed by Wayne, with the help of the Cortica 3 AI platform. It consists of a map showing the proposed route as far as Bozeman, Montana, and a brief text:

I come to you this evening with a message of utmost importance. The time of reckoning is now upon us, and we must heed a call from the keepers of the Final Truth. The heavens have spoken, and I've been instructed to lead us north on a journey of discovery out onto the plains, where our faith will be put to the ultimate test and our final destiny revealed. It is here that each of us will find salvation as we seal the final chapter in the history of humanity. Put aside your jobs, your duties, your earthly obligations and join us. We will depart one day hence, so make your way by whatever means along our path of travel. Your very soul demands it!

A hint of cannabis lingers in the air, and Kranz can only hope it hasn't compromised Nathan's performance. He'd suggested to Wayne that this particular task was best left to the professionals, but Wayne emphatically disagreed. When Kranz asked him why, he got a one-word reply:

"Loyalty."

Kranz had simply nodded and carried on. After his 20 years in military service, he understood implicitly. In the constant struggle for the next toehold in the hierarchy, loyalty frequently trumped competence as the vehicle upward. Those above needed a solid foundation secured by those below, regardless of their individual merits. Bauer, now widely known as Terminus, was no different, and the more tangible his power had become, the more devotion superseded dedication in his decision-making.

Nathan leaned back after he pushed the message out on all the major social media channels, and a few minor ones as well. "It's going, but it's slow. I'm telling you, man, it's a fucked-up telecom world out there right now."

"I'm sure it is," Kranz says absently. He's already moved far ahead, skipping over the logistics of the journey and on to the final encounter at Ingomar. He can do it. Better yet, he can do it well. For years, he effectively ran an infantry battalion of 800 marines. He did so as the outfit's ranking non-commissioned officer, answering only to the commanding officer, a colonel with highly questionable leadership skills. The man preferred political maneuvering on the golf course to the arduous complexity of directing men and material on the field of combat. Kranz, on the other hand, had mastered this end of the profession and sees himself as eminently qualified to guide his men through the most harrowing of battle scenarios.

. . .

"Morning. You folks up and about?" Fanno asks Tracy. The open trailer door frames him against the cool morning light. His eyes leave her as soon as the words are out. Why does he seem so distant around me? She wonders. "Sure. Would you like to come in?"

"Thank you," he says and steps up into the interior, where Gavin has come forward through the kitchen and sleeping quarters in the rear.

"Frank," Gavin says. "Have a seat. Would you like a little coffee?"

"No thanks." Fanno wears military fatigues done in a camouflage pattern and combat boots of an earthen tone. A pair of captain's bars signify his rank on a patch on his right collar. "I've just got a minute or two, and something came up that I thought you should know about. I've got some old friends at the Montana state police, and they just told me about an ambush north of here on Highway 87. Pretty bad. Two bodies and a burnt-out van. Looks like they were transporting a load of cryo-tanks. Later on, my pals contacted Omega, and confirmed it. Two dozen of 'em."

"Which were supposed to come here?" Gavin asks.

"That they were, but that's not the problem. The cops found two bodies but only one cell phone. Omega told them that the route to here may be on the one that's missing. In other words, we've probably got a target pasted on our backs."

"Swell," Gavin says. "For starters, this place is well on its way to being the most contested piece of real estate on the planet. And now its location has been compromised. You're right. It's only a matter of time before someone pays you a visit."

"To tell you the truth," Fanno says, "When I took this gig, I expected nothing less. You two should get out while you still can." He turns to Tracy. "Especially you."

"You don't mean because I'm a woman, do you?" Tracy asks. "I mean, you've got women here with you right now."

"Yes, I do. But they're trained to deal with something like this. You're not."

Tracy declines to comment. He has a point. Still, there's something else residing in the recesses of his demeanor, something offstage and wandering somewhere in the wings.

"And just who do you think might come calling?" Gavin asks Frank. "I mean, by now you've got biker gangs, rogue militias and God knows what else."

"You've got the Order," Tracy speaks up. "The Order of Atonement. They have a huge following, especially in the rural west. I've read some of their stuff. They're devoted to personal purification though the total destruction of humanity, which obviously includes everything in those tanks. If they get their act together, they could be real trouble."

"That they could," Fanno agrees. "Real trouble. I've seen my share of religious fanatics in my time overseas. Death comes easily."

"Now I know this might not be a popular suggestion," Gavin says. "And I know you have no use at all for the federal government. But in this case, you're both on the same side of the fence. You both want to see all those eggs and embryos survive to reseed the nation. Maybe you could talk it through and come up with a partnership of sorts, at least for the time being."

Frank closes his eyes and shakes his head, even as Gavin speaks. Slowly, calmly, rhythmically, as if in sync with some force unseen, unheard and unfathomable.

"Not gonna happen," he pronounces when Gavin is finished.

Gavin chooses not to pursue the subject. "If it's all the same to you," he says, "I'd like to stick around and see what happens." He wraps his arm around Tracy's shoulder. "I think Tracy can speak for herself."

"I'm in." Why did she say that? She feels several universes away from spinning numbers in the comfort of her cubicle at NCHS, where she was embedded in a pedantic yet reassuring bureaucratic certainty. Now humanity is being swept along by an inexorable tide pulling it toward a sudden twilight, and she's out on the plains of Montana in an armed enclave, where the final struggle for survival may play out.

She simply can't pass it up.

48

Kranz leans back in his folding chair atop Wayne's motorhome and beholds the vast sprawl of vehicles parked atop an ocean of prairie grass that spills to the horizon. He can't quite arrive at an accurate count due to their chaotic arrangement, but it must be in excess of five hundred. It's grown by at least a hundred since they pulled into Twin Falls shortly after noon. A looted high-wattage speaker system has been set up on two pick-ups parked adjacent to the home. A few minutes ago, Wayne used it to blast out his latest exhortation to the motorized flock. If you removed the vehicles and replaced them with horses, it could easily be Genghis Kahn addressing his hordes on the Mongolian steppes.

"...And so now we gather in the shadow of a world gone wrong, a world that must atone in full for its nearly unforgivable sins. Oceans choking on plastic. Forests reduced to blackened stumps. Migrants wandering on their way to nowhere. We can no longer seek personal redemption anywhere on the face of this mortally stricken earth. We must look ahead to salvation in a new world, one given to us by powers beyond our limited reckoning. In death, my friends, we shall find life anew..."

Earlier, Kranz had sketched a rough plan of their incursion into Twin Falls, where they met very little resistance. The town had about 70 police officers, eight of whom turned out to be followers of the Order. The rest had no intention of taking on the hundreds that poured in off the highway, many of them armed. Several firefights ensued as the faithful fanned out to loot the town's numerous gun stores, including a large sporting goods chain. The owners quickly realized that while the constitution gave them the right to bear arms, it did not guarantee they would prevail in the face of superior firepower. Next, they moved on to the supermarkets and grocery stores to replenish their food stocks. Finally, they drained all the gas stations dry by taking on fuel for their journey north.

Campers, pickups, sedans, motorcycles, motorhomes. All painted a pale copper by the setting sun and quickly coalescing into a social organism built on the fire of a newly minted faith that reflects the tenure of the times. Thin columns of smoke rise from barbeques and improvised campfires. Swarms of people move in a Brownian dance. Kranz has put out a call for those with military backgrounds to gather here within the hour. He will quickly assess their worth and build a command hierarchy on the fly. That done, he will start working on how to apply it when they reach Ingomar.

Wayne climbs up and seats himself in a folding chair next to Kranz. He looks out at the encampment and smiles. "You've done well, James. You're a practical man, and that's precisely what's needed right now."

Kranz nods thoughtfully. "Maybe so." Both of them know the truth of the matter. While Kranz may steer their burgeoning vehicle, Wayne remains the engine. And while drivers can be replaced, engines cannot.

Frank Fanno pulls off his combat boots and stretches his feet in relief. He sits with Gavin and Tracy in front of a television in the control room of the communications building across from the bunker. The screen displays an over-the-air broadcast from the ABC network affiliate in Roundup. It is running a lengthy and hastily edited account of a major civil disturbance in Twin Falls, Idaho, with video shot by a local news crew. It shows parallel streams of vehicles pouring down several main avenues in the core area. They ignore traffic lights, and their occupants hop off randomly and perform smash and grabs on local retail stores. Broken glass litters the sidewalks and the pop of rifle fire can be heard. Police are nowhere to be seen. One reporter has managed to identify the invading force as the Order of Atonement, a radical religious group from Tonopah, Nevada headed by a charismatic Wayne Bauer, also known as Terminus. The motive for their violent migration to this staid community 400 miles north remains a mystery.

The news cuts to a commercial. Fanno kills the sound and turns to Gavin and Tracy.

"Here they come," he declares.

"How long have we got?" Gavin asks.

"Day after tomorrow, by the looks of it," Fanno says. "You'll have to excuse me," he apologizes as he pulls his boots back on. "Looks like I got a little work to do."

Billings, Montana. Not a place Mark Stennis had ever anticipated spending any time at all. But here he is, all because its airport sits within helicopter range of Ingomar. His hotel offers a room service menu of stunning mediocrity, so he's taken to ordering out from a couple of the town's most reputable restaurants. Tonight, he methodically works his way through a dinner from Jakes featuring a bacon-wrapped filet mignon and spicy potato cake with a bottle of California Cabernet for good measure.

He turns on the TV for entertainment, which immediately ruins his dinner.

ABC informs him that a motorized horde has just descended upon Twin Falls, Idaho and plunged the place into civil anarchy. They've been tentatively identified as the Order of Atonement led by an eccentric spiritualist from Nevada. There is no immediate explanation of their decision to surge northward toward some unspecified destination.

Oh yes, there is. He got a call a few hours back from Hallock at the Omega Group, who thought he should know about an ambushed van and a missing cell phone that described the route to Ingomar. The assailants had torched the van and wantonly destroyed its cargo of cryo-tanks, which fits nicely with the online doctrine of a group called the Order of Atonement. They're amateurs, Hallock warned, but they're crazy and growing exponentially.

The Order. So here they are, on the march, heading north toward the bunker at Ingomar and its assets of nearly incalculable value. His assets. Before he can think it all the way through, his cellphone rings. His father.

"You watching the news?" Roger Stennis asks before his son can even answer.

"You mean Twin Falls?"

"Of course I mean Twin Falls. I got a courtesy call from the Omega Group and put two and two together. These Order people have pegged your location and now they're on their way. So, what's your plan?"

"I'm working on it."

"Jesus! I most certainly hope so. Where are you right now?"

"I'm in Billings."

"Unbelievable! You've left our entire future in the hands of some boy scouts and a guy who runs a machine shop? Get your ass back up there and take charge."

"And what if the place turns into a combat zone?"

"Then so be it. Your family didn't get this far by turning their backs on a fight when the chips were down. Get up there. Now."

Stennis puts his dinner aside and pours more Cabernet. He has to go. He can stall for maybe a day, but that's it. Any longer, and he risks banishment. For good. A dismal prospect in a collapsing world where power, money and guns are sure to carry the day.

He would like to pray for deliverance but doubts he has any working capital in that particular account.

49

The Idaho State Patrol sets up the roadblock on a stretch of Highway 191 that hugs the Gallatin River on the way north to Bozeman. The cohort tasked with this operation demonstrates a distinct lack of enthusiasm. Intelligence from points south describes a massive convoy of vehicles, as many as three or four hundred. It appears that newcomers are joining at every major junction along the way. It also appears that many are armed with a random assortment of hunting and combat rifles and God knows what else.

The officers, numbering a dozen, confer among themselves as they wait. The standard procedure is to place a few vehicles across the roadway and to supplement it with a chained link of sharp spikes to blow out the tires of errant traffic. But in this instance, such a ploy could prove extremely perilous. The spikes might disable the first few vehicles, but they would quickly be replaced by even more from the massive stream behind them. Any attempt at making arrests might provoke a potentially deadly firefight with a force vastly superior in numbers.

Ultimately, they decide to offer token resistance by placing a pair of patrol cars across the northbound lanes and to forego the tire spikes. That done, they take shelter in a copse of nearby pine trees adjacent to an irrigation ditch.

Thus, the first and last line of defense of the town of Bozeman is set in place.

The afternoon grows hot and muggy as they keep their vigil. A vaporous haze erases the overhead blue, and the sun turns a sluggish yellow. They first spot the convoy several miles off, where it spills down out of the hills and onto the valley floor. Immense. As it approaches their position, the tail end has yet to appear. When it draws closer, they scan the head of the column with field glasses. A large dump truck serves as the point, followed by a motorhome flanked by two more dump trunks, all moving at a brisk pace. The heads and shoulders of men riding in the trucks' gray metal bins come into focus, along with a thin trace of gun barrels pointed skyward.

When they reach the roadblock, the three trucks arrange themselves in a triangle, all with no loss in velocity. They form a spearhead that collides with the three roadblock vehicles and tosses them aside in tangled heaps onto the shoulders. The men in the bins open fire on the wreckage for target practice.

The state patrol peers out from the tree line and realizes that their decision not to engage was both prescient and prudent. They settle back and watch the seemingly endless linear parade. Sedans, pickups, motorcycles, sidecar rigs, campers, fifth wheelers, vans, small trucks. Many near the end of their mechanized lives but still rolling, their trunks, beds and cargo areas stuffed with booty from Twin Falls.

When the tail of the convoy finally passes, the officers come out from the tree line and watch its departure. The air has an urban stink about it seldom encountered in eastern Montana. Carbonized exhaust, heated rubber, fast food remnants, stored gasoline, spent oil, baked metal.

The officer in charge radios headquarters and tries to describe the scale of the incident she's just witnessed. She fails.

Sgt. Marion Davis is a 20-year man with a year left to go. Starting next fall, his retirement kicks in and he will feast off the state of Montana for the rest of his corpulent life. His post as administrator at the state's National Guard armory in Bozeman might be lacking in gravitas but offers a wealth of long-term security. Just to make sure, he's run a little side scam through a bogus "athletic fund" that nets him an extra five thousand every year, which he's stashed in an account owned by his wife in her maiden name. Enough to buy a nice little cabin cruiser for prolonged fun in the sun, with a Sapporo and a roast beef sandwich thrown in for good measure.

His idyllic vision took a small dent when he arrived at work this morning and the TV said that a religious mob in Twin Falls had pulled up and headed north, first on Highway 15 then on 20.

He relaxed and made a cup of coffee. They were still more than 300 miles away, and state patrol would be waiting to kick their ass, and that would be the end of it. But just to hedge his bet, he went down the hall onto the main drill floor and into the supply room where the arms vault was located. He spun the combination to the heavy metal door and methodically scanned the interior. Multiple racks of AR-15s, two .30 caliber machine guns, one .50 caliber machine gun, a rocket-propelled grenade launcher and one mortar tube. To the rear, several stacks of metal boxes house the ammunition used to power all this weaponry. He closed the door, rotated the locking lever, and spun the dial to obliterate the combination. Mission accomplished.

Now, in the midst of this lazy afternoon, he feels a familiar bout of drowsiness come on and feels no shame about it. With the exception of monthly drills, he largely has the building to himself and floats along gracefully in solitude. Right now, the place is soaked in silence except for the rush of cool air through the registers. He leaves his office and saunters down the hall to a spare office, where he has a cot and pillow set up. After setting an alarm on the floor, Davis plops down and lowers his eyelids toward dreamland.

They're just barely shut when the crash of broken glass bounces its way down the hall. He bolts upright and cautiously moves to the door and peeks down toward the main entrance. He spies broken glass on the buffed linoleum surface and steps out into the open to get a better view. Three men suddenly appear, all armed with combat rifles. The one in the middle is heavy set with a crewcut and has a definite military look about him.

"At ease, sergeant," he says in a gravelly voice. "We won't take much of your time."

The trio advances toward him, weapons trained on his midsection. He doesn't dare turn and run. They might take it as provocation and shoot him in the back. He feels sick with dread.

"No need to get excited," the military man tells him. "We just need you to take us to the arms vault. That's all. Nothing to it. Let's go now." He motions with his gun barrel down the hall behind them.

"Okay, okay," Davis hears himself whispering as he leads them on the same path he followed earlier. When they reach the vault, he twirls in the combination without them even asking. "Now step on in," the military guy commands. Once all three join Davis inside, the military guy breaks into a mean grin. "Good job," he says and points to the rear wall. "Go ahead and have a seat and we'll handle the rest. You wouldn't happen to have a hand cart or two around here, would you?"

Davis points toward the supply room. "Out there."

"Alright then," then military guy says. "Just relax. We've got it from here."

Davis spends the next 30 minutes watching them remove the entire contents of the vault. Fully aware that they are also removing his job and a goodly portion of his retirement.

They work silently, and when they're done, the military man shuts Davis in the emptied space. "Thanks for your service," he says just before he closes the door and twirls the lock.

"You've done well, James," Wayne Bauer tells Kranz. "Very well, indeed." The cool air of early evening wraps around them as they survey the formidable array of weaponry laid out on a dozen green tarps stretched out over the straw-like mat of shortgrass. Their view is bounded by a series of highway rigs arranged to form a secure area in the midst of the Order's latest encampment just east of Bozeman. Many citizens fled the town after hearing what happened in Twin Falls, leaving the streets open to brazen theft and looting – all in the name of the Final Truth. Unfortunately, there were several armed skirmishes before the local police gave up and melted away. Several Order members were wounded and three were killed. The dead were buried on the edge of the encampment, and Wayne personally attended their internment, reciting an improvised rite of passage.

"We'll hold the heavy weapons from the armory in reserve until we see how the battle shapes up," Kranz tells Wayne. "They just might be our ace in the hole."

Together, they watch four lines of men, plus a few women, approach the tarps where they receive a platoon number, a rifle, and ammunition to carry in backpacks pilfered from a sporting goods chain. "We're not going down to the squad level of command," Kranz comments. "Too much room for confusion. Not enough time for that."

"How much resistance do you anticipate?" Bauer asks.

"A lot. We know from our intel that the Sigma Group is involved, which means it's a military installation of some kind. We'll scout the place with drones as soon as we get close enough."

"In the end, it doesn't really matter," Wayne says.

"Oh yeah?"

"All of us must be prepared to make the ultimate sacrifice. If that's what it takes to destroy the abomination held there, then so be it. The divine order of the Final Truth demands it."

Kranz expels a frustrated sigh. "You look at this thing in terms of saved souls. I look at it in terms of lost combatants. I've gotta tell you: Dead men won't win you a war."

"Yes, but each will win a great personal victory and be set free to journey as they wish."

"And your abomination will remain untouched."

"For the time being, yes. But we'll have lit a torch that can't be extinguished. Others will take it up. They won't rest until the will of the Final Truth prevails."

Kranz doesn't respond. Bauer has gone over the top. Up until now, there was always some path, however tortuous, that linked his weird spirituality with tactical reality. No longer. Kranz has to wonder if the AI in Cortica 3 is somehow involved. Has it captured Bauer's soul and bent it to its will? He'll never know. What he does know is that it's time to start devising an exit strategy.

50

Stennis tries to ignore the insistent beat of the rotor blades and focus on getting a connection on his cellphone. No luck. They are either out of a service area, or the service is undergoing sporadic failure that is now common throughout the system. He pockets it and sits back in the front seat of the turbine-powered chopper.

"How much farther?" he asks the pilot through the mic extending from his headset.

"About thirty miles," comes the answer. "We're going to follow the river a little longer and then turn north. From there, it'll be a straight shot."

Stennis feels he is dressed appropriately for the trip. A Bally leather flight jacket over a quarter-zip sweatshirt. Brioni denims and hand-tooled cowboy boots. Prada aviator sunglasses. It's the kind of attire that should speak of authority to the pseudo-military people he will soon encounter at Ingomar.

Below, the Yellowstone River snakes to the east within an irrigated green buffer where it encounters the barren plains. The rotors continue to pound out their mechanical mantra. Stennis closes his eyes and fights off the temptation to replay the savage mandate of his father.

"Holy Jesus!" comes the exclamation over the headphones. "Look at that!"

Stennis yanks himself out of his self-imposed stupor and gathers in the view out the windshield. The convoy below takes the shape of a very long segmented insect as it travels along next to the river.

"That's it for sure," Stennis says. "Take her on down for a better look."

"I dunno," the pilot worries. "They might not like strangers."

"Well then, keep a little distance. Get us up closer to the front."

The pilot silently calculates the risk, then complies. He's getting triple time for this trip. They close to within a few hundred yards along one side of the rolling menagerie and speed toward the front, where they see a Class A motorhome flanked by pair of dump trucks with men in their bins, now in agitated motion.

"That's close enough," Stennis warns. Too late. A loud ping reverberates through the cockpit. A bullet hole appears high on the windshield on the pilot's side. A second ping puts the craft into a slight shudder. Red warning lights dance frantically across the instrument panel. The pilot instinctively pulls up and away.

"Are we okay?" Stennis asks through a flood of adrenaline.

The pilot skims the panel and flips some switches and punches some buttons. "For now," he says. "But not for long."

A heavyset man deep into middle age steers Bauer's motorhome at a steady pace that matches the dump trucks. He drove a Greyhound for 21 years before the Final Truth reached out and touched him. His new calling makes him one of four dozen men assigned to the Eternal Gate, which now travels in a string of vehicles directly behind the motorhome. Assembled by Kranz, the Eternal Gate reflects Bauer's mounting paranoia since the assassination attempt, a fear he shares with numerous historical despots: Hitler's Escort Battalion, Saddam's Special Republican Guard, Napoleon's Imperial Guard and Stalin's Red Guards, and so on. Ironically, Wayne would never consider himself a tyrant of this sort. He imagines that he operates from a purely spiritual perspective, free from any worldly designs.

A few feet behind the driver, Evelyn Gossart, Bauer's communications person, sits in a generously padded armchair, reading yet another paperback. It's one of many she's consumed since Bauer gradually quit seeking her counsel. She glances over at him in the dinette, where he and Kranz sit opposite each other with a laptop between them.

They're fucking crazy, especially Bauer. They weren't at first, but that seems like years ago now. She thought it would be a standard marketing communications gig, something well within the confines of professional practice. A little silly, but highly lucrative. Wrong. Yesterday evening, she watched Bauer deliver an improvised eulogy for someone who actually got killed in pursuit of his grandiose vision. Killed. Dead. Now what? She knows the pair is planning something far more violent involving a big cache of frozen embryos and eggs, and she's along for the ride – with nowhere to bail. She pictures herself trapped in a horror movie where she tries to climb out of the screen, run down the aisle and sprint through the lobby out into the merciful light of God's own day. Good luck with that.

Kranz looks at the laptop display and its aerial view of Ingomar shot by a long-range drone they launched during a brief rest stop. He takes it all in, the support buildings, the behemoth bunker, the surrounding ditch.

"Here's how it happens," he tells Bauer. "First, it's an open space, so we need to cover our approach. Otherwise, we'll get mowed down before we even get close. We do it with some drones dropping smoke grenades between us and the perimeter. That'll give us enough time to take them on point blank. They'll be overwhelmed and have to fall back to that big ditch around the bunker. Then we hit them with some mortar rounds, which will force them to retreat inside the bunker itself. After that, we can take our time, and rig enough explosives to blow the door open. Then they can either surrender or die in battle. Whichever way it goes, we got what we came for."

Bauer takes a long look at the image before he speaks. "It might work. But I see a weakness."

"Where?"

"Do we know their strength in numbers?"

"Not exactly, but we can assume…"

"We can assume nothing. We'll only get one chance at this, and then we face a catastrophe."

"So, what do you suggest?"

"If they have the numbers to match us head-on, we might not overwhelm them. We need to make absolutely sure that doesn't happen."

"And how do we do that?"

"We send in everybody except those with children, who might experience a crisis of faith and rebel."

"What?"

"We mix the faithful in among the fighters. That will give us maybe six or seven hundred attackers. Those who perish will experience a joy we can't even begin to imagine."

Kranz feels the motorhome's big tires hum on the pavement beneath them. He hears the relentless air blast streaming over the flat windshield. He floats free in the moment, in a vacuum of disbelief. Slowly, the ultimate horror of it all intrudes. He knows he has to comply. Quitting is out of the question. Once outside the Order, he'll be hunted down like an errant dog and held accountable for the sacking of two towns and the deaths that followed. If he stays on, he lacks the power to challenge Bauer's decision. The man holds a biblical sway over his people.

"Are you sure about this?" he says. It's the best he can do.

"I'm beyond sure," Bauer replies. "You have to remember that I act as a portal between this world and a level of intelligence far beyond our comprehension. The decision is not mine. It comes from somewhere beyond what we call infinity."

"Okay then" Kranz says. "Your call."

Bauer knows the call resides far beyond his mortal confines but declines to comment. Kranz doesn't dwell within the tent of the faithful but does serve a necessary purpose. So be it.

Evelyn Gossart puts down her paperback and stares at the tiled floor of faux marble. She heard it all. She sincerely wishes she hadn't. She quietly rises, goes to the bathroom in the rear and throws up.

Gunfire erupts from outside, off to the left. A quick series of closely spaced explosive pops. Bauer and Kranz snap their attention to the view out the dinette window. A row of men in the dump truck flanking them thrust their weapons skyward and expel round after round. Their shoulders shudder from the recoil. Above them, a chopper comes into view, a small one. As it twists up and away, a thin trail of smoke from the engine compartment stains the sky.

"Well," observes Kranz, "there goes our element of surprise."

51

They call the drone the MQ-9 Reaper, a veteran of several wars and numerous conflicts in the more contentious regions of the globe. On this particular day, it traces lazy circles over the plains of Eastern Montana at the behest of the President of the United States. Its hi-res cameras follow the northward progress of the Order's caravan as it closes in on the base at Ingomar. The larger the caravan grows, the stronger the consensus that they intend to attack the installation in an attempt to destroy its frozen cache. Their apocalyptic doctrine demands it, no matter what the cost.

The President is well aware of this. She is also aware that deploying the nation's formidable combat weaponry to attack a convoy composed entirely of civilians will be unprecedented in the nation's history.

"Looks like they're close enough to start forming up for an assault," the secretary of defense tells her as they stare at the output from the Reaper's camera. "Our nearest assets are about 200 miles off. If we don't deploy now, it could be all over before we ever get there. We have a half dozen combat helicopters standing by. That should be enough to do the job if the bunker's being threatened."

The President scans the faces around the table in the White House briefing room. "Anybody disagree with that?" Silence. "Okay, nobody pulls any trigger whatsoever unless I give the go ahead. Understand?" A collective nod. "We're not going to take any action unless they're right on the brink of breaching the bunker." A resigned sigh from the President. "All right then, send 'em out."

"See anything yet?" Fanno asks over the portable two-way radio from where he stands just outside the bunker's front.

"Checking," Tracy replies over an identical radio 50 meters away inside the blockhouse contained within the bunker. She scans four displays from four cameras mounted on the upper stretches of the bunker's curved, earthen roof. They give an elevated view of the surrounding terrain in all its sparseness and flatness. Her scan catches no movement on the first camera, which points southeast. Not so with the second camera, which points southwest. She adjusts it to a maximum telephoto shot.

"I've got movement on the road coming from the south. A big string of vehicles. Maybe even hundreds. It's got to be them."

"Okay, keep me advised of their progress."

"Got it." Tracy wound up in this role because she's the most technically adept among them. In addition to her math degree, she took numerous engineering and computer science courses. In a world thoroughly saturated by digital electronics, it's served her quite well. Like right now, when her very survival may depend on it.

In addition to their concern for each other, Gavin and Tracy feel the pull of ideological considerations. As a journalist, Gavin feels a historical obligation to record the coming events as thoroughly and accurately as possible. And Tracy considers it her duty to help defend this wellspring of future life from mindless and brutal destruction.

Tracy adjusts the magnification on the southwest camera, which shows the long string of vehicles generating a giant dust cloud that blows eastward on the prevailing wind. Her position here in the blockhouse not only gives her a bird's eye view of the potential battlefield; it also lets her monitor the communications gear, their last and increasingly tenuous link with the outside world. Their best option is some kind of link to the vast constellation of telecom satellites orbiting overhead. But to establish such a link from her end without dedicated equipment would be extraordinarily complicated. She can only hope that someone at a place like the National Security Agency will take the initiative and figure out how to hook them up.

"Let's start with what we know," Fanno tells Gavin from where they stand on the concrete apron outside the bunker's armored metal doors. "From the size of the convoy, they've probably got several hundred people they can throw at this. We've got about eighty. Then you have to add all the combat gear they seized in Bozeman plus the stuff they've looted along the way. That amounts to some respectable firepower."

Gavin looks over to the edge of the concrete, where the excavated trench starts. A machine gun nest guards the entrance as Fanno's troops file down into it. The same thing is happening on the opposite side. Expressions of worry, fear and doubt have replaced their previous swagger. They're no longer just playing army. Some of them might actually get hurt. A few of them might actually get killed.

"It's all on you, isn't it?" Gavin says to Fanno.

Fanno appears puzzled. "What do you mean?"

"If wasn't for you, most of these people would cut and run. You're the only thing holding all this together."

Fanno stares out to somewhere close to infinity. "You might be right. But anymore, it doesn't matter. Truth is, we're not fighting to save the stuff in the bunker. Not exactly. Right now, we're fighting to save each other. And I'm no exception."

"I thought you said this was all about God's property," Gavin reminds him.

"It is. And I've got good reason to believe He's on our side, but we won't know for sure until this thing is all over."

"Well until then, what's your plan?" Gavin inquires.

"We've got four platoons, about twenty people each," Fanno says. He points to the buildings opposite the bunker. "We deploy one platoon over there to defend the west side. If things go bad, they pull back over here and into the trenches. We can cover their retreat with machine gun fire. The other three platoons are dispersed around the bunker. The trenches are deep enough we can move around without much exposure to enemy fire. If it looks like we'll be overrun, we retire back into the bunker, and that'll make us a really tough nut to crack." He turns to Gavin. "So that's it."

"I'm counting on you, Frank," Gavin says with a trace of humor.

Fanno picks up on it. "So am I," he grins.

"Captain!"

Fanno turns to one of his platoon sergeants, who points to the southern sky from where he stands on the edge of a trench. A helicopter is headed their way, a relatively small one of the civilian variety. A slender trail of black smoke traces its path against the overcast sky.

"Well, what do you know," Frank says with a disgusted smile. "Here comes the money."

"Be right back," Gavin says. He turns and sprints back into the bunker and on into the blockhouse.

As Gavin enters, Tracy has picked up the ailing chopper on the display from the southwest camera. "Let me guess," she says.

"No doubt about it," Gavin says. "The chickenshit comes home to roost."

"Normally, that would be funny. Not so much right now. Got any ideas?"

"We engage him on our terms. For right now, you stay in here and out of sight with the door closed."

"Okay. And what about you?"

"He doesn't know we're connected, and he's really got nothing on me, except that I'm a nosey reporter. I think I can handle that, especially in front of Frank. Right now, what I need is a little protection."

He spots a storage locker where he finds a strap-on Kevlar vest and a helmet. He looks over to the monitors while donning them. The northwest camera shows Stennis's chopper attempting a very wobbly landing on the helipad next to the parking area.

"Gotta go," Gavin says and hurries out the door. "Love you."

"Love you." Tracy wishes she'd touched him. Every simple moment seems so very large right now.

By the time Gavin reaches Fanno out front, the chopper is down on the pad across the way. Its turbine issues a prolonged sigh as its rotor blades lose their momentum. The pilot hops out, fire extinguisher in hand, and heads back toward the engine compartment where a small lick of flame issues from one of the vents. Stennis comes out on the other side, spots Fanno and Gavin, and strides in their direction in his faux-military attire.

Fanno shakes his head. "Un-fuckin-believable."

"And that's just the start," Gavin adds.

"I don't wanna know. At least not right now."

Stennis is just a few steps away when he recognizes Gavin. He pulls off his sunglasses and squints to confirm it. His face falls.

"Mr. Stennis. We meet again," Gavin says.

Stennis turns to Fanno. "What the fuck is *he* doing here?"

"Mr. Gray and I are working on a book," Fanno replies calmly.

"Not right now he's not," Stennis says, "This is my operation. I'm taking charge. He's out of here."

"You're taking charge, huh?" Fanno says.

"You heard me. Now bring me up to date."

Gavin has to stifle a laugh. Under the circumstances, the man's arrogance is close to astounding.

Fanno takes on a bemused smile, looks down, and idly kicks a pebble across the concrete. And then another. When he senses Stennis approaching a full boil, he looks up.

"Way I see it, this is a military operation in a war zone. So, consider yourself a conscript. Which means you're not in charge of shit."

Stennis loses it. "You redneck piece of shit! Don't you get it? I *own* this place. Which means I also own *you*. Now get real!"

By now, two of Fanno's platoon sergeants have joined the group. Fanno's face turns to steel. "By the time this is over, you'll be lucky if you even own your own ass. Now get out of my sight."

Stennis opens his mouth to shoot back but finds himself speechless. He reels slightly, spins, and strides back toward the helicopter.

"Well done," Gavin comments.

"Got no time for that kind of shit," Fanno says. He turns to the two sergeants. "Now let's get back to work."

He expands on the plan he outlined earlier. One of the platoons goes to the far side of the buildings across the road to cover the western perimeter. Piles of construction material sit between the buildings and the unfinished outer fence, so the attackers will become vulnerable as they channel through. If his troops meet an overwhelming force, they will fall back and use the buildings for cover. If that fails, they will retreat to the trench around the bunker, with the machine guns providing cover fire. Fanno orders the other three platoons to be evenly dispersed along the length of the trench, which provides an excellent defensive position. It also allows him to rearrange the defenders according to where the assault is coming from.

He gathers all four platoon sergeants for a final briefing. "Here's the deal. We know there's a hell of a lot of 'em. But we also know they've had no time to train or organize. They're just one step above a mob, and that's why they're going down. All we have to do is stay tight and stick to what I've taught you. Now go out there and kick ass."

"You've gotta fix it," Stennis yells at the pilot. "We've got to get out of here." The pilot, a stoic fellow somewhere in his forties, has the engine casing open and stares at the smoking innards. He gives the bill of his cap a habitual tug before addressing Stennis. "Not gonna happen."

"It *has* to happen," Stennis exclaims. "Look, you were out there. You saw what's coming. All hell's going to break loose."

The pilot methodically shuts the engine cover. "Yeah. Well, not much I can do about that."

"So just what are you gonna do?"

"I'm going to get the fuck outa here." He leaves Stennis cowering against the fuselage, walks around to the opposite side, and heads for the gate that borders the highway.

He's gone about 20 meters when the mortar round explodes right next to him.

Stennis instinctively dives for cover and burrows his way between chopper's landing runners. His eardrums reel in concussive shock, rendering him nearly deaf. His pulse pounds its way up to heights never before realized. The smoke and dust lift enough that he can see the shredded remnants of the pilot staring up at a sky of dirty gray.

. . .

Fanno knows that it's a 60mm mortar the instant it explodes out toward the gate. He's heard the sound many times before and witnessed the carnage that often follows. "Mortar round," he yells down the length of the trench on the bunker's south side. "Keep down!"

"That was way wide. They haven't got us dialed in," he yells to Gavin. "They need a spotter to do that, or more likely a drone." He turns to a nearby platoon sergeant. "Watch the sky. Shoot anything that moves!"

Fanno starts down the length of the trench with Gavin behind him. "Just stick with what you've learned," he keeps telling the troops embedded in the packed earth. "You'll be okay." Gavin notes that it brings at least some measure of relief to the stricken young faces.

A second mortar explodes. Its attendant flash and smoke place it somewhere down around the trailer area.

"They're shootin' blind," Fanno tells Gavin. "Let's hope it stays that way."

Fanno's two-way radio comes alive with Tracy's voice. "They're spreading out across the plain to the south of you, maybe two hundred meters out. Same thing to the west."

"How many?"

"It's hard to say at this distance. A lot. Hundreds, for sure."

"Okay, let me know if they start to close in."

"I don't get it," Fanno says to Gavin. "You gotta wonder just how many combat-worthy people you'd have out of a group that size. Something's not right."

"I don't know," Gavin replies. "But I think their idea of who's combat ready may be a little different than yours."

The tell-tale hornet buzz of a drone intervenes. The .50-caliber gun opens up with its pump-pump-pump. The buzz stops.

"I see smoke," Tracy says over the radio.

"How much and where?" Fanno asks.

"About fifty yards out, maybe less. Dense white smoke from several locations. The wind's pushing it west to east."

"Get ready," Fanno tells the nearby platoon sergeant. "Everybody locked and loaded. Pass the word." He turns to Gavin. "Smoke grenades. They're putting up a screen so we can't pick 'em off out on the flat terrain. By the time we get a clean field of fire, they'll be almost on top of us." He looks at Gavin's body armor and helmet. "We better get you a gun."

They're being herded, Tracy realizes. The monitor feed from the south-facing cameras shows a mass of tiny squirming dots all across the field of view. Behind them, a group of utility vehicles bounces over the plain and channels them into a broad front that covers the south and west. "It looks like they're lining up to attack," she radios Fanno. "It's crazy. Just crazy."

"It's war," he responds. "Let me know when they start through the smoke."

It doesn't take long. The utility vehicles all turn toward Ingomar and prompt the mass of attackers in the rear to surge forward. Their action sets off a ripple all the way to those in front, who plunge into the billowing smokescreen.

By now, she can make out a hint of torsos and limbs, and occasional red specks of some kind. A shiver of dread runs through her. They're actually going to do it.

"Here they come." Gavin turns to the filtered sound of Tracy's voice on the two-way radio. He beckons to Fanno, who passes it to him.

"Tracy, can you hear me?" he says while punching the call button.

"Gavin, yes."

"Don't worry. I'll be okay. We've got good cover. Stay safe."

"I will. Yes, I will."

Gavin hands the radio back to Fanno, who peers up over the top of the trench. "Everybody into position!" he yells. Up and down the trench, the troops bring their rifles up to rest along its top. They stare out into a white fog that lingers around the large gaps in the security fence along the perimeter. The machine guns at either end cock their weapons amidst a sudden silence. Then a manic roar starts from somewhere out in the whiteness. Softly at first but building rapidly. Dissonant madness. The pop of small arms fire joins in, dotted by brief star-like flashes.

They first appear as ghostly silhouettes coming out of the smoke, each wearing a red headband. They flood through the gaps, like pent-up water through the vents on a dam.

"Aw shit," Fanno says. It quickly becomes apparent that only a minority carry firearms. The rest brandish an improvised arsenal of axes, pipe wrenches, crowbars, shovels, weeding hoes, baseball bats, and whatever else has presented itself.

A few brandish nothing at all.

"Same as always," Fanno mutters as he stares out at the advancing wave. He turns to Gavin with his face steeped in sorrow. "Them or us."

"Fire!" he yells down the trench. Twenty rifles and the two machine guns open up in a deafening volley. They pour a withering fire into the flood of attackers, who twist and shudder and collapse. Still more flood through and trip and stumble over the fallen.

There has to be an end to it, Gavin thinks. There just has to be.

But on it goes.

The platoon defending the buildings to the west confronts its own rush of attackers streaming in from between the piles of construction material. With only four squads of five rifles each, they face hopeless odds and fall back to the far side of the buildings. After a brief holding action, they begin to sprint across the open space to the front of the bunker. A few are hit, but their comrades drag them to the safety of the trench. Once they're clear, the machine guns open up on the attackers, which slows but does not stop their advance.

A killing field, built on the beliefs of a maintenance man from the Comfort Inn in Tonopah, Nevada. Yet another faith rising out of yet another desert and spilling over into the annals of history. In times to come, many would term it insane while others would define it as simply the latest expression of the divine will. Still others would lock horns over what precisely divine will might actually be. And so on.

From his prone position under the belly of the helicopter, Stennis cringes and winces at the report of automatic rifles and the random detonation of mortar rounds. The attackers, with their red headbands, are now coursing through the rows of vehicles in the parking lot and turning to join the slaughter in front of the bunker. Unbelievable.

Sooner or later, they will discover him here. He with no headband. An infidel in their midst. They will most surely kill him. No clever propositions, no bribes, no debit cards, no premium watches will save him.

Unless, of course, he can become one of them.

The thought no sooner presents itself than one of the attackers goes down in close proximity to him. Since they are out in the periphery of the battle, if you could call it that, the man must have taken a stray bullet. He lies still, bleeding from a neck wound and still clutching an aging golf club, his weapon of choice.

Stennis weighs the alternatives. He can risk being caught as an apostate, or he can expose himself to gunfire while getting the headband. He chooses the latter. Bullets kill you fast, zealots kill you slow.

He slithers out, dashes to the shelter of a nearby pickup and peers into the lot. A few attackers jog by with their eyes already in heaven, but not many. This is it. He sprints out to the downed combatant, rips the band off his head, and flees back into the lot. He relaxes slightly after cinching up the headband, which feels all warm, damp, and sweaty. He can now meander among the parked vehicles and merge into the chaos of the moment and its relative safety while he charts his escape.

They've brought up a machine gun, probably from the armory in Bozeman. More critically, they've found someone who knows how to use it. A row of .50-caliber bullets laces the lip of the trench where Fanno and his men hunker down. Several are hit, and pitch back into the dirt, which is now littered with empty ammo boxes. A moment later, a mortar round explodes where the trench rounds the rear corner of the bunker. Several more combatants fall, one howling in agony.

Fanno gets on the radio to Tracy. "How many more out there?"

"Hard to say with all the smoke," comes Tracy's voice. "Hundreds, maybe."

Fanno needs to see the front line of the assault. He times his peek to start after a second machine gun volley marches down the trench top and passes him by. It doesn't look good. The attackers are on the verge of a human stampede, and Fanno has only a single machine gun at the front corner to oppose them. He turns to the nearest platoon sergeant.

"Everybody into the bunker! Single file. Wounded first. Pass the word!"

Gavin marvels at how the soldiers make way for those carting the wounded before filing out themselves. None of them will ever get a medal, nor will Fanno, who probably wouldn't take one anyway.

Fanno turns to Gavin and points his thumb to a gap in the line. "There you go. Get the fuck outa here."

"Nope," Gavin replies. "I think I'm gonna stick around for a while." He knows precisely why he said it. He's a writer, a journalist, a bearer of stories, and each story has a life all its own. Whatever the tale, you can't end it shy of where it wants to go.

"Suit yourself," Fanno responds with a grim smile.

Gavin looks behind them to the bunker's earthen roof. Little clouds of atomized dirt start to appear across its rounded surface as the attackers concentrate their fire. The end of the retreating line in the trench files past. He and Fanno fall in behind them. They round the corner to the front of the bunker, where the last of the troops mount a crude set of wooden steps that takes them up onto the paved apron leading to the massive metal door, still swung open. A single soldier covers their retreat with fire from a sandbagged machine gun nest atop the concrete surface.

Gavin goes first, and as he climbs out, he sees the boiling churn of the assault, now only a short distance off. Its leading edge reminds him of the sputtering, foaming surge of agitated sand produced by the collapse of a breaking wave at the beach.

"Move!" Fanno climbs out behind him and points toward the bunker entrance. He turns to the machine gunner. "You too!"

The young soldier needs no further prompting. He abandons his weapon and runs toward the entrance, with Gavin right behind.

After just a few steps, the machine gun starts up again. Before he even turns to the sound, Gavin knows what it means. Fanno has manned the weapon to cover their retreat. Which leaves no one to cover Fanno's retreat. He fires in arc wide enough to suppress nearby return fire. But not quite enough. A single bullet catches him somewhere near his shoulder, knocking him to the ground. He tries to get up and man the gun again, but crumples onto the ground.

"Gavin, no!" Tracy watches in horror on the monitor as Gavin races out over the pavement to where Fanno has fallen. He locks onto the fallen leader's wrists and drags him backward as incoming rounds dig wicked little pocks along their path. Their image disappears off the bottom of the monitor, and Tracy bursts out of the blockhouse, just in time to see Gavin gently laying Fanno down while two of his soldiers swing the door shut with a tremendous thud. A series of metallic spangs pierce the ensuing silence as bullets strike the door's outer surface.

"Get a medic," Gavin instructs the pair, who run off to somewhere in the recesses of bunker.

Tracy can't help the tears that well up as she reaches Gavin. "They could've killed you," she tells him.

Gavin smiles as he gathers her in his arms. "But they didn't."

Stennis cautiously inches along the primed quarter panel of an old Dodge pickup. His fingers glide over its mildly abrasive surface as he peeks out at the core of the conflict near the front of the bunker. The attackers press forward through the scattered bodies of their fallen comrades, some with firearms, most not. At the bunker, two figures scramble toward its open doors while a third mans a machine gun that keeps the advance at bay, at least for the moment. Here in the parking lot, only a trickle of the faithful now pass on through on their way to eternal bliss. He pans over to the front gate and the remains of his pilot. No one in sight. It's time to go. He steps out from behind the pickup to plot the best path toward the gate and freedom.

"You need help, don't you?"

Stennis whirls to meet the voice. It's a woman of the kind he's always rendered invisible. They simply don't register when he navigates the streets of Manhattan. Her red headband circles a grizzled forest of gray hair above a sagging face devoid of makeup. She peers out at him though glasses absolutely archaic in style. A faded flannel shirt attempts to hide her ample belly but fails. Her one truly distinguishing feature is the 12-gauge pump action shotgun she grasps with pale, knobby fingers.

Stennis freezes. If it was an ambassador's wife, a sleek female attorney, or an aspiring actress, he could have easily launched into spontaneous dialogue both charming and substantive. But not with this utterly alien creature, this hardscrabble spawn of circumstances far beyond his comprehension.

"What kind of help?" he warily asks.

"I can see what's happening with you. You're having a moment of doubt. You're not letting the Final Truth into your soul, which is the rightful place for it to dwell. But we all know that only through death will we find our true life."

"Our true life, yes. We all need to find our true lives," he ventures.

"And now that time has come," she announces, and pumps a round into the shotgun's chamber.

"No!" he yells and raises his hands in surrender. It doesn't work. She moves the shotgun up toward her shoulder.

He pivots and sprints toward the gate. His legs become pistons powered by a panic beyond measure. He barely hears the report of the shotgun when it deposits a load of buckshot into his buttocks. He screams and pitches forward into the dirt, ruining his supple flight jacket and fracturing his premium sunglasses.

He writhes under the cloud-soaked prairie sky in a profound state of pain. The woman chambers a second round on her walk out to meet him.

"I'm so sorry," she tells him. "I hit you low. You should have been off on your journey by now."

And then she blows his face off.

52

"There's no exit wound," the medic informs Gavin. "The bullet's still in there somewhere. And he doesn't look good." Neither does the medic, who is less than twenty and steeped in anxiety. His training consisted of a few field manuals and a brief set of online videos. None have prepared him for what he now faces.

They both turn toward Fanno, who lies out of earshot on the bunker floor of buffed cement, his head elevated by a few rolled up blankets. The medic continues: "I think there's some internal bleeding, probably from an artery that got nicked. Not much I can do about that."

"Understand," Gavin responds. It reminds him of the old Hollywood cliché where the hero takes a bullet in the shoulder but carries on anyway. Not always so in the jungle of blood vessels, nerves, muscles and bone buried beneath the skin, where a bullet can find limitless opportunity to cause disaster.

"Stand by. I need to talk with him," Gavin tells the medic. He walks back to where Tracy kneels beside Fanno, who has the pale, distant look of someone slipping into serious shock. "Frank, you with me?" Gavin asks.

"Yeah, I'm with you," Fanno replies through closed eyes. "I want to know our casualties."

"Counting you, Sixteen wounded and four dead. Seven of the wounded need an ER as soon as possible, you among them."

"Jesus," Fanno whispers. "What a mess."

"Well, there might be a way out of it," Gavin says.

"Oh yeah?"

"Tracy thinks maybe the feds have the means to reach us by phone. If they do, we could have them intervene here and clear out the crazies in no time at all."

Fanno takes a deep breath. His skin glistens from shock-induced sweat. "Oh yeah? And then who clears out the feds? Who keeps them from grabbing God's own property and calling it their own?"

"Hard to say. But without them, you've got people in here that are going to die if they don't get help. You okay with that?"

Fanno closes his eyes and shakes his head, very slowly. His mouth opens in silent deliberation, but no words come. Tracy tugs Gavin's sleeve and motions him aside. A sudden volley of spangs and pings strike the door on its outer side. The Order of Atonement is here to stay.

"I want to speak to him alone," Tracy insists.

"Why? I think it's pretty obvious…"

"Trust me, okay?"

"Okay." Gavin shrugs and walks back toward the blockhouse. From the start, Tracey has had some ineffable connection with the man. So be it.

Tracy once more kneels beside Fanno and rests her hand on top of his, which has gone cold and clammy. His eyes open and fix on her.

"There's something I think you need to know," she says.

"What?"

"Not everything stored in here is God's property. Some of it is mine."

"What do you mean?"

"When I was in school, I hit a rough patch in my final year. My parents had some investments tank on them, so I was on my own financially. I saw a promotion that gave me a way out. I could sell a few of my eggs to an egg bank and make enough to get through the year. I did it. Some of them went to couples for in vitro fertilization, but I had a few more frozen and stored for my own use – just in case I couldn't conceive when I was ready."

Frank's eyes slide shut, and he takes shallow breaths through his slack mouth.

The stars come out. Thousands of them. They fill the void and give it meaning.

"You with me?" she asks.

"I'm with you," he whispers through closed eyes.

A woman appears in the sky above. A beautiful woman in a shifting gown of bluish green.

"What you need to know is that I'm not alone in this. A lot of other young women have done the same. And a lot of it is still here right now in those tanks, waiting to become babies when the time is right."

The woman raises her right hand with infinite grace and extends her index finger. Tiny, brilliant points of light begin to rise from the earth below. They quickly form a river, a migration of epic proportion...

"The lights," Fanno murmurs. "Can you see the lights?"

"I'm not sure..." Tracy begins.

"I need to see all my platoon leaders. Now."

Tracy looks behind her. All four of them stand nearby, looking on anxiously at their fallen leader. She motions them forward, and they gather around him on bended knees.

"Here's what I want," he says in a small but clear voice, resonant in its conviction. "If those savages outside blow their way in here, you fight to the death. You'll have done your duty in the service of God and life itself. Understand?"

They all nod solemnly. He surveys each face and takes in their tacit assent.

"Now there's at least some chance the feds will show up and shoo them off," he continues. "If that happens, stand down and let 'em in. For once, they're doing the right thing, and we have to respect that. Got it?"

He scans each face once more, slowly this time. He peers deeply into each set of eyes and extracts their implied consent.

"Yes sir," one of them finally answers for all.

"Good. Now go get your people ready." His head sinks back into the rolled blankets and his eyes close once more. There's a transcendent weariness to him.

The four leaders rise and head into the interior. Tracy motions to the medic, who comes back in close. "Make him as comfortable as you can, okay? And let me know if anything changes."

"Yes, ma'am."

Gavin appears at the blockhouse entrance just as Tracy arrives. "Something's happening outside. Take a look."

She moves to the TV camera monitors and sees an improvised motorcade coming up a road from the south to where it turns into the western perimeter. A dozen or more SUVs surround a large motorhome and start to penetrate a gap in the security fence. The motorhome holds back while the smaller vehicles move ahead into the large open area between the support buildings and the bunker. Here they encounter an exuberant throng of the faithful who pump their weapons into the air, drunk with victory. The bunker is theirs. They have only to breech the big metal doors and the vile contents within will be destroyed in accordance with the dictates of the Final Truth. The SUVs spread out and start to steer the mob away from the center, like vehicular cowboys herding human cattle.

Tracy directs one of the cameras in tight on the motorhome, which remains stationary. A diaphanous coat of dust covers its deep black exterior and tinted windows. Overhead clouds make a reflective bounce off the windshield, concealing its occupants.

"And there's the alpha," Gavin says.

"How long before we can breech the door?" Bauer asks. He sits in the passenger seat where he can look out at the massive bunker on the far side of the clearing. Kranz crouches next to him. The Eternal Gate has the space partially cleared, revealing scores of bodies scattered about.

"Depends," Kranz answers. "First, we need to round up enough explosives. And as you can see, things are a little disorganized right now."

"I need to speak to them," Bauer says. "I need to give them direction. I need to give them guidance."

But he and Kranz both know he also needs protection. There's always the possibility that some misguided member of the faithful will misinterpret the Final Truth and decide that its leader and originator should set the ultimate example for all to follow. Before the great Terminus can speak, they need to clear sufficient space around the motorhome so that no one can get a clean shot when he climbs on top to address the multitude.

Kranz peers out the windshield. The cloud cover gives the scene a slightly bluish gray cast; and the bunker, with its sod-covered roof, rises out of the prairie like some enormous creature from depths unknown.

"I think it's clear enough," Kranz observes. "Let's go."

On the monitors, Gavin and Tracy watch the motorhome creep out into the cleared space, working its way through the fallen brethren. "Here we go," Gavin says. "The victorious leader makes a triumphal entry into the conquered city. Been done before, God knows how many times."

"Yes, but this time is different," Tracy comments.

"How so?"

"It's the last time."

She's right. He knows it the instant she says it. Their immediate struggle suddenly snaps into true perspective. Even if they save the frozen store of life out here on the edge of nowhere, humanity at large still staggers about wildly on the brink of oblivion. No more triumphs, no more defeats, no more celebrating, no more mourning, no more stumbling ahead into the unknowable. All gone.

Gavin's cellphone rings, causing Tracy to whip around and stare at it. He checks the caller ID, which shows only a cryptic string of numbers. "Hello," he responds.

"Yes, who am I speaking to?" a female voice says.

"My name's Gavin Gray. I'm talking to you from Ingomar in eastern Montana."

"Right. We've been able to identify you through INN."

"And just who might you be?" Gavin asks.

"I'm Glenda Blume, the US deputy secretary of defense. It hasn't been easy to reach you. There've been multiple telecommunications issues, but this link is satellite-based and should be okay. We put a drone overhead and have a general idea of what's happened. How are you holding up?"

"So-so. I'm going to put you on speaker. I have a Tracy Pallas from the CDC here with me who's handling the electronic stuff. We also have what's left of the paramilitary outfit that defended the place, with both dead and wounded."

"Sorry to hear that."

"Look, I don't have to be a military genius to tell you what comes next. They're taking a break right now to do their victory dance, and then they're going to round up whatever they need to blow the front door open."

"We concur with that, and we've dispatched two combat choppers from Malmstrom, which should be arriving at your location any time. They've been instructed to stand off while we consider our options."

"Options? Like what?"

"The President is concerned about the use of deadly force against a large gathering of civilians, no matter how weird their religious convictions might be."

"Got it. Now, what about her concern for a group of seriously wounded amateur soldiers – no matter how weird their political convictions might be?"

"That's a tough call," the deputy secretary says.

"Maybe not," Tracy intervenes. "Look."

On the monitor, the motorhome has come to a stop in the middle of the cleared area. One of the SUVs has pulled alongside and is unloading what appears to be a PA system.

"It looks like you might be able to remove the head without harming the body," Gavin observes.

"Put your phone on video and show me what you see outside," the secretary asks.

Gavin switches to video and homes in on the monitor showing the motorhome, where a ladder is being placed on the side. "You're right," the secretary says. "Stand by."

"Terminus! Terminus! Terminus! Terminus!"

Bauer waits calmly while Kranz sends two armed guards up the ladder to positions fore and aft on the vehicle's roof. The chant of the crowd washes over him in a most exhilarating manner. He soaks up every decibel and makes it his own.

"Okay," Kranz tells him. "You're on."

Wayne mounts the bottom rung. He knows from within the depths of him that when he reaches the top rung, he will never again be Wayne Bauer. He will be only Terminus, so simply beautiful and infinitely complex.

Kranz looks about anxiously as Wayne clears the ladder and steps onto the roof. The potential for disaster is beyond calculation. The mob could break its bonds and crush them in its mad embrace. A good marksman among them could get off a fatal shot, even at this distance. Bauer might get carried away and topple off and break his neck.

Terminus walks slowly to the middle of the roof while the crowd bellows his name, his one and only name. He raises both arms above his head and rotates ever so slowly. All must see. All must venerate. That done, he gently lowers his arms in a gesture commanding silence. A hush comes over the faithful, like water descending from a boil to a simmer. Terminus begins to speak through the wireless mic attached to his collar.

"We stand here on the threshold of a great victory. Soon this giant door will spring open, and we will enter and destroy all that stands in defiance of the Final Truth. We will not be denied!"

"Terminus! Terminus! Terminus! Terminus!"

"We will clear a path for all that have fallen here, for all those who have cast off into the waters of eternal salvation. We will clear a path for all those who will soon follow. The hour of our complete and utter atonement is at hand!"

"Terminus! Terminus! Terminus! Terminus!"

A dip in the noise follows before Bauer can speak again. And in the midst of this dip, Kranz's ears take in the faint but unmistakable sound of a helicopter. It comes from the north, like an agitated insect.

Kranz sprints to the ladder and bounds up to the roof. "Get him out of here!" he screams to the nearest guard. "Now!"

A quarter mile away, the chopper gets its final clearance. Its rotors churn the thick afternoon air as it ascends to a height where it can see the bunker, the clearing, the crowd, the motorhome. One of the two crew adjusts the aim of a 20mm rotary cannon hung beneath the ship's sleek snout.

"Target locked," he announces over the intercom.

"Fire," the pilot in command orders.

The cannon's three barrels spin madly in an angry snarl. In just a few seconds, it spews out 125 rounds in a closely packed cluster. It pauses, as if to catch its breath and lets loose a second volley, a little more widely spaced.

Both volleys scream in over the heads of the faithful and tear into the motorhome.

Kranz clears the ladder and runs toward Bauer, who has ignored the first guard and opens his mouth to continue his oration, his best ever he thinks.

But nothing comes out.

Instead, he shudders and crumbles under the impact of multiple rounds tearing through his torso. Kranz and the two guards suffer the same fate. The second volley peppers the vehicle's side and sets it to rocking. Several rounds penetrate the fuel tanks and trigger a violent explosion, a billowing orange ball brilliant against the cloudy sky.

"Amen," Tracy says as they stare at the burning vehicle on the monitor. The faithful appear motionless, too stunned to move. No one tries to extinguish the burning motorhome. The multitudes keep their distance.

"You got that?" Gavin asks the deputy secretary on the phone.

"Yeah, we got it. Can you confirm the target has been terminated?"

Yep, she's definitely in the defense business, Gavin thinks. "Not quite yet. I'll have to go out there and count the pieces – and I don't think I'd be very welcome just yet."

"Understand. We've got a convoy from Malmstrom coming to get you. Once we close in on your position, we'll assess the situation and take it from there."

"Ma'am?" The medic has appeared at the blockhouse door.

"Yes?"

"It's the captain," he says solemnly. "He's, uh, not doing very well. He wants to see you."

Gavin and Tracy exchange glances. "Go," Gavin says. "It's his call. I'll take it from here."

The medic is right. Fanno is not doing well. His face has gone mushroom pale. His breath alarmingly shallow. He looks out at her through eyes drenched in sadness. Tracy's not sure how to respond, but he saves her the trouble.

"I need to know what's happening," he tells her. "Where are we at?"

She once again kneels before him and puts her hand over his. His eyes close, as if in relief of some kind. "First of all, how are you?" she asks.

"Doesn't matter," he says weakly. "What's going on out there?"

"We're okay for the time being, anyway. You made a good decision about the feds. They sent in a chopper and took out Bauer, the leader. His people seem pretty stunned. Hopefully, that's the end of it. Basically, you won."

His eyes come open. "Nobody won," he says. "Nobody ever wins."

"I have to disagree." She points back into the bunker. "There are thousands and thousands of potential babies back there. And when they're born, each and every one will owe their life to you."

"God's property," he murmurs.

She gently squeezes his hand. "And yours, too."

The faintest of smiles glides across his face and his eyes go to half-mast. "You'll never know who you really are," he tells her.

Before she can ask why, his eyes slide shut for the last time.

A woman appears in the sky above. A beautiful woman in a shifting gown of bluish green. She gazes down with a beatific smile lit by the yellow brilliance of the distant sun.

A crow, a large one, pumps its jet-black wings to clear the top of the bunker's earthen roof. It spreads them wide as it glides over the open space where the motorhome burns its way into the late afternoon. It circles the ascending column of black smoke and rides the updraft generated by the mechanized pyre below. As the bird traces an upward spiral, it issues a series of sharp caws. An incantation, perhaps? An encoded eulogy? The faithful take it as neither and read it as a call to disperse. The crow leads the way by peeling off and disappearing to the south.

Many hundreds of people begin a wordless trek back the way they came, toward their vehicles parked a few miles off. From there, they will retrace their recent migratory path and branch off into smaller tributaries as they withdraw. In the end, they will go the way of a mountainous snowpack working its way down the landscape to the shore where it surrenders itself to the boundless expanse of the sea.

A random gunshot sounds here and there. Wayne Bauer's doctrine of the Final Truth still holds at least some sway, even now.

53

They saved the dead for morning. The wounded were taken out by medivac choppers in the early evening hours as soon as a drone sweep in the infrared confirmed the area secure.

Now the dawn sky waxes cool and cloudy as the black body bags come out on olive drab stretchers to be loaded onto trucks in the waiting convoy. Fanno's body is the last to emerge from the bunker's interior. It is carried by two of his men, who walk at a slow and solemn pace. The remainder stand off to the side and spontaneously break into a salute as he passes by. Many struggle to hold back tears.

"I can't quite make up my mind," Tracy tells Gavin from where they stand nearby. "He really wasn't a bad guy. But he wasn't exactly a good guy either."

"I don't know," Gavin says. "That describes a whole lot of us. Maybe all of us."

"Are you going to finish your book on him?"

"Absolutely. He's one of the key figures of our time. It's kind of ironic: You've got all these people who've tried to scratch and claw their way into the history books, and here you've got this guy who could have cared less. All he wanted was to be left alone, really."

"Does he have any family?"

"Not that I know of. His wife died some time back." Gavin nods to the makeshift formation, which is now dissolving. "They were pretty much it."

"They could have done worse," Tracy notes.

"Yes, they could have."

All the young men, and a few young women, start to drift across to the parking lot, where their vehicles await them, the same ones they arrived in just a short time ago, the ones that will carry them back into a civilian world that will never seem the same. The naked horror of real combat has embedded itself within them, like a virus biding its time, looking for opportune moments to rise once more.

Gavin learns from the convoy commander that a larger force is being assembled to secure the base permanently. It will arrive within 36 hours and soon face a problem of horrific dimension. Hundreds of bodies lie scattered across the area. Already, birds are alighting on them, and other creatures are beginning a cautious approach. In response, a massive field morgue will be erected, the kind usually reserved for epidemics. Families will be able to identify the remains and have the option to transport them for local burial. Those that remain will be incinerated in a mass grave marked by a stone monument bearing their names, if known. No mention of the Order of Atonement will be included.

Tracy and Gavin walk back into the bunker for one last visit to the heart of the matter, the cryo-tanks. They travel down the rows between the metal racks and look up at the dull gray containers with their blue lids and handles that protrude like cartoonish ears. Hardly what you would associate with the frozen sparks of life that slumber within.

Tracy senses this is the moment to let him know. "I'm in one of those," she tells him.

"You're what?"

She grasps his hand and tells him what she told Fanno on his way to eternity.

"Wow," is the best Gavin can do.

"I would have told you sooner, but I had to be sure."

"About what?"

"That you're the one."

"And now you're sure?"

"And now I'm sure."

As they fall into each other's arms among the dormant vessels, a slight stirring settles in, more a feeling than anything else.

Tiny, brilliant points of light begin to rise from the earth below. They quickly form a river, a sparkling channel that gently curves past her toward the waiting sun.

Epilogue

FIVE YEARS HENCE

"Where did the kids go?" Athena asks her mother.

Just a few months past her third birthday, she's become an inexhaustible font of questions. She stands hand in hand with Tracy as they gaze at the empty yard of a vacated daycare center a brief walk from where they live. The play structures stand intact, with slides, tunnels, ladders, and miniature roofs done in cheerful reds, yellows, greens and blues. All empty. Athena clearly understands their purpose and feels their allure. Everything is as it should be, except for no kids, no laughter, no squeals of delight. A puzzling void.

"They went out for a while," Tracy answers. "But they'll be back."

"When?"

"I'm not sure. We'll just have to wait and see."

"Can we come back then?"

"Of course we can." Tracy gives Athena's hand a gentle tug to guide them on down the street to the heart of this small town, with its grocery, drug store, hardware store, medical offices and so on. Its scale makes it easier to secure against intrusion, which is a perpetual concern. Athena and her peers number about 300,000 in the US, the result of a massive effort to convert the national store of frozen embryos and eggs into pregnancies over the past four years. A microscopic sliver of the population, compared to times past. Before the Plunge, as it's now referred to, their age group numbered about 23 million. This latest and possibly last generation is the object of great love, hate, hope, envy and obsession by the world at large.

Thus, the need for 24/7 vigilance. Tracy knows that a pair of security people lurk nearby, courtesy of a federal force set up specifically for this purpose. She appreciates that they've become adept at staying out of immediate eyesight, thereby creating the illusion of normalcy. Starting next year, Athena will begin attending a special school with her contemporaries, as they gradually and gently come to terms with their extraordinary place in the scheme of things. The curriculum is still a work in progress and the subject of considerable debate.

Sometimes, in reflective moments, Tracy spins the numbers in her head much as she did at the CDC. She's managed to construct a scenario that offers at least some measure of hope. By the time she turns 75, the world population will have dropped from 8 billion to 2 billion as the Plunge marches forward through successive age groups. The resulting decline in human consumption levels will substantially reduce environmental stress, and perhaps violent conflict as well. Most significantly, it will trigger a gradual drop in the PFAS levels, and within 35 years natural pregnancies might once again be the norm.

They've reached the town square, a single block centered on a neatly tended garden and lined with wooden benches and elm trees. The spring sun drenches the flowers and saturates their various hues. A squirrel surrenders one of the benches to them.

"I want to go home now," Athena announces as they sit.

"You do?"

"I want to see daddy. He's going to read to me. He promised."

"Well then, I'm sure he will."

Tracy pictures Gavin at home in their townhouse as he types away on his book, an epic account of the fertility plunge, all the way from Tracy's detection of a minor statistical aberration to the post-Ingomar disposition of the embryos and eggs. His publisher anxiously awaits the final draft, but Gavin remains acutely aware of its significance and won't let it go until every detail is properly resolved. After all, it may be the last significant historical document produced for a very long time – and possibly forever.

On the bench, Athena rises and crawls into Tracy's lap, where they cuddle up into a comfy embrace.

"You okay, baby?" Tracy asks.

"Okay," comes the reply, so soft and small.

Tracy closes her eyes and wraps her arms around this precious child, more precious than she will ever know.